"Mutie ants!" Ryan yelled. "Our only hope is the tree."

The horrifying creatures were more than a foot long, and their mandibles were huge, disproportionate even to their grotesquely mutated size. Longer than a man's finger, they clicked together in a deafening warning as the ants became aware of the six companions.

As Ryan led the charge, the front row of insects retreated, then regrouped in a solid phalanx of glittering death.

To hesitate was to die.

The crunching of delicate skeletons beneath bootheels almost drowned out the clicking jaws. Ryan could now see the main body of the killer army beyond the mangrove, and not an inch of ground was free of the iridescent horde that swept toward him.

Ryan gained the mangrove. Several low branches were within easy reach, and he made a running dive, swinging to safety with prehensile agility. When he was four feet above the carpet of ants, the one-eyed man finally looked for his friends. All were winning the desperate race. Except the old man.

Then, only a few strides from safety, Doc Tanner stumbled....

**Also available in the
Deathlands saga:**

JAMES AXLER

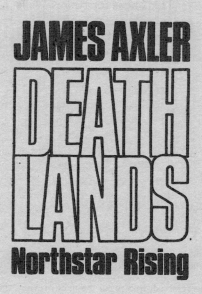

DEATH LANDS

Northstar Rising

A GOLD EAGLE BOOK FROM

WORLDWIDE®

TORONTO • NEW YORK • LONDON • PARIS
AMSTERDAM • STOCKHOLM • HAMBURG
ATHENS • MILAN • TOKYO • SYDNEY

This one is for Angus Wells
who has been, and still is,
one of the very best of friends.
All good things.

First edition December 1989

ISBN 0-373-62510-3

There's night and day, brother, both sweet things; sun, moon, and stars, brother, all sweet things; there's likewise a wind on the heath. Life is very sweet, brother; who would wish to die?

—Lavengro
by George Barrow

CHAPTER ONE

BLACK.

Blackness.

Blackness.

Laughter.

The hands on his throat remorselessly strong.

Someone laughed.

A voice breathed in Ryan's ear. "You who are about to die . . ."

Pocked skin.

Circle of silver and bald head.

A smell of burned cloth and hair.

MAJOR COMMISSAR Gregori Zimyanin, of the Internal Security Section of Moscow, felt as though someone had pushed a brass-hilted bayonet into the center of his skull, then stirred it around, puddling his brains. The Russian was immensely strong, and he was recovering from the jump with remarkable speed.

As consciousness began to creep back into the blurred fringes of his mind, so shards of memory also lurched out into the open. There had been a dreadful firefight, with many corpses; a body of one of the enemy, flaming like a beacon of defiance; the Yank flag; a winding staircase, shrouded in choking smoke.

The brawl had ended with swirling blackness and his fingers clawing at the throat of the leader of the terrorists. With a massive effort of will, Zimyanin managed to open his eyes.

Something was wrong. Something had changed in the glass-walled chamber. The colors had altered and the air tasted different. The thick choking smoke was gone, and the air was thin and cold. The Russian had lived at altitude in winter and knew the sensation well. Somehow, while they were all unconscious, the Americans had succeeded in transporting the whole mysterious complex to a mountain.

In his attempts to master the language of his bitter enemies, the officer had been secretly learning the English tongue, using a book with a publication date of 1911, nearly two hundred years earlier—*The English Tongue for the Benefit of the Russian Gentleman Abroad*.

"I beg your pardon, but could you inform me as to the whereabouts of my entourage?" he whispered through dry lips.

Where could all of his men have gone? Dozens of troops couldn't just disappear into space. He fumbled for the pistol at his belt, feeling the familiar shape of the 9 mm Makarov blaster.

Now his eyes were focusing, settling on something opposite him that was colored dazzling white and vivid crimson.

"By the anvil and the hammer," Zimyanin muttered.

It was a young, skinny albino boy, his hair like the tumbled snow around the hamlet of Ozhbarchik in the far, far northeast. A thread of fresh blood inched from the lad's nose, his mouth sagged open and his eyes were shut tight.

Next to him lay an old man with wild, silver hair, clutching a small, unconscious puppy.

A woman with hair as red as blazing pitch was stretched flat on the floor, but she was moving, fingers opening and closing as she approached consciousness.

Ryan Cawdor blinked, opening his one good eye. The patch over his ruined left eye had shifted during the fight with the Russian, and he lifted a hand to straighten it.

And saw Zimyanin.

The stocky Russian was crouched on the far side of the gateway chamber, like a beast waiting to spring. His heavy features were smeared with soot, and a worm of dried blood from the corner of his mouth had clotted in his drooping mustache.

"Bastard," Ryan said quietly. His own blaster, the 9 mm SIG-Sauer P-226, was holstered in his belt and he began to reach for it.

Zimyanin had a glacial moment of frozen time to make up his mind. Somehow the Americans had disposed of his men and moved him to a different location. The one-eyed killer was fumbling for his pistol, and at least one of the others was coming around from the sleeping gas. Or whatever it was they'd used to knock everyone out.

He made his decision, diving for the door to the glass-walled room. If he was to escape this could be his best and only chance.

A hand grabbed at Zimyanin's ankle, and he kicked out, his heavy, ash-crusted boot hitting Jak Lauren on the side of his pale skull. The fingers relaxed their grip and the Russian was at the door.

Ryan's pistol had cleared its rig and his finger was tightening on the trigger when the Russian darted through the doorway. There was a glimpse of the room beyond, then the door slammed shut.

"Fireblast," Ryan cursed. "He's triggered the jump mechanism again. Everyone down and get ready."

Already the disks in floor and ceiling were glowing, and a ragged spray of gas was filling the octagonal room.

Zimyanin hesitated outside the gateway chamber, puzzled by what he saw. There was a small room, with a larger room visible beyond it, behind a barred door. The wall to his left had broken down into fragments of powdered rock. But the peculiar thing was that the floor and walls were covered with a thin layer of pinkish slime.

And there was a gut-churning smell of sickly decay.

An urgent, rustling sound emerged from beyond the broken wall. Coming toward him.

Ryan was slipping into unconsciousness again, struggling to keep a hold on his pistol. His mind tried to blank out the bizarre appearance and disappearance of the Russian sec man.

He could hear someone in the chamber making coughing, choking sounds, but there was nothing he could do to help. The floor was vibrating beneath him, and he could feel a rumbling, clear through the marrow of his bones. The heavy blaster dropped from his fingers and clanged on the metal plates with a harsh echo that seemed to go on and on.

Beyond the thick arma-glass walls, Ryan thought he could just make out the figure of Zimyanin. But his vision was blurring and nothing was certain.

There seemed to be the crack of an automatic pistol, flat and sudden, a yell, starting off with surprise and shrilling quickly into raw terror.

Another shot.

A third.

The yell had become a scream, high and thin like a stallion at the gelding.

As blackness gripped him, Ryan's last doubtful vision was of something moving beyond the walls of the gateway, something that was pale yellow and immeasurably huge.

CHAPTER TWO

JAK LAUREN LAY facedown in a stinking pool of his own vomit; Doc Tanner was bleeding copiously from the nose, the streaks of crimson dribbling over his neck and chest; J. B. Dix was even more sallow than usual, his eyes rolled up sightlessly in their sockets, and he was breathing fast and light through his open mouth; Krysty Wroth had managed to slide into a self-induced trance, deliberately putting herself into a coma to take away the overpowering pressures of a mat-trans jump. Her breath was shallow and slow, and her heartbeat had dropped to less than a quarter of normal.

Ryan Cawdor's powers of recovery were astounding. His body was honed to a razored perfection, ready for any threat, but even he suffered badly from the jumps. And to have to make a second jump so soon after the first was devastating.

His brain felt as if a high-velocity .44 had entered through his right temple and exited somewhere near the base of his skull, blowing a section of bone away and sucking most of his brains out through the exit wound.

He coughed, then groaned softly at the agonizing pain it caused him. He tried to open his eye, but the lancing white light made him close it again immediately. All he wanted to do was to curl up in a ball and lie there on the floor for a few weeks. His fingers were numbed, and his teeth felt loose in the gums.

Very cautiously he eased his eye open again, wincing at the light. This time he managed to keep it from closing. The walls of the chamber were a dull brown color, and there seemed only a dim light beyond them. The disks in floor and ceiling were already fading, and he could taste the bitterness of iron on his tongue. Ryan glanced around at the others.

Krysty looked fine. Pale and drawn, but clearly under control. As he tried to sit up, she moved, shuddering slightly and opening her eyes. Her tumbled mane of bright red hair was curled tightly about her neck and shoulders. The hair was sentient and reacted to whatever was going on. Once Krysty was recovered from the jump it would uncurl and fall naturally down her back.

"Hi, lover."

Ryan risked a nod. "You?"

"Been worse." She paused. "Been better. How about you?"

"Same."

Krysty looked around. "What in Gaia's name happened, Ryan? The Russkie?"

"Zimyanin attacked me during the first jump. Both blacked out. Came around. He got out and slammed the door shut."

"And we jumped again? No wonder I feel so lousy. Like a mutie rattler's been sleeping in my head for three months."

Ryan managed to lever himself up until he was sitting with his back flat against the cold glass wall of the chamber.

"Heard a coupla shots as I went under and saw some kind of...something real big. Mebbe the Russkie's bought the farm this time."

"Guess we'll never know." The voice came from J. B. Dix, who'd also come around. "Wouldn't much like having that mean Red mother hiking around Deathlands after us."

"Assuming we're *in* Deathlands," Krysty said. She sniffed the cool damp air. "Don't much like the smell of this place. Like coming around in the middle of an old, buried tomb."

Krysty's mutie sense picked up on "feelings," and Ryan had learned over their months together to trust her.

"Danger?" he asked.

"Mebbe. Not close. I reckon we should see to Jak and Doc."

The albino boy was showing signs of coming around. His legs moved feebly, like a drowning kitten's, and he struggled to open his pale red eyes. As Krysty stooped to help him, he coughed and spit, clearing his throat of the clogging bile. He sat up un-aided and wiped at his smeared face with the sleeve of his fur coat.

"We jump two times or dream it? Head feels dead inside."

"We jumped twice. One of the Russians came in with us then escaped when we made the first jump. He shut the door and sent us off again."

Jak nodded at Ryan's explanation. "Yeah," he muttered. "Fuck him."

"Doc doesn't look in fighting shape," J.B. remarked.

"The old man always takes a jump hardest of all," Krysty commented. "Good job Rick went the way he did. He'd never have made another jump in that kind of shape."

The memory of the man who'd briefly lived, traveled and fought with them brought a silence. Rick Ginsberg had been a freezie, someone who'd suffered from a serious illness and had been surgically frozen in the last months before the long winters began. Ryan and his friends had been able to revive Rick. The freezie had told them about two other cryonic centers in Deathlands, and Ryan's wish was to try to locate one or both. It was possible that the companions would benefit from these freezies' skills, if more of them could be successfully thawed.

"Oh! By the three Kennedys! Have I been bingeing with a bottle or two?" The rich, sonorous voice of Doc Tanner broke the stillness.

"You got bloodied nose, Doc," Jak said. He stood up unsteadily, bracing himself with a hand against the wall.

"Could be, sonny. Could be." Doc touched his lips and peered shortsightedly at his crimson-slobbered fingers. "Indeed you are correct. Tapped the claret, have I not? First blood to Theophilus Algernon Tanner, Esquire. Upon my soul, but I fear that someone has removed my poor head and replaced it with a miniature maelstrom."

"Your mouth, Doc," Ryan said.

"Yes, my dear friend?"

"Wipe the blood off of it. Then close it."

IT TOOK BETTER than half an hour before Ryan was convinced that everyone was well enough to take the chance of opening the heavy door. Previous experiences had quickly taught them the need for extreme caution when moving out into one of the redoubts, hidden fortresses that had been keystones in the defense system of the old United States. Gateways within the redoubts had the capability of transporting human beings instantly from one location to another by means of mat-trans chambers.

But the nuclear holocaust of 2001 had destroyed some of the redoubts and buried others. Still more had remained hidden among the glowing hot spots of the Deathlands.

Though Ryan and his comrades had made many jumps, they still had found no way of actually controlling their destinations. To use a gateway was, in every sense, to leap into the darkness.

"Ready?"

They all nodded. The chamber felt dank, and breath misted in the cold air. Everyone kept on the furs they'd acquired during their time in Russia. Zorro was still whimpering and when put down would huddle against his master. Eventually Doc picked up the puppy and stuffed him inside his coat.

"Ride along with me, little fellow," he said. "Though I confess that those who have been close to me have met a sorry end."

"Blasters ready?" Ryan held his own SIG-Sauer in his right hand. The automatic G-12 Heckler & Koch caseless rifle was slung across his broad shoulders, and the long-bladed panga was sheathed at his belt.

Krysty, standing next to him, held her silvered, thirteen-shot P7A Heckler & Koch pistol; J.B., the Armorer, had his trusty Steyr AUG 5.6 mm blaster; Jak held his enormous satin-finish .357 Magnum, which looked too big for him to handle; Doc, intent on the dog, left his Le Mat in its holster.

"Let's go," Ryan said.

The door swung open on stiff hinges, revealing a small bare anteroom. The room beyond that was also closed, and Ryan pushed at it with his hand.

"Black dust!" J.B. exclaimed, wrinkling his nose. "That's a corpse stink, if ever I smelled it. Long dead and long rotted."

Krysty touched Ryan on the arm. "There's bad news out there, lover. I can feel it, real strong. And not far away."

"Muties?" he asked.

"Could be."

"Air itself tastes dead," J.B. said. "Don't relish another jump, but I've been better places than this."

"I was once privileged to be present at the opening of the catafalque of some ancient Egyptian priest. Apthak...something or other. I disremember his name. It had been sealed for centuries. This redoubt has much the same odor." Doc shook his head. The blood had clotted, dark brown, on his grizzled chin, making him look as though he'd been in a fight. He was trembling with fatigue as he stood with the others.

"Me first?" Jak asked.

"Yeah. Watch your step. Door's real stiff. Could be anything behind it."

The hinges were damaged and squealed alarmingly as the teenager heaved against them. The door opened a few more inches then stuck again.

The nuke-plant that ran every redoubt was still ticking over, somewhere deep in the bowels of the military complex, supplying power and keeping the gateway functioning. Beyond the half-open door they could make out the same kind of control room that they'd seen in other redoubts. But it was poorly lit, and the smell was growing ever stronger.

"Give it a good big push, kid," J.B. urged, and received a glare from the boy.

"Don't call me fucking kid, old man!" Jak snarled, white hair pasted to his forehead.

He set his scrawny shoulder to the paneled metal and braced himself against the concrete floor, gritting his teeth and straining at the task. Ryan took a half step forward to help the boy, but a sideways glance from the crimson, feral eyes stopped him dead.

Steel grated on stone, and the door moved slowly back, revealing the control area, with its familiar banks of chattering comp-consoles.

"Some of them aren't working," Krysty observed. "I don't much like the look of that."

Doc followed Jak into the larger room, staring around with an expression of fascinated horror and amazement.

"How in tarnation did we make this jump? Pile of rusting scrap like this shouldn't have jumped a fly across three inches of tabletop. Half these contacts are blown." He ran a finger across some of the banks of dead machinery. "Tell you what, my dear companions. If we ever leave here and arrive anywhere safely it will be the greatest miracle since Teddy's election. Dreadful neglect here."

"Hasn't been dusted in the best part of a hundred years, Doc," Krysty said, tapping one of the displays of flickering, fading lights with the barrel of her blaster.

Immediately the entire row of digital displays went blank. There was a sound like a distant turbine running down and shedding blades, and half of the overhead strip lights went dark.

"Don't do that again!" Ryan snapped. "That's double-stupe, Krysty!"

"Sorry. Looks like you're ace on the line, Doc. This place is ready to lie down and die, right here in front of us."

"Think we should wait here and recover some strength? I got me the feeling that whatever's out beyond the main entrance door isn't going to be smiling news."

"I think we all got that feeling, J.B.," Ryan agreed. "Doesn't look like there's any food or water around here. And we're not exactly overloaded."

"You want to go out there, lover?" Krysty asked.

"I don't *want* to. If you got a rock and a hard place, you pick the hard place. Let's move out of here. J.B., take the main door."

There was a note of bleak determination in Ryan's voice that they all recognized.

"Sure." The Armorer moved light-footed between the rows of long-abandoned desks, toward the heavy double doors that sealed off the mat-trans unit from the rest of the redoubt.

Stenciled on the wall beside them was the faint message: 352 Open. 253 Close.

"Nothing like a secret code that no son of a bitch can remember." Ryan grinned. "Green lever's down. Lift it and press the buttons."

"Here come the discards and retards," Doc muttered. "Gentlemen rankers, all out on... Can't recall. Just remember that we were to be damned for all of eternity."

The rambling stopped when he caught Ryan's glance. It was a worry that the old man's mind still sometimes slipped a couple of notches, though he was better than when Ryan, Krysty and J.B. had first met him. Then it had been ten parts madness to a smattering of sanity.

The scientists who'd established matter-transmitting had also dabbled in temporal transfer—time jumps. In years of ultrasecret experiments there had only been one successful trawling of a live human being from the past... and a lot of hideously pulped abortions of failure.

The one success, nearly, had been Doc Tanner, picked out of November 1896 where he'd been a happily married man with two young children and dumped a century, then two, later. He made himself such a nuisance that he was eventually retrawled forward another hundred years.

None of that made for a well-balanced, incisive mind.

Doc nodded to himself, lost in some half world of his own, as J.B. threw the lever and coded in the numbers. The door, operated by its antique mechanism, began to move slowly upward.

"Fucking stink!" Jak gagged.

As the door made its ponderous ascent, the stench came seeping in below it, almost like a visible tide wave—rotten flesh and endless nauseating decay.

"No," Krysty whispered. "No, Ryan. Something's out there."

"Yeah, but it's gotta be long dead."

The door shuddered to a halt, about three-quarters open. Beyond it they could see only that the passage was completely dark. The light from behind them spilled out, then was swallowed by the stygian blackness.

"Need lamps," J.B. said.

"Nothing." Jak looked at Ryan for orders.

"You all wait here. I'll go a ways up the corridor and see what I find."

Within five paces the darkness absorbed him.

"Let it lie, lover," Krysty called, her voice muffled.

Ryan turned to reply, and was instantly knocked to the cold damp floor.

CHAPTER THREE

THE SUDDEN SHOCK of the fall knocked the breath from Ryan, but he automatically tried for the best defensive position. The Trader used to say that if you couldn't hit, then you tried to save yourself from getting hit. Trader was always a man who looked for the best option.

Ryan curled up tight, hands between his legs to protect his groin, head tucked in to keep his face from being too vulnerable, muscular shoulders hunched against a strangler.

Hands grabbed at him, soft flesh against his body. Breath hissed and slobbered in the darkness, with the same nauseating taste of decay as the air in the redoubt.

Almost instantly Ryan realized something very strange. The fingers that moved over him were feeble, almost tender, with no strength or power to them. In seconds he was recovered from the shock of the attack and began to resist.

"Ryan!" someone yelled. "What's happening?"

In the pitch blackness, he heard something that might have been speech, a wet, whispering sound, like someone whose tongue was too large for his dribbling mouth. Ryan kicked against the enfolding bodies and found himself easily upon his feet again.

Blunt teeth nibbled at his calf and he punched down, feeling spongy flesh that seemed to part under his fist, smearing his skin with a clammy ichor. There was a bubbling cry and something fell away from him onto the stones.

"Ryan!" It was Krysty's voice.

"It's okay! Got me some of the weakest muties the world ever saw. Stay there."

He could see the spillage of yellow light from the gateway control room, with four figures silhouetted against it. But where he stood was still inky gloom, with hands that pulled at him and tried to draw him down to the floor. He felt for the hilt of the panga at his hip and drew it in a muted hiss of promised death.

His eye had become accustomed to the blackness, and he could make out the dim figures of four attackers. One was already rolling on the floor, clutching at his face and moaning. The other three seemed torn between the desire to flee and the desire to attack. One stood off and the other two were groping at Ryan with hopeless, pawing gestures.

The muties were naked, and none was taller than five foot two. Their bodies were thin and weak. It was difficult to be sure, but there seemed to be an odd, shimmering phosphorescence about them. As far as Ryan could see, they were completely hairless and had no visible genitals.

The panga hissed once, lopping an arm off the nearest mutie. Blood pattered around Ryan's feet, and the creature went down like a gut-shot child.

"Want help?" Jak yelled.

"No. Stay there and get ready to drop the doors once I come back in."

A second hacking blow from the panga opened a huge gash across another mutie's lower abdomen, and its intestines spilled into the dirt. Now only one mutie remained up and interested.

"Coming!" Ryan yelled, his boots slithering in the puddled blood.

As he moved toward the beckoning light, the mutie suddenly hurled itself at him, fastening its puny grip around his leg, just below the knee. Ryan hardly checked his stride as he dragged the creature behind him, hearing the slimy scraping of its skin on the concrete floor of the passage.

Jak glided into the shadows, reaching for one of his concealed throwing-knives. He drew the delicate, leaf-bladed weapon and waited for Ryan to reach him so that he could stoop and slit the mutie's throat.

The smell, unbelievably, was becoming even stronger.

"Leave him, Jak. Bastard's weaker'n a half-drowned kitten."

Ryan finally reached the pool of light and could actually look down at his clinging opponent. It was the first time he'd seen the face of one of the subterranean muties.

The creature's open mouth was tiny and lipless, and possessed a single row of stunted, filed teeth. Its nose barely broke the blubbery plane of the cheeks, and its ears were relatively large, sticking out on either side of the hairless skull like the doors of a war wag.

But the creature's eyes won the spare mag prize.

They were huge—boggling and bulbous, watering profusely even in the poor light that seeped into the corridor. The irises were colorless, and Ryan couldn't make out any sign of a pupil. Not that he was interested enough to peer too closely into the mutie's distorted face.

"Disgusting, pathetic little thing," Doc observed. "Don't harm it, Ryan."

"Let cut neck?" Jak asked eagerly, still gripping his honed blade.

Ryan reached down and plucked the mutie off his leg, heaving it out of the ring of light into the malodorous darkness. With an expression of disgust he wiped his hands on his pants.

"This redoubt must be sealed off from ordinary light," Krysty said, instinctively moving closer to Ryan. "They've evolved like that because of living in darkness. No hair, big eyes. Feeble."

"Heard of some out in the big Rockies," J.B. said. "Heard they call 'em troggies. Don't know why that is."

"I suspect that it might be an abbreviation for the word *troglodyte*. One who creeps into a hole. A dweller within caves," Doc offered.

"If there's no light, then there's not a lot of point in going on," Ryan said. "I know they're no threat in a firefight, but I wouldn't like to meet a hundred or so down a dark hallway."

Krysty had stepped away from him, out into the corridor. She stood with her head on one side, listening intently. "Quiet!"

"What?"

She looked at him, her emerald eyes glittering in the half-light. "I just have a feeling, lover, that you're going to meet what you didn't want."

"You mean there's..."

"Hundreds, lover. I can hear them shuffling this way. And I do mean hundreds!"

They could all hear a sibilant bubbling sound, and soon they were able to make out movement in the black corridor.

"Got the firepower to chill 'em all," J.B. said.

Ryan shook his head. "No. No way, folks. If Krysty's right, and there's a hundred or more, we can just about take them all out. But it'll mean using almost every round we got between us. Can't waste bullets on muties like that."

"Not fuckin' gateway again!" Jak exploded. "No. Let's chill 'em."

"You want to go against me, Jak, then go ahead. Want to fight? Okay. The rest of us are leaving."

"Didn't..." the young boy began, his red eyes downcast.

"No time for talk, Jak. Let's go. Drop the sec door and we're safe. Those triple-poor sons of bitches couldn't open it in a year of rest days."

Ryan was last in from the corridor. He glanced out and saw that the nearest of the muties had crept within twenty yards of him. He considered firing a warning shot, then dismissed the idea.

"Lower it. Press two five three. Drop the green lever.

"Drop the door!" he snapped, seeing the muties suddenly rush closer.

Once the entrance was barred, they could at least rest for a few uncomfortable hours before facing another jump.

"Stuck!" the teenager grunted.

"Yeah, it's stuck fast," J.B. agreed, trying to help Jak.

"Fireblast! Cover the corridor, J.B., and I'll try it."

The Armorer hefted his Heckler & Koch MP-7 SD-8 and put it onto semiautomatic. Ryan joined Jak, struggling to move the heavy green lever that operated the controls of the sec door.

It moved an inch or two, then they heard the ominous grinding of stripped gears. The door fell about seven inches, then stopped again.

"Once more," Ryan said through gritted teeth, putting everything into a last effort. The lever moved again, but with the doughy softness of a broken mechanism. Ryan stepped away from it. "Coupla bursts, J.B. Then follow us in."

"Not another jump, my dear fellow! I beg you, Ryan, to reconsider. I have the gravest doubts that I shall be able to—"

Doc was interrupted by two triple-round bursts from J.B.'s weapon, the sound effectively muffled by the integral silencer.

"Hasn't slowed them much. Figure if I had a burner-gren it'd keep them back."

Ryan led the others back through the faltering control room to the gateway. The cacophony of the advancing muties was much louder. Their naked skins rustled against one another in the press of bodies, their gobbling, bubbling speech rising into a menacing crescendo.

"Inside," Ryan snapped, pushing the chamber door open. Doc, Krysty and Jak filed in.

"They're coming for real," J.B. called, firing a double burst as he ran. At least one of the bullets ricocheted into a control panel, and two rows of lights went out.

"Come on. Move it, before you wreck the whole joint," Ryan urged.

The slight figure, fedora perched perilously on the back of his head, darted inside the arma-glass walls.

"Could we not hold them off, Ryan?" Doc called plaintively. "A third jump, so devilishly close to the others..."

"No choice," Ryan insisted as he jumped into the chamber and started to close the door.

The hinges were stiff and it moved slowly, giving the mutie in the lead just enough time to slither across the anteroom and throw its body toward the shrinking gap.

Ryan saw it coming, figuring its puny strength could do no harm. The ponderously heavy door slammed shut, triggering the jump mechanism in the defective gateway. And the troggie's arm was trapped in it.

The arm was almost severed at the wrist, and the slightly webbed fingers fluttered and tapped on the nearest metal disk. Blood, virtually colorless, flowed along the side wall.

"Clear the damned door!" Doc croaked as the vaporous gas began to fill the room and the metal plates in the floor and ceiling started to glow.

"It can't get in," Ryan said, slipping to his knees.

"Not the point. Blocks contacts so micros won't properly inter..." The old man's voice was fading away.

Ryan could feel his own mind already slipping from his control. He tried to crawl across the chamber to where the fingers danced, thinking he could still manage to free the severed arm and close the arma-glass door properly.

Someone was pushing him and he heard a single, piercing yelp. "Zorro," he whispered, though his lips had become numb and rubbery.

The lights were painfully bright and he had a sudden, agonizing ache across his temples. Sensation was draining from his extremities as he reached the mutie's hand and tried to move it.

But the mat-trans process had already gone too far. "Malfunction!"

Ryan couldn't decide if the voice came from Doc Tanner or if it was some doomsday warning from the gateway controls.

"Malfunction," he breathed.

Then the nightmares began.

CHAPTER FOUR

JAK LAUREN WANDERED through a green-leafed forest. Shafts of summer sunlight darted between the gently swaying branches, dappling the winding path ahead of him.

Every now and again the rich balsam scent of the overhanging pines filled his nostrils. Around him stretched the high, clean meadows, speckled with Indian paintbrush, like speckles of spilled blood. Delicate bear grass, tipped with abundant white lace, nodded along the edges of the trail. Purple asters, harebells and the tiny false Solomon's seal filled his vision.

Somewhere down to his right he caught glimpses of a large lake, crystal clear, with the faint tint of turquoise that whispered meltwater. And up the slope to the boy's left was the distant thunder of a high falls, tumbling over starry quartz into a spray-fringed pool.

The animal appeared from nowhere.

A massive silver-tip grizzly sow, with the characteristic hump of muscle across its shoulders, was weaving its head to and fro, and bloody spittle frothed from its muzzle.

An arrow thunked into the bole of a lodgepole pine at Jak's side, a small strip of white parchment tied around it with purple ribbon. Keeping a cautious eye on the bear, the boy unpeeled the paper and read the message.

Yellow cottage, quarter mile behind you. Turn left at lightning-hit live oak.

There was a distant crackle of thunder somewhere over the lake, and the wind was beginning to rise.

Constantly looking over his shoulder, Jak paced out a quarter mile. He gripped the bow in his right hand, an arrow notched and ready to loose. But the silver-tip had vanished.

For a moment he thought he glimpsed a couple of people, on a parallel path—a tall woman with startlingly red hair, and a man who wore a white bandage over his eyes.

There was the tree, its top splintered and torn by a lightning bolt. "Turn left," he muttered to himself.

The path grew wider, winding uphill, twisting and turning, with a cairn of white stones to mark each bend. Jak saw a fluttering scrap of yellowed paper held against one of the piles of rock by a piece of rusting iron.

Nearly home, Jak. Your mother and me are looking forward to welcoming you safe back. Not far to go, lad.

The bow was becoming cold and wet. He looked down at it and found the stout yew had turned into polished ice. The arrow was straw with a tip of smoldering red ash.

Ahead of him, something gray and scaled waddled across the path. It looked like a mutie alligator. The sun was gone, and dark clouds swooped over the stark mountaintops all around him. But he could see the cottage. The walls were painted golden yellow, and a lamp hung in the front window to guide the weary traveler home.

"Home," Jak said, and found that the word wouldn't fit properly inside his chilled lips.

He was less than one hundred paces from the trim little house. Behind him he could dimly hear the howling of a hunting pack of wolves. The bow was melting fast, running through his fingers and blazing like molten silver.

The cottage door opened and he could see a tall man, dressed in a green jerkin. "Come in, son. You're safe now, with us."

The door closed, and Jak found himself in a cheery room with a log fire crackling in the hearth. Copper pans winked from the shelves and a spread of food was laid out on a dazzling damask cloth—fresh-baked bread and crisp salad, with slices of smoked ham as thick as a man's finger.

Jak picked up one of the china bowls and saw that it held a mass of pulsating white maggots.

"Your mother's favorite, Jak. Made them special, she did. She'd be here herself, but she's dead and gone these fifteen years."

There was another burst of thunder that seemed to shake the whole building. The lights dimmed, and the fire died away. Jak suddenly began to feel very sick.

"You don't look too good, son. Mother's kept your room nice, waiting for you to come on back. Safe and secure, Jakky. Go and have a rest. Your own little bed in your own little room."

The nausea was growing like a bubble of rotten air, filling his stomach, rising through his chest and squeezing his lungs. It surrounded his heart and made it pound faster. The idea of lying down and sleeping seemed attractive.

"In there, son." His father pointed to a low door in the corner of the room. Jak noticed that the man's fingers were crooked, ending in thick, jagged nails that curved back on themselves.

The room was growing darker, and the sickness was surging into his throat. "Lie down," he whispered.

"Safe and secure, Jak. Insecure and unsafe, Jak. Which?"

The door opened without his touching it, and he stepped through.

"No," Jak whispered.

His feet slipped away, and he began to fall down a long, polished tunnel.

"No!"

Faster and faster he fell, and he tried to grab at the sides of the tunnel, his fingers blistering from the speed and heat of his fall.

"No!" Jak screamed.

Infinities below him he could make out a speck of silver-white light, rushing toward him at a dizzying speed.

"No!"

THE DESERT SANDS were red with blood.

John Barrymore Dix lay flat behind a low bullet pocked wall, pressed to the warm earth, waiting for the stickies to come at him again.

The sky was pale orange, scarred with the drifting remnants of a fearsome chem storm of scarlet and jagged silver. The air still tasted of ozone from the force and power of the tempest.

The rest of the war wag's crew were dead, butchered by the ceaseless attacks of the gibbering muties. They'd come in waves from the sun-baked arroyos, their suckered hands tearing and ripping at the bodies of the defenders. Bullets scarcely checked the stickies with their rubbery flesh. Lead went in and out, and left only a small hole and a trickle of what passed for blood. You had to shoot a stickie in the head and pulp its ferocious residual brain. J.B. knew he'd sent a dozen or more out on the last train to the coast, but there were hundreds more, waiting out there.

His friends lay around him.

The white-haired boy had most of his face missing, exposing the glistening pallor of bone. His satin-finish Magnum was by his side, its barrel clogged with blood and mud.

The woman had taken her own life, kissing the muzzle of the 9 mm Heckler & Koch pistol. Her bright blood was invisible against her matted crimson hair.

Maybe that was the best, cleanest way to buy the farm.

All J.B. could see of the old man was the cracked knee boots protruding from under a pile of mutie corpses. The silver swordstick, blade snapped jaggedly in two, lay nearby, the blade reflecting the fire of the nuke-ravaged sky.

A dead puppy, head missing, was flung against the bottom of the wall.

''Ryan?'' J.B. called, knowing that there wouldn't be an answer. Not this time. Not anymore.

He could feel bile, hot and sour, churning in his guts. The sun beat down on his head, despite the protection of his dented fedora. His eyes blurred, and he blinked to try to clear them.

''Come on, you bastards,'' he muttered, risking a look over the wall. Nothing. Just the purple sand dunes that stretched out toward the shimmering horizon.

J.B. knelt and reviewed his arsenal of weapons, laid neatly in front of him. He'd fieldstripped, oiled, polished, greased and loaded dozens of them. Each had a round snug under the cocked hammer. All he had to do was heft them and squeeze the cool, curved triggers.

He squinted, then rubbed at his eyes. There seemed to be some movement to his left, near a half-burned Joshua tree.

J.B. laid down his Colt Navy pistol and pressed his forehead with the tips of his fingers. His glasses were smeared and dusty, and he wondered whether he should try to clean them before the attack came. His headache was getting worse, and he realized that he was feeling sick, as if someone had kicked him hard in the balls.

He wondered which gun to use first. He looked in front of himself again and saw that there were literally hundreds of different blasters. Right by his boots was a stocky silenced Sterling Parabellum submachine gun. J.B. didn't recall having noticed that one before.

A pair of elegant rifles were propped against each other—a Ruger M-77 and a Steyr-Mannlicher, each with a polished walnut stock and a scope sight. Hunting guns.

J.B. couldn't remember where they'd come from. From some of the other dead, he supposed. But as he looked around, the Armorer realized that all the bodies had disappeared, both norms and muties. The land around him was full of blasters and empty of anything else.

The army of stickies was advancing slowly toward him, their bare feet shushing through the hot sand.

He couldn't make up his mind as to which blaster to use to defend himself. Something old, like the jumble of wheel lock and flintlock pistols? Or the long .50-caliber Sharps? Maybe its classic rainbow trajectory was what he needed to begin picking off the muties at long range.

If only his head didn't hurt so much! It was making it difficult for him to think straight.

J.B. closed his eyes and let his head sink forward onto his chest. He tried to steady his breathing, fearing he was going to start throwing up.

When he opened his eyes again the stickies were across the river, pouring up the steep valley toward the ruined church where he was hiding. The sky was darkening fast, and he wondered whether night would fall quickly enough to help him.

''Time to start throwing some lead,'' he said to himself.

He picked up the nearest blaster from the polished steel racks in front of him. It was a Parker-Hale M-94, equipped with a folding bipod and a Smith & Wesson Startron 800 passive vision night sight. The Armorer worked the bolt and steadied the rifle on the sill of a broken stained-glass window. The sight brought the nearest stickie almost within touching distance. J.B. gently squeezed the trigger.

And heard the dry click of a misfire.

He dropped the blaster and snatched up the Nambu, hearing the same hollow, empty sound.

The French rifle, the same result.

A Walther PPK, plated with a thin layer of pure gold. Misfire.

J.B. dropped the last of the useless, malfunctioning weapons and turned to face the doorway of the church. The headless remains of a crucified man hung above the lintel, one leg missing. The stickies came silently walking through the dark entrance. Creepily they weren't hurrying, and some of them seemed to be smiling.

They reached out toward the helpless man with their spread, suckered hands, ready to draw the skin from the flesh, the eyes from the sockets, the flesh from the bones.

The life from the body.

The churning pain in J.B.'s head was close to unbearable. It was like having the needle tip of a scalpel drawn slowly around the inside of the skull, slicing tiny wafers of tissue from the brain.

The Trader stood near the shattered remnants of the altar, watching as the muties surrounded J.B. for their butchering.

"Help me," J.B. croaked, licking his dry lips.

The suckered hands were everywhere, bringing a sucking blackness.

"Help me?" J. B. Dix looked toward the gaunt, remote figure of the Trader.

"No."

DR. THEOPHILUS TANNER beamed as the puppy came bounding up the dusty street toward him, its tail wagging furiously. A speeding brougham bowled by, driven by a liveried negro, narrowly missing the eager animal. Doc glimpsed a beautiful, cold-faced woman, sitting back on the maroon velvet cushions, ignoring the common people.

The dog went to him, and he stooped to pat it. "Friendly little chap, isn't he, Emily?"

"He is, my dearest," Doc's pretty young wife replied.

The dog began to tremble.

Emily Tanner backed away from it, lifting the hem of her skirt. She turned a worried face to her handsome young husband. "What's wrong, dear?"

The dog rolled on its side, legs jerking as if it were trying to run on the air. Its eyes were open wide, and it made an alarmed, whining noise.

"I guess it's hungry," Doc replied. "Best leave the animal, or someone could come along and set it ablaze. Happens all the time."

There was a moment of sickening blackness.

When it cleared away, Doc was strolling down Fifth Avenue with Emily on his arm. She was pushing a wicker perambulator that held baby Rachel. Emily was heavily pregnant. It was a beautiful summer morning, and the street bustled with horse-drawn carriages and cabs. A hansom had lost a wheel on the corner of Thirty-Second, and a sweating, swearing Irish policeman was struggling to clear the jammed traffic.

Doc took out a kerchief with a swallow's-eye design and dabbed at his brow. "By the three... something. Hot."

"When do we leave for Omaha, my prince among men?" Emily asked.

"Dog has too many heads, my dear. Cerberus by name and Totality by nature."

She smiled up at him, infinitely gentle. "Don't leave me, Theo."

"Of course not. Never and a day. Safe here, aren't we, Ryan?"

The one-eyed man was walking on the far side of the pram. He wore a patch over his left eye, but the other socket welled with black blood.

"Today's not safe, Doc," he replied. "Tomorrow's worse. Only safe place is yesterday."

The picture of nineteenth-century New York trembled and Doc fell to his knees, holding his head and rocking back and forth. The pain was appalling, swirling around inside his mind. Dark shadows sucked at all of his memories.

"Yesterday's safe," he muttered.

Emily, the baby, the pram...they'd all vanished. There was a gleaming horse tram, with walls of turquoise arma-glass. People were inside it, sitting upright and facing the front: a woman holding a little baby near the rear; a man in a hat and a young boy with stark white hair, carrying a puppy in his arms; a tall woman whose hair blazed like a New Mexico sunset. All were moving away from him.

"Come back to yesterday," Doc shouted, starting to run toward them.

But a swordstick of demonic agony tore into his head and he fell down, blood coursing from his nose. The blood ran over the sidewalk, which was built from patterned tiles that made up a star-spangled banner.

A mop-headed youth holding a battered guitar patted him on the shoulder. "Something's happening and you don't know about it. I'll let you be in my past if you'll let me be in yours."

It seemed like a good offer to Doc, but by the time he'd struggled to his knees the boy had vanished.

"Someone dug the dog a tomb," Doc said, nearly weeping from the sickness and his own weakness.

Emily kissed him on the cheek. "Stay here with me forever, my love."

"Yes," he whispered as the blackness enveloped him.

KRYSTY WROTH COULD usually control what happened to her mind when she was sleeping, or when she was making a mat-trans jump. The training that she'd been given by her mother, Sonja, back in her home ville of Harmony, meant that she possessed a variety of arcane skills. But even her mind was torn into the ether by the third, faulty jump.

She knew that the lover in her dream was Cort Strasser, knew him for one of the most evil beings to blight the Deathlands. Jordan Teague had been Baron of Mocsin, a notorious frontier pesthole, with fester-

ing alleys, gaudies and bars. To control somewhere
like Mocsin meant "no more Mr. Nice Guy." But
Teague couldn't have done it alone. He needed a sec
boss who would be ten times more vicious and cruel.

Cort Strasser.

Krysty lay back in the soft, warm bed and moaned
as he touched her. His long, strong fingers sought out
the hidden places of her body, making her writhe with
an overwhelming sensual delight.

She clasped the tall, gaunt figure to her, reveling in
the lean tension beneath the corded muscles. He rolled
above her, spreading her thighs with a brutal jab of his
knee. One hand gripped her wrists and held them ef-
fortlessly still above her head. Sweat beaded the near-
bald head. Thin eyes stared deep into her face, thin lips
peeled off broken teeth.

"Ryan did that," she whispered. "Threw a blaster
into your mouth."

For a moment Strasser hesitated, poised above her.
His thick, powerful erection shrank between his
thighs, and he lifted a clubbed fist threateningly.

"Keep your mouth shut, redhead slut," he hissed.
"I'll tell you when to open it, and I'll tell you what to
do with it. Understand?"

Krysty nodded. "And you'll give me a son?"

"If you're good to me, bitch. If you're not, it'll be
one of my toys to remind you of how to obey your
master."

A log fire was dying in the open hearth. A small
brindled puppy was sleeping in front of it, head on its

paws. And on the table by the fire was a selection of Cort Strasser's toys. A whip with a short, stubby handle was studded with nails. The thongs were plaited wire, and the tips were splinters of jagged glass. Next to it was a longer whip, with a single, cutting lash. There were knives on the table, as well as a number of sexual aids—phalluses of differing sizes and shapes, but all with some unexpected and cruel refinement.

"You ready, whore?"

Strasser's narrow mustache was glistening with perspiration, and he licked his lips. By lifting her head a little Krysty could see that he was once again fully erect.

"This isn't right."

He laughed, his breath foul in her face. "Not right? You triple-stupe slag! Don't tell me what's right."

"Gaia, help me!"

Krysty's head was hurting, and the weight of the sec boss on her stomach was making her feel sick. But she felt powerless against the man's strength.

"Gaia don't do shit, lady," he cackled, bracing himself between her thighs.

"Let her go, Strasser."

Ryan stood in the doorway, a silvery automatic pistol in his right hand. Doc and J.B. were with him, and in the corridor behind, Krysty glimpsed the sparkle of snowy hair.

"Go fuck yourself, Cawdor," the sec boss snarled, unmoving.

"Sure thing," Ryan replied, turning on his heel.

"Ryan!" Krysty called.

"What?"

"Wait!"

"Going, lover. Got to keep moving. Mebbe stop one day."

"Let the back-shooting bastard go," Strasser urged, pressing the tip of his engorged maleness against her body.

"Ryan, I want you."

"Cort there'll give you what you want, lover," Ryan said wearily. "Child, family, place to settle and live."

The headache was electrifyingly painful, throbbing to the beat of an unseen drum. Krysty struggled against Cort Strasser, but her normal power had gone.

"Only with you, lover," she yelled.

But she and Strasser were alone on a hillside, above a shallow valley. Beneath them she could see the polluted waters of a vast rancid lake. The sec boss still held her beneath him, about to complete the rape.

"Gaia, help me."

"I'll help you with this." He laughed, making Krysty sure she would vomit at any second.

A little dog, barking its brave defiance, hurled itself at Strasser, distracting him for another, blessed moment.

The dog received abrupt punishment from the murderous man. He reached out with his free hand and caught the pup around the throat, squeezed once and dropped the twitching little body to the warm earth.

"Killer!" she spit.

"Yeah, you believe it."

"You'll die."

He stroked Krysty's long red hair with his free hand and smiled with a shocking gentleness. "Yeah. We all will."

"I can't stand it."

Cort Strasser's face shimmered like a reflection in a wind-tainted pool. The grip on her arms weakened, and Krysty tried again to pull away from him. Her eyes felt as if someone were trying to push them from their sockets with white-heated pistons.

"Gonna give you what you want, slut. Give you what all women want."

He thrust then, and she screamed at the terrible ripping, rending pain in her loins that tore through her body and made her black out.

"Noooo!"

KEEPING A HOLD on his sanity was one of Ryan Cawdor's toughest struggles.

Three jumps, back to back to back, the last from a defective gateway, were enough to scramble anyone's brain. He fought as hard as he knew how to hold the sweeping tide of blackness at bay. But it rose and rose about him, until even his mental and physical powers were drained.

He was in an abandoned ocher quarry, endless ravines and canyons of multicolored clays that ranged from the palest gray-white to the deepest, richest vermilion. Ragged trees lined the tops of the sheer cliffs, and the remnants of rotting wooden ladders were pinned to the walls.

The air was heavy and sulfurous, weighing down on Ryan's head and shoulders. His steel-toed combat boots slithered in the orange clay, making it hard to progress in any direction. And all directions looked the same. His coat was sodden with his sweat, and he wasn't carrying any kind of weapon.

Ryan felt there were other people somewhere in this Technicolor wilderness, but he couldn't quite see or hear them. He saw the marks of feet, sometimes fresh with moisture still seeping into them, and twice he thought he heard a voice behind the next twisting turn. But when he rounded the blind corner nobody was there.

As he eased the patch from over his left eye, he was assaulted by a sudden memory of his murderous brother, Harvey. The livid scar etched across his right cheek flared at the thought.

There was a doorway in the bright wall of stone ahead of him and a barred gate with a huge, brooding figure standing in front of it—an armored man, holding a strange weapon of polished brass with a gaping muzzle. It was like no blaster that Ryan Cawdor had ever seen, and he knew instinctively that it possessed a dreadful megacull capability. Nothing he could do would enable him to beat this sinister sec guard.

Yet the gateway presented him with his only chance of escaping from the ocher maze.

"What's your sec clearance, outlander?" the sentry asked in a booming voice.

"B 100."

"Name?"

"Cawdor. Ryan Cawdor."

The giant consulted a piece of white parchment in his mailed fist. "Cawdor. Cawdor. Cawdor. Did you say Cawdor?"

"Yeah."

"Did you say Richard Cawdor?"

"No, Ryan."

"You said Richard!"

"No."

The weird weapon lifted toward the one-eyed man, its barrel reflecting the pink of the sky. "Ryan Cawdor, are you saying?"

"Yeah, and you'd better not point that blaster at me, unless you aim to use it."

The guard roared a rippling belly laugh. "Well, now. I call that mighty big talk for a one-eyed thin man like you, Ryan Cawdor."

Ryan winced at the noise, finding it made his splitting headache even worse.

"You going to let me through, or do I chill you where you stand?"

"No need, outlander. My list has your name on it. This door is only for you. And now I'm going to open it."

THE CORRIDOR HAD walls of pale gray, a floor of black tiles and a ceiling of peeling yellow paint. It stretched away ahead of Ryan, as far as he could see.

Above him he could hear the noise of countless feet, marching in a stumbling dissonant rhythm, the sound muffled by the ceiling. On either side of the passage were rows of identical doors, each with a tiny peephole.

Ryan paused and looked in the first one, then the second and the third, moving to the other side and finding that each peephole revealed exactly the same thing—a square concrete cell, with a bunk bed and an enamel chamber pot. The rooms were seven feet across and had a barred window of opaque arma-glass six inches wide.

And in each room stood a naked person—alternately male and female—with their backs toward the doors. Their hands were manacled behind them, and bags of rough hessian covered their heads, knotted at the sides with purple cord.

None moved or made any sound, nor was there a sign of anyone who might have been a guard.

Ryan turned away and walked farther along, finding another corridor that opened to his left. It was a blind alley with only five doors, and these doors, like the others, had peepholes.

In the first cell stood an old man, his head hidden under a sacking hood. On the bunk lay a folded kerchief, bearing a swallow's-eye design.

The next cell held a man close to middle-age, but lean and muscular. On the bunk was a pair of rimless spectacles.

A teenager stood motionless in the third, the hood revealing a trickle of snow-white hair beneath it. On his bunk was a dish that held a mess of pallid creatures that writhed and twisted about one another.

In the second last Ryan saw a tall athletic woman, whose fiery hair had escaped beneath the hessian mask. On her bunk was a riding crop with a handle of carved ivory.

There was nobody in the last cell, but on the narrow bed lay the corpse of a small puppy. From the angle of its head, Ryan could see that its neck had been broken.

THE MAN WHO SAT across the table from Ryan was aged beyond measuring: his scant hair was without color and clung to the shrunken skull like moss to a boulder; his eyes were veiled and blind, lost beneath layers of pale wrinkled skin; the mouth was toothless, lipless, and seemed possessed of a strange ticking life of its own.

Spittle dripped ceaselessly, running over the chin and down the scrawny neck, which was wattled like an ancient turkey. He was dressed in a collarless shirt that was tucked into baggy pants, and he smelled of urine and last week's stew, in roughly equal proportions.

"You passed the gate built only for you. You passed without the word. And now you will witness the last and greatest mystery of them all."

"No." Ryan swallowed hard to contain the vomit that he could taste rising from his churning stomach.

"Indeed, yes, Ryan Cawdor, late of the ville of Front Royal. I will reveal to you what all men desire and all men fear."

"What?"

"The manner of your passing."

Ryan tried to shake his head, but the pressure on his brain was too severe. "Don't fucking want it, old man."

The tabletop between them was made of cold dark glass. As Ryan leaned forward to rest his head on his hands, it seemed that he could see flickerings of light and fire within the somber shadows. Once he thought he glimpsed the face of Krysty Wroth, twisted like that of a tormented soul, with a grinning, thin-lipped skull at her shoulder.

"No man wishes it, but you are valued above all men, Ryan Cawdor. And this shall be your suitable reward."

"Why?"

For some reason the question amused the smirking dotard and he giggled, his voice high-pitched like a little girl's. "Because you are the meanest bastard that ever walked through the valley of Deathlands. That's why."

"I have never taken pleasure in killing." Even as he spoke, Ryan knew in his heart that it was a lie. He'd killed men who deserved to die, and women. And to leave the earth a little cleaner was always a good thing.

"That don't signify doodleysquat here, Ryan Cawdor. Now, look into the middle of this here table and you'll see how you get chilled, when you get chilled and where you get chilled."

Ryan looked away, trying to make out what kind of room they were in. All he could see were folds of heavy material, draped in the corners. It could have been a tent, but it felt colder and the echoes didn't sound right.

"Don't you want to know?"

"No. Who are you?"

"I'm *now*. I want to show you *soon*. Want to know if you marry? Have kids? I can show you all that. If it's there. But you have to see the end as well as the beginning. Might not be so bad."

"No."

"Could be you go in your sleep on your 120th birthday, your kin all around your bedside, weeping."

"Could be it's in the gutter of some pesthole, looking up at the sky while the rain bounces off my eyes."

The old man laughed again. "Look into the table, Ryan Cawdor, and find out."

Unable to resist, the pain blinding him, Ryan leaned forward over the darkness.

And watched.

CHAPTER FIVE

THE NOISE FADED AWAY.

The metal plates set into the floor and ceiling of the chamber gradually ceased glowing and became cold to the touch. The vague mist that had flooded the red-walled arma-glass room dissipated.

In the control room, filters and thermostats kept the temperature even. The comp-wheels spun, powered by the eternally vigilant nuke-generators.

All things were as they should be.

The triple jump had gone bitterly hard for all of the companions, but one by one they began to claw their way back from the swamping nightmares that had enveloped them.

Ryan came out of it first. He blinked into consciousness, feeling as though he'd been fighting for hours, hundreds of feet deep in water. He was soaked with perspiration, and a jackhammer thumped ceaselessly behind his temples. His fingers crabbed across his face, and he felt the stickiness of drying blood over his chin. Wisely he made no effort to sit up. He sensed it would be impossible. The best he could hope for was to open his eye and see how things went with his four friends and the little dog.

"Fireblast," he whispered through dry, cracked lips. Ryan had seen enough of death to know that Zorro had booked himself a ticket up the chimney. It wouldn't help Doc Tanner's always tenuous hold on reality.

The others all looked as if death had been visiting with them.

Krysty was moving, hands folded between her thighs, head shaking as though she were refusing an unwanted invitation. Ryan had never seen her red hair so tightly and defensively coiled about her head. Her angular face was gray with the pain of the most recent jump.

Jak was curled into a ball, his hair tangled and stained with specks of vomit. Nothing could be seen of the boy's face, though Ryan thought he glimpsed the red coals of Jak's eyes behind the veil.

J.B. lay flat on his back, as stiff as an oaken plank, hands at his side. He, too, had been bleeding from nostrils and mouth.

Doc jerked awake as Ryan watched him. The old man looked appalling. His face and clothes were smeared with a mixture of blood and sickness, and his deep-set eyes didn't seem to focus. He stared wildly ahead of him with a frightening lack of comprehension.

"Doc," Ryan called, but there wasn't the least sign of recognition.

"I've felt worse," Krysty whispered, her voice cracking.

"Yeah?"

"Just can't recall when."

"Bad jump that. I really don't think I'd make it through another one."

She nodded, and cautiously pulled herself into a sitting position, against the dull red walls of the chamber. "I had some triple-bad dreams this time, lover. Real dark side."

"Same with me."

"What'd you see?" She closed her eyes and drew in a long shuddering breath. "I saw things I don't ever want to see again."

Ryan considered a long time before he answered her. "Old man showed me . . . showed me pictures of what he said was. . . No, I can't even tell you, lover. Sorry."

Krysty nodded slowly. "I understand."

There was a groan as J.B. struggled to reenter the land of the living. He rolled over on his side, boots scrabbling on the floor, while he fought himself into a huddled crouch. "That was about as bad as I want it, Ryan," he muttered.

"I won't argue with you. Least we made it to someplace else."

"The walls are a different color, and it feels a whole lot hotter than last time," Krysty remarked. "Hey, lover. I don't like the look of Doc."

"He's come around," J.B. commented as he rolled over so that he sat next to the unconscious Jak Lauren.

"His eyes are open, but he's not seeing anything. Give the kid a shake, J.B., and get him upright. He's puked a lot. Could choke."

The Armorer pushed at Jak's shoulder, making him stir. The albino tried to sit up and flopped sideways, coughing and spluttering. Blood and half-digested food spilled from his white lips over his camouflage jacket. J.B. held him firmly, patting him on the back. The boy's eyes eased open, unfocused, like a newborn rabbit's.

"Been sick, Pa. Sorry. Tell Ma... where the fuck are... What?"

"Bad jump for us all, Jak," J.B. said gently. "Looks like we mostly made it. But the dog died, and Doc's not flea-jumping well."

"No jumps, Ryan," the boy gasped. "Or make 'em on ownsome."

Ryan turned his attention back to Doc. The lined face seemed somehow younger, as if most of the worry lines had been smoothed away during the horrendous jump. The old man pulled himself to his knees, smoothing his frock coat with gnarled fingers. His breathing seemed surprisingly slow and steady.

"Doc?" Krysty asked.

His eyes stared straight ahead, and there was no visible sign that anyone was home inside the leonine skull.

"Doc? I know you can hear me. Tell us how you feel."

Ryan had a little more success. At least Doc turned slowly in his direction.

"He's in shock, lover," Krysty said quietly. "Mebbe best to leave him awhile."

"Tomorrow's so devilish dangerous," Doc said, his voice as rich and deep as ever. But the eyes still didn't budge from gazing at some invisible point in a limitless distance.

"Want sick," Jak muttered, easing himself away from J.B. He retched again, managing only to bring up a few threads of scarlet blood.

"Shall we open the door?" J.B. suggested. But Ryan shook his head.

"Give it awhile. I reckon all of us can do with a rest for a few minutes.

RYAN TOUCHED the red walls, feeling the warmth that seeped through the heavy arma-glass. He wondered where in Deathlands they'd ended their jump, or if, in fact, they were in Deathlands at all.

After their last adventure there was no longer the certainty that all of the gateways were within what had once been the continental United States. Perhaps the one in Russia had been unique. But they'd already seen some evidence, admittedly circumstantial, that there might even have been a gateway on one of the space stations that had circled the Earth before darkday and the end of civilization.

It was a thought that nagged at Ryan Cawdor, intriguing him with the possibilities, as did the thought of finding other cryonic centers and maybe, just maybe, managing to thaw out more freezies.

"Guess it's time we made a move," he announced. "Everyone ready?"

They all nodded or muttered their agreement. All except Doc Tanner.

"C'mon, Doc."

The old man sat still, as though he hadn't heard Ryan's voice. Krysty knelt at his side and touched his arm. "Doc?"

He looked up then, squinting as if he couldn't quite focus on her face. "What is it? Who are... Is that you, Emily, my dear?"

"No, it's Krysty, Doc. It's time we were moving on out of here."

"Why?"

"Get some food and drink." She winced as she stood up straight. "And a wash if we're lucky. Time's wasting, Doc."

"And let it waste, we are no longer... You know that our yesterdays are ever present. Tomorrow is another now. We cannot say when life will end, and no man can say how." He smiled and nodded to himself.

"Nice verse, Doc," J.B. said. "Won't load no mags for us."

"Nor butter any parsnips, will it, my dear brother Cyril?"

"Cyril! Who the—"

"His mind's gotten locked way back," Ryan said. "He was like this when we first met him. Back in

Mocsin. Best we can hope is that it was the third jump. Pushed him too hard. Should recover.''

''But we have to go,'' J.B. pressed, the edge to his voice showing his growing irritation. J.B.'s philosophy of life was that a man didn't show weakness, nor let down friends.

In the Deathlands that often came down to the same thing.

''Get up, Doc,'' Krysty said, helping him as he got unwillingly to his feet.

''Very well, Emily. I shall be guided by you in this. Are we to take a promenade?''

''Sure. All of us together.'' She nodded to Ryan. ''I think we're ready as we'll ever be, lover.''

Ryan glanced around, motioning for Jak to move over and help Doc on the other side. Then he reached for the handle on the chamber door and turned it.

CHAPTER SIX

THE HEAT outside the chamber was even more striking and oppressive.

"Feels like home," Jak said. "Good Louisiana warm and wet."

"Hot as the hobs of Hades." Krysty sighed. "Don't rightly know what that means, but Uncle Tyas Mc-Cann used to say it in summer back in Harmony."

Ryan led them into the anteroom that they'd come to expect. Most of them had been evacuated and bare, showing signs that there'd been warning in some redoubts of the sudden conflict of 2001.

But this particular room looked as though it had been abandoned about ten minutes ago. The small square table held four hands of cards, and a shelf contained some mugs and a tattered book. There were posters on the walls, faded and torn, revealing their age.

The friends paused and looked around. Only Doc showed no interest, head drooping on his breast, eyes dull. It looked as though he'd have slumped like a discarded puppet if Jak and Krysty hadn't been supporting him.

Ryan always felt a buzz of excitement at a moment like this. To find some sort of time capsule, undisturbed for a century, meant a thrill of glimpsing the lost past through this peephole.

He looked first at the posters. One showed a Russian hammer and sickle, both dripping gobbets of blood, descending toward the skyscrapers of an American city. A young man stood legs apart, fists raised, ready to try to combat and deflect them. The caption beneath the picture was vaguely familiar to Ryan, who'd seen it before:

"Ask not what your country can do for you—ask what you can do for your country."

Two of the other posters were what he knew used to be called pinups. One depicted a tall blonde, sitting astride a huge black and chrome two-wheel wag. She wore a pair of thigh-length boots in dark green leather. Other than the boots she wore only a bright smile. On the other wall was a life-size poster of a heavily muscled, bronzed man, wearing a smile similar to the woman's. But he wasn't even wearing boots. The caption simply said: Stud Study X.

Doc was near collapse, and Krysty helped him to sit down at the table, where he immediately laid his head on his folded arms.

Ryan looked at the table. On one corner was a pile of small change that looked as if it had gotten rained on—the metal had sprouted a mold. "They were playing poker when the sirens sounded. Or the bells.

Or whatever it was that told them dark night was on
its way."

Jak picked up one of the hands of cards. "Two
pairs. Queens an' fours."

Krysty smiled. "This hand won't beat you, Jak."
She turned the cards over. "Pair of threes. Like I
always say. There's some you lose, and there's some
you draw."

"I win," J.B. said, flipping over the third hand of
cards. Three sixes. "Beat that, Ryan. If you can."

One by one Ryan picked up the moist, rotting playing cards and turned them over. "Eight of clubs, ace
of spades, eight of spades, ace of hearts."

"Still not good enough," the Armorer told him,
wiping moisture from his glasses. "Come on, Ryan.
Turn it and see what you got."

"I reckon it'll be good enough to beat you. Want a
bet on it?"

"With what? Last time I had a fistful of jack
was...was so long ago I can't even remember."

"Bet you first go at the next hot water we find,"
Ryan suggested. "How's that?"

"You got it. Turn the card."

The rectangle of pasteboard was clammy to the
touch. "Ace of clubs. A full house. Aces on eights. I
win, J.B., I win."

"Dead man's hand," Doc Tanner announced in a
frail, uncertain voice.

"How's that?" Krysty asked.

"Same hand Bill Hickok was holding when he was gunned down from behind. I saw him once. Out in Deadwood. I was about seven years of age. Didn't look like a hero to me. Blind as a bat, though bats see fine in the night. Dark glasses. Held aces on eights when he was shot down. Mount Moriah cemetery, if I recall it right."

The voice faded away into stillness. Ryan sat down opposite the old man and tried to catch his eye. "Doc, you feeling better?"

"Dead man, Emily, my dear. Only alive in the dear days of the past."

"Doc?"

This time there was no reply.

At a word from Ryan, Jak slipped back into the chamber and removed the corpse of little Zorro, tucking it out of sight behind a corner cupboard in the anteroom. It seemed best to do what could be done to ease Doc's mind. His seeing the puppy dead wasn't going to be a help—though Ryan was concerned that the body would stink and rot too fast in the humidity and heat.

Krysty and J.B. helped the old man to his feet again, receiving a puzzled smile for their efforts. They led him into the control room.

"Don't know how all this still works," J.B. stated, shaking his head. "Must be damned well sealed to keep dry."

Doc was propped up at a desk, where he immediately fell deeply asleep. The others wandered around the large room, past the display boards, gauges and dials, the dancing arrows and whirling comp-wheels. The thousands of lights—green, amber, red and blue—and coded displays of digital activity suggested to Ryan that this might also be the control room for the entire redoubt, and linked to the deep-buried eternal nuke-power source.

The one-eyed man ran a finger along the top of one of the master consoles, wrinkling his forehead and sighing as he looked at the smear of green lichen on his skin. As the Armorer had said, it was astounding that everything seemed to be working as well as it was.

"Dump all the coats here," he said.

"From the icebox into the frying pan," Krysty commented as she dropped her fur coat.

After some consideration, Ryan shrugged off his beloved fur-collared coat and discarded the silk scarf with its weighted ends, which left him in a brown shirt and gray pants. J.B. was dressed identically. Krysty had on her brown overalls and chisel-toe Western boots. Jak wore gray pants and his ragged vest, made from different-colored strips of canvas and leather. Fragments of razored steel had been sewn into it.

Doc kept on his frock coat and knee breeches.

All of them retained their assorted blasters and steels.

The main doors that would open into the rest of the military complex operated on the same code as all the others. But this time they worked with an impressive silent efficiency, the green lever producing the faintest hiss of pneumatic power as the hugely thick door slid upward.

Leaving Doc slumped in his chair, the others ringed the entrance, blasters cocked and ready. Though it had been warm enough before, the wave of air that battered them through the open doorway was positively tropical in its heat and humidity.

"Wow! Fucking triple-hotter'n home." Jak whistled.

"Where do you think we are, lover?" Krysty asked. "Inside a volcano that's ready to blow?"

"How about Hawaii?" J.B. suggested, tasting the air like a questing lizard. "Could have jumped the Pacific?"

Ryan shook his head. "Let's move real careful, people. We can find out where we are, once we get out into the open."

The air felt slippery, instantly bathing all of them in sweat. Krysty heard a thin, high-pitched buzzing, and slapped quickly at her arm. "Gaia! That little bastard bit sharp." She showed the others the smear of blood, just above the wrist, and the pulped corpse of an iridescent insect. It was more than an inch long, with wings of veiled lace.

"Better get Doc out and close the sec doors again," Ryan said. "Don't want to open it up to any mutie creature out here. Jak, help Doc. J.B., throw the lock."

The sec door slid softly into place, making the gateway section of the complex secure against intruders. Of any sort.

The corridor was much like those they'd encountered in other redoubts. The arched ceiling, with concealed lighting, was twelve feet high and about fifteen feet wide. As they began to follow a slight rise, their boots slithered through the green mold that coated floor, walls and ceiling.

There were no side passages and no entrances to the main corridor. Twice they walked beneath sec cameras. At one time the video equipment would have been in motion, constantly swinging up and down and from left to right. Now the cameras seemed locked in place, immovable. Ryan's guess was that the green moss had built up on the mountings over the years and had clogged their mechanism.

Doc had been leaning heavily on Jak's arm, his feet dragging, slowing their progress. But he suddenly shrugged off the boy's help with an imperious gesture of dismissal. "I have no need of your aid, my good man! If I had a few copper coins I would give them to you in order to rid myself of your importuning. Are there no workhouses for the poor?"

"An' fuck you too, Doc," the albino spit.

"Jak," Ryan cautioned.

"What?"

"His mind's been pushed sideways by that last jump. He doesn't know what he's saying. Just keep a careful eye on him."

"Yeah, yeah. Sure."

The air felt hotter, and the slime around their feet grew thicker and wetter. The corridor dipped, and the companions found themselves wading in several inches of tepid water.

Something wriggled and splashed just ahead of J.B., making him stop and probe the dimness with the barrel of his Heckler & Koch. But the movement ceased.

Several times they heard the humming of insects, but the attack on Krysty wasn't repeated.

They traveled another few hundred yards without encountering side passages or doorways. Ryan wanted to try to get into the main part of the redoubt, so that they could scavenge for food and drink, maybe top up on ammo. And it would be so good to have a long hot wash.

Over the years Ryan had seen quite a few old vids and read books and mags from the predark times. It constantly amused and amazed him how often people seemed to bathe, and wash their hair. Women in some of the vids seemed to do nothing but wash their hair and then strip off to shower or bathe. Often a preliminary for lovemaking, Ryan had noticed.

Generally the only place in Deathlands to be sure of a hot bath was in a gaudy house with a whore to scrub at you with a cake of lye soap. But the nature of the business meant that you might be the thirtieth person using the same scummy water.

"These caves are becoming tedious, Emily," Doc said loudly. "I shall endeavor to obtain egress for us as soon as I possibly can."

"He might be part-stupe at the moment," Krysty said, grinning, "but I reckon I wouldn't mind getting out of here. Another half hour and I'll be growing mold on the inside of my eyes."

Jak was in the lead and he stopped suddenly, holding up a hand.

"What is it?"

"Think see lighter ahead. But...hear weird noise."

Krysty half closed her eyes, concentrating on listening. She shook her head for a moment, then, her whole body stiffening, turned to Ryan.

"Insects."

"What? Like these little bastards around us?"

Jak answered. "No. Lots!"

"He's right, lover. Lots. Sounds to me like the largest swarm of something coming our way. Sounds like the biggest bees ever spawned."

"Bees?" Doc asked with a note of bland curiosity in his voice. "Does this mean there will be honey for tea?"

Everyone ignored him.

The moss-lined walls of the corridor seemed to close in on them, as if trying to suck them into a dark maw. In the silence, Ryan could finally hear the noise, which was a deep and insistent hum with a high overtone of urgency to it. The corridor began to vibrate, and Ryan could even feel the hum deep in marrow of his bones.

There was a prickling of the short hairs at his nape that was the closest he'd ever come to feeling fear.

"Killer bees," J.B. said flatly. "Seen them before. Remember that ville down on the Gulf, Ryan, five years back?"

Ryan remembered the frightening silence and the bloated corpses, bodies covered with a mass of lethal stings. Men, women, children and animals—all dead, victims of predators less than an inch long. Ryan recalled once seeing an old mag story about the way the bees had been bred someplace in South America and had come raiding north.

"What do we do?" Krysty asked. "They'll hit us way before we get back to the mat-trans."

Ryan nodded. "Back's no good. Can't get over or around. Only chance is a door ahead somewhere. J.B. and Jak, take Doc. Carry him if you have to."

He led the way at a fast trot, his rifle looped over his shoulder. One thing was sure—that a blaster wouldn't be much help against millions of murderous insects.

The humming grew louder.

Doc had virtually collapsed, hanging between Jak and the Armorer, the toes of his boots furrowing through the clogging lichen.

"There," Krysty panted at his shoulder, pointing to the right-hand side of the corridor. Even in the dim light Ryan could make out the rectangular shape of a doorway, with a comp-control panel recessed in the concrete halfway up.

The humming rose in pitch, as though the swarm could scent intruders in their warm, green world.

"It's number-coded," Krysty stated flatly.

It was also hopelessly blocked with the intruding fingers of feathery moss.

J.B. and Jak arrived at the doorway, hauling Doc Tanner between them. Both looked at the sec lock, neither said a word. The noise of the insects was almost deafening. The corridor ran straight ahead for a couple of hundred yards before it forked left. Ryan stared into the shadows, suddenly realizing that the advance flight of the swarm was in sight. A shimmering blur of vicious movement raced toward them, heartbeats away.

CHAPTER SEVEN

"IN CASE OF EMERGENCY, break glass."

Against the triumphant screeching of the insects, Doc Tanner's voice was barely audible. Though his head was still sunk on his chest, his eyes were glinting brightly in the gloom.

"Emergency override," Ryan shouted. "Fireblast! Of course."

He smashed the glass over the buttons of the comp-lock, ignoring the cuts to his fingers. Over the top of the numbers and letters was a single red switch. Dimly from behind the door they could all hear the sirens blasting out the warning that the manual override had been triggered.

Ryan flicked the switch, enduring the half second of agonized doubt as microcircuits that had been barren for a hundred years finally clicked into startled life. The bolts rattled back, and the door began to open.

Krysty slipped through the gap first, turning to help pull Doc into safety. Jak and J.B. followed immediately. Ryan was last through, throwing his weight with the others to close the door behind them. Doc was dropped to the floor as the other four all heaved to narrow the gap.

The humming was overwhelming.

"Throw the locking levers, Jak!' Ryan gritted as they fought against the heavy door.

The gap was down to twelve inches, to eight and then to four.

The first, fastest bees hit the gap when it was a shrinking two inches, but their attack was so ferocious that dozens of them squeezed through before the door crunched shut.

"Black dust!" J.B. cursed, taking off his beloved fedora and swatting at the bees.

The insects were longer and slimmer than the bumbling honeybees that Ryan knew well from various parts of Deathlands. These were more like aerial torpedoes, with scaled bodies of turquoise and silver, narrow wings that beat with dazzling speed and stings like hooked barbs, their tips glistening with a highly toxic venom.

Jak slammed the bolts on the door. Though Ryan knew it had to be imagination, he actually thought he could hear the millions of ferocious projectiles pounding on the other side of the arma-steel barrier.

A jagged burst of pain struck Ryan on the back of the neck, just above his collar. He slapped at it, feeling a fluttering body pulped under his hand. Another bee stung him on that same hand, making him curse and spin around. He waved his fists and tried to club them away.

Each of the companions was under attack by at least ten of the killer bees. Unlike some other insects, these bees didn't lose their lives when they used their stings.

Ryan didn't have time to take in his surroundings; he simply realized that they were in a bare entrance hall with other doors opening off it. The siren continued to blare, but seemed to be running down, the tone gradually growing deeper.

Krysty had a livid swelling just below her left eye and another at the corner of her mouth. J.B. was best off, his hat proving a lethal weapon against the mutie insects. Ryan had five separate stings before the bees were finally all killed and crushed to the floor. Doc sat against a wall, sunk once more into his catatonic state, stings disfiguring his hands. Jak had been stung only once, but it was on the inside of his nose, causing him excruciating pain.

"Found the door in time," Ryan said, touching one of the tender swellings on his neck. "I guess another fifteen seconds and half the swarm would have been in here with us."

"And 'Goodbye' would be all she wrote." J.B. sniffed.

Krysty nodded. "If just a few stings from these mutie bees hurts this much . . ."

There was no need for her to finish the sentence. Everyone knew what she meant.

ONE OF THE OTHER DOORS led them into a section of what had once been a huge redoubt. Unlike in the gateway part of the complex, it looked as though the withdrawal here had been more leisurely and thorough. They found little evidence of private possessions that had been left behind. But they did find a residential section that had nuke-powered cooking facilities with stocks of all sorts of food and drink.

"Which should mean some ammo around the place," J.B. suggested hopefully.

Krysty pointed to a large sign with an arrow, pointing toward Ablutions.

"That's for me," she said.

"Me too." Ryan grinned. "Mebbe take some of the shit out of these stings. And I get first go at the hot water, if there is any."

J.B. took off his spectacles and polished them on his sleeve. "Fair 'nough, Ryan. Me and Jak'll try and rustle up some eats. And get Doc to rest up. Dormitories are down that way."

Krysty laid a hand on Ryan's arm as they walked off together. "Could be what we all need, lover. A chance to rest and recreate some. Acclimate to this damp heat. Sleep, eat and wash."

He reached to pat her on the backside. "And this, Krysty. In a bed with clean sheets and blankets. If the place seems safe-sealed we can lie together without a blaster in our fists."

She stopped, lifted her face and kissed him gently on the lips. "Sounds good to me, lover, real good."

In fact it was wonderful.

They passed through several hissing automatic doors, the pervasive green algae disappearing and the air becoming cooler and cleaner, until they reached a changing room, with rows of cubicles and piles of white towels. Most had rotted, and disintegrated when picked up, but Krysty and Ryan found a few near the bottom that seemed in better condition.

"Automatic wash and dry machines," Krysty called, "with fluff'n fold option."

"Hope they work. I recall putting a good pair of pants into one of them in a redoubt and getting back a handful of wet khaki ribbons."

The showers were immaculately white tiled, with drain plugs of polished chrome and gleaming taps that offered controlled temperatures from Icy to Scalding. Ryan was undressed first and chose plain Hot. He turned the handle and waited, not really believing that anything would happen.

He finally heard a faint sound, like the whisperings of the long-dead. Cautiously he moved out of the way of the glittering nozzles, not knowing what to expect. The hissing grew louder, and Krysty joined him, looking up at the shower head.

"Think it's working, lover?"

Ryan waited. With a splutter of trapped air, water suddenly came gushing out, hot and clear, steaming as it splashed on the white tiles.

"Yeah."

"Better'n self-heats," J.B. said, stirring a huge copper caldron of tinned soup and stew and sniffing it proudly. His hat was pushed to the back of his head, and his glasses had slipped down to the tip of his nose.

"What's in it?" Krysty asked.

"Beef, kidney and more beef, tomatoes and sweet corn, peas and beans. Okra and some grits to thicken it up some."

"Doc's sleep," Jak said. "Think head'll ever come back, Ryan?"

"Can't tell. Losing Lori was a mind toppler for him. Then the triple jump and the dog getting chilled pushed him over the edge. Old bastard's come back before. Hope he will again."

Doc appeared in the doorway of the big dining room, bleary-eyed.

"Come back, did I hear you say? Back. Back is safe, but forward is most perilous. A darke tower to ride against."

"Want to eat, Doc?" J.B. asked. "It's about ready."

"Most kind, my dear chap. I trust you've received the table reservation for my wife and myself."

"How's that?" J.B. caught Ryan's glance. "Oh, yeah, sure."

Doc walked stiffly across the room and sat down with a sigh of heartfelt weariness. "I don't suppose any of you good people have seen my brain anywhere around, perchance? I know it was a small and poor thing, but it was my own. If anyone should happen to stumble across it . . .''

Ryan, Krysty and Jak sat down around the table. J.B. ladled out the soup, which was almost thick enough to slice with a knife. He'd also found some deep-freeze rolls and revived them in one of the long banks of microwave ovens. There was steaming coffee to drink, and a variety of ice cream for dessert.

"My compliments to your chef," Doc said, barely stifling a belch. He'd pushed away his dish after a third helping of peach-and-pecan ice cream. "Good a meal as I ever enjoyed. Yes, Theophilus Tanner is himself again, gentlemen.''

"Glad to hear it, Doc," Ryan replied as he finished off a second portion of strawberry and quince dessert.

But the old man completely ignored him, wiping his mouth with his kerchief, eyes drilling past them into a different world.

J.B. broke the silence. "Found some jolt, tucked away behind the cans. Guess one of the cooks must've left it when they pulled out.''

The Armorer unfolded the frail paper bundle, revealing the powdery white crystals, a lethal mix of smack, coke and mescal that had been popular before the long chill came. Jolt was now enjoying a rebirth in the Deathlands.

"Not for me," Ryan said. "Dump it in the cans, J.B.''

Jak put down his spoon and looked as if he were going to say something about the drug, but he caught Ryan staring at him and snapped his mouth shut.

"The fountain of youth flows with poisoned water," Doc rambled, but nobody took any notice of him.

"Krysty and me'll clean up here. You and Jak take Doc along and try to wash him up some. If he objects, let it lay. Not worth the sweat to upset him any more. Then I reckon the dormitory sounds like a real good idea."

RYAN WOKE EARLY. He glanced at his chron and saw that it was just after five. Something had tugged him from sleep, and he reached automatically for his pistol. Without disturbing Krysty he slipped from their tousled bed, pulled on his pants and quietly padded into the main section of the dormitory. Jak and J.B. were sleeping in one of the side rooms, and Doc was next door to them.

Ryan pushed open the green-painted door with the muzzle of his pistol and glanced around. Doc's bed had been slept in, but now it was empty.

He could hear a noise, and he followed it through the dining room and down a short corridor, which came quickly to a sort of crossroads.

Doc Tanner was there, walking in stuttering, jerky steps. He advanced a few paces down one passage, then went back. The old man tried another, then retreated again. Ryan moved closer, recognizing the sound that had pulled him out of sleep.

Doc was crying quietly to himself, gobbets of tears furrowing his cheeks. His eyes were red and swollen, and Ryan wondered how long the old man had been out there, alone.

"Hey!" he called. "Doc?"

He turned around, and Ryan was concerned at the madness he saw in the face, a shapeless, loose quality, as if the features had been pushed out of focus.

"Doc?" Ryan almost whispered the syllable. "Want to go back to bed, Doc?"

There was no recognition in the staring eyes, and the mouth was slack and drooling. At that moment it came to Ryan that Doc Tanner might have finally taken one jump too many and wouldn't be rejoining the rest of them.

"Who's there?"

"Me, Doc. Ryan Cawdor, your old friend. Can I help?"

"I fear I have not—" the voice faltered "—had the pleasure of your acquaintance. But I would be grateful for your assistance."

"Sure. How can I help you, Doctor?"

Ryan moved a few steps closer. Behind him, he heard footsteps and recognized the sound of Krysty. But he didn't turn around, not wanting to risk losing this tenuous contact.

"Help me," Doc pleaded with a desperate urgency. "Tell me where I am, Mr. Cawdor. Where am I? Why am I here? How may I be free? And where, oh, where in the name of mercy, are my wife and children?''

Ryan was just in time to catch the old man as he fell to the concrete floor in a dead faint.

CHAPTER EIGHT

"FULL EVACUATION by 00.01 on Day Four of Schedule 01/PrOv/Ce/TC. Redoubt to be sealed throughout and only Ltd sec force remaining in approved external watch section."

Jak had found the piece of paper from which he read, crumpled in a corner of one of the corridors, near what they guessed was a triple sec door leading to the open air. It was the only clue to the speed and organization of the evacuation.

"That's why it's all left running and stocked. Like they just sealed it for a couple of days, and figured they'd return when the scare was over." Ryan handed the paper back to the albino boy, who scrunched it between his hands and threw it onto the floor.

"Only the scare was never over." J.B. shook his head.

"Best get back to relieve Krysty," Ryan said. "Least we got enough ammo to last us a while. Except for Doc's cannon."

The redoubt had been kind to them in most ways. Apart from food and drink and the good hot water, it had also allowed them all to top up on self-lights and grens. J.B.'s dark brown leather jacket concealed a whole mix of the tiny, lethal grenades: implodes and frags; burners and shraps; lights and delays. All were color-coded for maximum efficiency. Jak and Ryan had also helped themselves to a variety of the grens, hooking them on their belts.

All carried mags of ammo, some of it loose in pockets.

Ryan had been delighted to come across some of the scarce caseless rounds for his beloved Heckler & Koch G-12 rifle. The blaster held a clip of fifty of the 4.7 mm rounds, and he'd been getting low.

Since that quality of ammunition wasn't manufactured anywhere in the Deathlands, he'd started to resign himself to dumping the gun and picking up something that fired a more convenient 9 mm bullet. They had loads of 9 mm—for his own SIG-Sauer P-226, for Krysty's P7A-13 H&K, for the Armorer's MP-7 SD-8 Heckler & Koch rifle.

J.B. had also topped up his supplies of 5.56 mm ammo for his Steyr AUG pistol, and Jak's pants pocket bulged with extra rounds for his massive .357 Magnum.

The friends were ready again to take on anything that moved—other than swarms of killer bees.

KRYSTY STOOD in the passage, waiting for them. "Doc's woken up," she said. But the look on her face made it patently clear that this wasn't necessarily good news.

"But?"

"See for yourself, lover."

The old man lay on his back, boots stacked side by side on the floor, the sheet pulled up under his chin. With his hands folded on his chest, he looked like the carved figure of a crusader in an ancient church memorial.

Ryan perched on the end of the bed, the other three behind him. "Hi," he said.

Pale blue eyes turned slowly toward him. "Good day to you."

"Know who I am?"

"I fear not."

"Know where you are?"

"Some hospital for the poor and needy?"

"Do you know what the year is?" Krysty asked.

"Of course. It's 1896."

Krysty nodded. "Right on."

Doc made an effort to sit up, then relaxed and lay back on the double pillows. "Please, will one of you take a message to my dear wife? She will be so worried at my absence."

"Absence?" Ryan queried.

"I've been away from home for...let me see. It must be very close to two hundred years now, and she will be beginning to become concerned about it. Do you not think?"

Ryan kept his face schooled not to show his deep worry. "We'll do what we can. I didn't catch your name, I'm afraid." He'd fallen into the older man's old-fashioned and stilted way of speech.

"Theophilus Algernon Tanner. Doctor of Science at Harvard. Doctor of Philosophy at the English university of Oxford. A pleasure to meet you. Pray forgive my not rising."

"Course. Can we get you anything to eat, Doc? Drink?"

"Thank you. A glass of water, and perhaps a Bath Oliver, if you have such a thing."

Ryan nodded, hiding his total ignorance of what Doc wanted to eat. "Sure. Listen, me and the others have to talk some. Then we're going out for a kind of...of a walk. The nurses have all gone home so you better come with us."

"Delighted, my dear fellow. And you won't forget to inform my sweet Emily of my temporary indisposition, will you? My card is in my waistcoat."

"EVERYONE READY NOW? I'll just trigger the main doors for a few inches. Jak, get down and have a look under it. See anything you don't like...just say 'close,' and we'll shut it again. We don't need any more of those bastard bees. I can still feel the stings in me."

The boy lay down, his newly washed white hair spreading out on the concrete like spilled foam. Ryan punched in the number code and threw the green lever up. Almost immediately he returned it to a central position to stop the sec door about eighteen inches from the floor. Jak took his time, looking all around outside. "Nothing," he said finally.

"Nothing?'

"Fucking big trees. Fucking hot. Nothing."

Cautiously Ryan allowed the arma-door to slide all the way up.

The heat swept into the redoubt like a tumbling wave, carrying with it an overwhelming smell of *green*.

The entrance was set back into a hillside, behind what had once been a turning area for large military wags. But that was now a plateau of solid, waving grass, speckled with clusters of the most colorful flowers Ryan had ever seen. Crimsons, golds, purples and vivid yellows seemed even brighter against the swaying emerald backdrop.

"Paradise," Krysty murmured, shaking her head in admiration and wonderment.

Beyond the flowery carpet they could see the tops of luxuriant trees, some of them resembling monstrously big palms. The air was heavy with moist scents and languorous perfumes from the flowers, some of them verging on the sickly.

"Got be Hawaii, or someplace in the Pacific," Ryan said. "Seen an old sec vid about Hawaii. Called *Fifty* it was. Weird name."

"I think Hawaii had big mountains," Krysty offered doubtfully. "This looks like it's too flat to be Hawaii."

"Africa," J.B. suggested. "Or India. I've seen pics of jungles looking like this."

"Tell you one thing," Ryan said. "This surely isn't any place in Deathlands."

Doc was wandering around in small circles, head up, staring at the vivid pink clouds that scarred the orange sky. "Red sky in the morning, then shepherds take warning," he said, looking around at the florid walls of the tropical jungle. "Here be tygers, I fear. We must exercise care."

J.B. had taken the tiny microsextant from a pocket and was busily shooting the sun, checking his data on a comp-table of locations. He checked again. And again.

"Hawaii?" Ryan asked. The Armorer shook his head.

"Africa? Or India?" Krysty probed.

J.B. shook his head. "No. It's... According to this, we're in the middle of what was Minnesota."

Doc Tanner began to laugh.

CHAPTER NINE

RYAN CAREFULLY CLOSED the door into the redoubt. His knowledge of prenuke America wasn't vast, but there were still enough old books to be found around the Deathlands for him to be certain of one thing—Minnesota hadn't been a state that was filled with a wild profusion of tropical plants set amid a luxuriant forest.

J.B. had checked his sextant a fourth time, then a fifth time and had shown the reading to anyone who would look at it. "Yeah, Ryan," he finally admitted. "It's Minnesota. North, right up close to where the border with Canada used to be. But it's not supposed to be like this. It's supposed to be..."

"Bleak," Krysty concluded. "And look at these flowers."

"And that butterfly," Doc said, reviving his interest for a moment. "It must be the size of a soup plate." The insect's wings were a good two feet across, and fluttered lazily in the afternoon sunshine. Two tips trailed from the back of the orange-and-brown-dappled wings.

"Giant Yellow Swallowtail," the old man said admiringly. "Habitat's all over South America, right up to Mexico and into Texas. But the suggestion that such a beautiful creature could survive as far north as Minnesota is obviously absurd. Therefore we are not in Minnesota. *Quod erat demonstrandum.*" He smirked in a foxy way at the others. "Which means that which was to be proved."

"Great, Doc," Ryan said. "So we're in Minnesota, but we're not in Minnesota."

"Who gives fuck?" Jak asked. "We going look around, or not?"

"Okay," Ryan agreed, "let's go."

As they moved away from the entrance and down through the clinging vegetation, they saw that the hill was very short. Effectively the whole place was set in a shallow bowl of similar low mountains, making a flat-bottomed valley. Ryan guessed that it was this particular sheltered formation that kept the air so still and warm. But it didn't explain how such rare tropical trees and flowers came to be in Minnesota.

At the back of Ryan's mind, though he hadn't mentioned it to any of the others, was Rick Ginsberg's information about other freezie centers. One was near Big Bend, down in south Texas, and the other was somewhere close to the old city of Duluth, in northern Minnesota.

ONE OF KRYSTY'S AREAS of specialized knowledge was botany. In her birthplace of Harmony there had been a number of men and women with arcane skills. Dulcie Harrison had encouraged the flame-haired young girl to read in the ville's surprisingly extensive library on all aspects of horticulture and agriculture, pointing out to her that Deathlands was never likely to become industrialized again.

"The land, Krysty, my dear," she used to say, spluttering around her ill-fitting false teeth in her vehemence, "there has always been the land. And there will always be the land."

"Silver oaks and begonias," Krysty said now. "And that's a huge eucalyptus. No idea what that is, but I know that's a giant nasturtium climbing all over it."

They were following what had at first looked like the main trail down from the redoubt. But the many years' growth of lush foliage had obliterated almost all trace of what must once have been a well-kept two-lane blacktop. In the end Ryan was forced to draw his panga and hack away at the dense foliage with the hissing eighteen-inch blade.

"What are those wondrous blooms?" Doc asked.

"Hibiscus, Doc," Krysty replied.

"Thank you, young lady. I am much indebted to you. Hibiscus. It puts me somewhat in mind of the flowers that one might see strewn across a funeral bier. Now, what a dismal thought is that!"

The smell of the vegetation was overwhelming, and Ryan paused to draw breath and wipe the sticky mulch from the edge of the steel cleaver. Sweat streaked his face and body, and the hot shower seemed a millenium away.

Doc's voice floated to him again, but with a whining, querulous tone that was quite unlike his usual way of speaking. "Pardon me, young lady."

"What is it, Doc?"

"I would prefer a more formal response than 'Doc.' It makes me sound like a stock character in a cheap melodrama. But that is not what I was about to remark upon. You are wearing breeches, young woman, are you not?"

Ryan turned around at that and caught Krysty's expression of amused bewilderment.

"Yes, I am, Dr. Tanner. What of it? You want I should take them off?"

"Of course not! What a wanton and brazen reply!"

"You figure a woman should only wear pretty dimity dresses. Is that it?"

"I have no objection to working clothes for working women. But not breeches."

"And women shouldn't have the right to vote, either, Doc?"

He shook his head, and for a moment Ryan glimpsed a dreadful uncertainty in the old man's eyes. A spasm of doubt. "I thought they already... But not back when I've been... If it comes, then I shall support it, my dear. You have the word of Theophilus A. Tanner upon it."

Ryan grinned at that, and turned once more to resume his battle with the clinging, suffocating walls of undergrowth.

THE SUN HAD CLAWED its way through the layers of ragged cloud until it was nearly overhead. The companions had stopped three times for a rest and a drink from their supply of water. It seemed to Ryan, looking behind them, that the vegetation was growing faster than they could cut it down. Their beaten path was already becoming invisible. Fortunately J.B. had been taking bearings every two or three hundred yards to make sure they'd eventually be able to track their way back.

"How much farther are we going to go?" J.B. asked.

"Another hour, I figure. If there's no sign of getting out of this jungle by then, we can head back to the redoubt. Rest up some and then make another jump to get out of here."

"Terrific." Krysty sighed. "Just what I always wanted, lover. Another wonderful jump. It'll kill Doc."

"You know a better hole to go to?" Ryan asked. "Any of you? I don't know what this place has for mutie life, but I don't take to the idea of spending a night out in the middle of it."

"Go on longer" was Jak's terse comment.

"How about you, Doc?" Ryan asked. "You want to go on or go back?" He knew immediately that it was a mistake to use the word *back* to the befuddled old man.

"Back? I am already 'back,' as you call it, Mr. Cawdor. How can I return whither I am already bound? *Quo vadis?* as the classics have it. Whither goest thou? Where do we come from and where do we go? The eternal enigma.''

He continued to mutter to himself, making little sense. Ryan glanced at the other three. "Guess that's a vote from Doc for going on a ways," he said quietly.

JAK WAS BREAKING TRAIL, swinging Ryan's heavy panga with incredible speed and delicacy. A litter of hacked branches and broken plants marked the track of his passing.

"Houses," he announced suddenly, dropping to his knees behind a screen of reddish-purple bougainvillea.

Ryan gestured to J.B. and Krysty to keep Doc to the rear, while he wriggled forward on hands and knees to join the boy.

"Where?"

"There," Jak replied, pointing with the green-slobbered tip of the panga.

A small river flowed silently from left to right, behind the flowering shrub. Beyond it was a clearer area of long grass. A group of single-story concrete buildings lay behind the remains of a rusting sec fence that was topped with razored wire. As elsewhere in this peculiar region, the harshness of the concrete blocks was softened by a coating of pale green moss.

At first glance the installation looked like the ruins of a federal prison. Ryan had seen enough of them in his life. Not many places had survived a century after dark day, but prisons were the grim exceptions.

The friends crouched in total stillness for a long fifteen minutes, watching for any sign of human habitation. Or inhuman habitation.

Other than a swarm of myriad tiny golden insects, darting above the sullen, oily surface of the river, there was no sign of life. Ryan heard a muted clicking and glanced down at his shirt, where he kept a miniature rad counter pinned—as did most of the norm population of Deathlands. It had changed color from safe-green to somewhere between yellow and red, showing that there was a medium-hot spot not too far from them.

Jak looked at his own counter, which had remained stubbornly green. He tapped it, but nothing happened.

"Could be missile silos around here," Ryan whispered.

"Cross?" Jak asked.

"Wait a while longer. Don't like the feel of all this."

The buildings all showed signs of serious damage, either from the big nuking or from earth-shakes, or from the extremes of weather and rad storms that still raged around Deathlands. The windows were gone, as well as parts of some walls and several sections of the roofs.

While they watched there was a rippling in the thick grass beyond the river and a long, copper-colored snake emerged, holding a paralyzed bundle of fur in its gaping jaws. It slid silently into the dark water, head high, swimming downstream in long undulating coils of power. Ryan's guess put the reptile at twenty-five to thirty feet.

"Big bastard," Jak hissed.

"Swallow you in one." Ryan grinned.

A noisy, chattering flock of bright-plumaged birds was perched on the corner of the roof of the nearest building. At a distance they looked to Ryan like parrots or macaws, but their presence told him that there were, probably, no hidden blasters covering them from the shadows.

He turned and beckoned the others forward, motioning Doc to keep low.

"Why? Is this some sort of sport, Mr. Cawdor? Or are we under threat from hostile Indians? I speak something of the tongue of the Mescalero Apaches, you know. I spent time among them only...only the other...once."

"Krysty. You and me go across the river. Get to the buildings and have a quick recce. We'll call the rest of you over when it's safe. Keep us covered. Questions? No? Let's do it."

J. B. Dix unslung his Heckler & Koch rifle and steadied it in a notch of the bougainvillea. He switched on the laser-optic sight and scanned the silent buildings across the water. Jak drew his Magnum and waited alongside the Armorer. Doc had lost interest again in what was happening, and he sat down with cracking knees. He picked a tiny orange flower and inhaled the scent with his eyes squeezed shut.

Ryan led the way.

There was no way of knowing how deep the river was from its murky surface, nor what kind of vicious life it might contain. Ryan could still conjure up the sight of a man called Bob Duvall, who'd been a relief driver on War Wag Three. He'd bathed in a similar river up near the Darks despite Trader's warnings about caution.

A shoal of tiny fishes had taken him. The creatures were no more than three inches in length, but two and a half inches of that was teeth. They'd stripped old Bob to the bone before he could make the bank and safety. Ryan could still recall the sight: the whiteness of washed bone and the dangling strips of mauled sinew; the fish still biting at torn slabs of flesh, while the river filled with blood.

The screams hadn't lasted more than fifteen seconds.

"Could try to wade it," Krysty suggested.

"You never knew Bob Duvall, lover," Ryan replied. "We'll go upstream and find a safe place to get us across."

They eventually came to the tumbled remains of a stone bridge, with decorative little arches, some fallen, some still standing. It wasn't difficult to jump over the gaps, though Krysty stumbled as a piece of loose rock rolled from under her boot heel.

They followed a track winding near the edge of the forest. Between the grass and the nearest of the buildings they passed something that looked like a gigantic anthill. If the area held ants at least nine inches in length...

Ryan didn't let his mind dwell too long on that.

Krysty waved an all clear to the hiding trio across the river, receiving a clenched-fist signal in return from J.B.

"Want to go inside?" she asked Ryan.

He shook his head. "Nope. Wait for the others. Scouting ruins like this without taking all the care can bring a load of bloody grief."

They looked around, checking the blind windows and the hidden angles, but nothing moved. The birds had disappeared, as well as the insects.

"Look." Krysty pointed with the muzzle of her blaster.

Ryan took a cautious few steps toward the rectangular stone block that barely protruded above the lush meadow grass. "It's a sign," he called.

"From the Almighty?"

"Come again, lover?"

Krysty grinned. "Let it pass. What kind of sign is it?"

Ryan had knelt in the grass and was cutting vegetation away with his panga. "Looks like the name of the place. Got a shit-lot of moss all over the letters. I'll scrape some of it.... Yeah."

The others had crossed the wrecked bridge and stood in a half ring around Ryan, J.B.'s eyes constantly raking the buildings ahead of them and the river and forest behind. Gradually Ryan cleared the top half of the sign: "Wendigo Institute of Botanical Research."

"That's where all of these weird flowers and plants have come from," Krysty said excitedly. "When the nuking came, it must've blown seeds and stuff everywhere. And it's changed the climate in this big valley."

"There's more," Ryan told them. "Incorporating the Blackwood Center for Chemical and Neurological Research, Military Division."

"Germ warfare," Doc spit, anger and contempt fighting in his voice. "Swines. Gas and poisons, and blindness and madness. I've seen the vids. Volunteers that tore out their own eyes and devoured their own ripped genitals. Devils!"

"Sounds like a real good place to move away from," J.B. said finally. "That sort of stuff can hang around a thousand years."

"Make triple-muties," Jake said uneasily, looking around.

"There's another line of letters. Below the rest. Smaller. Grass is hiding them."

Ryan looked where Krysty was pointing. He etched at the lichen with the point of his panga, the steel making a harsh, scratching sound. He sat back on his heels to read the last line.

"With the Shelley Cryonic Institute—Private. This is it! The place Rick mentioned. More freezies are inside there."

CHAPTER TEN

RYAN'S HIGH EXPECTATIONS began to evaporate as soon as they set foot within the ruined complex. The devastation was worse than it had appeared from the outside. Many of the roofs had collapsed under nuke-waves of shock, and rain and humidity had done the rest.

The floors were rotted and slippery, and pools of warm brackish water had accumulated in doorways and at turns of corridors. Broken glass cracked underfoot, from the myriad windows and skylights. The interior had been totally ravaged, probably within the first few weeks of the center's destruction. It crossed Ryan's mind to wonder what kind of appalling chemicals had been set free at that time. The botanical complex had created this bizarre tropical oasis within rural Minnesota. So what could the germs, diseases, nerve gases and hallucinogens have wrought?

The companions picked their way through the linked buildings. The huge pharmacy was ankle deep in a mixture of mossy green sludge and smashed vials and syringes, which had once contained who knew what blasphemous obscenities?

"No freezies around here," Jak stated, shaking his mane of hair.

Ryan wiped sweat from behind his eye patch. "Guess you're right. Still, we know the institute was here once. Let's at least try to dig out where the freezies used to be."

A large hornet buzzed into the room, making straight for Krysty. Her reflexes were good enough to swipe it out of the air. It landed in one of the dirty puddles, swimming and whining in an infinity of crazed desperation. J.B. finally set his boot on it.

"Hope there aren't too many of that," he said. "I don't see many good hiding places around here."

The deeper they walked into the complex, the more the buildings seemed to have suffered. They walked out through a broken wall, facing nothing but dozens of piles of variegated rubble and a windowless rectangular concrete blockhouse, which looked relatively undamaged.

The structure was two stories high, and above the dark green doors they could all read the weathered sign that said: Shelley Cryonic Institute. Private.

Ryan's optimism inched up a few more notches.

THE SEC DOORS SHOWED signs of innumerable attacks on their titanium-vanadium steel exterior. Dents, scratches and chips marked the smooth green finish. When J.B. pushed at it, the lock seemed as solid as the day it had been made.

"Better and better," Ryan said quietly, squeezing Krysty on the arm.

"What?"

"If it's still locked and wired into the main nuke-power source of the redoubt, then there could still be freezies down there. Alive."

The woman shuddered. "No, lover."

"You mean you can't feel any life inside? That it?"

"No. I mean, I can't. But that wasn't . . . I can still remember too well what happened when we tried to thaw out those other poor folk."

"Rick made it."

"Sure. But I kept feeling there were a lot of times that he'd mebbe rather not."

"You think we shouldn't even try?"

She smiled at him. "Course not. I think you always have to try. Just hope it's not as bad as it was the last time."

"Got to get in here first," J.B. said practically.

"You got some fresh plas-ex yesterday?" Ryan asked.

"Yeah. Take a handful to blow this mother out of the way."

"Do it." Ryan took Doc by the arm and led him back among the ruins, to protect him from the blast.

The old man followed him without making any kind of protest.

Several minutes later J.B. joined them unhurriedly, as if he were going for an afternoon's fishing in a trout stream. He glanced at his wrist chron as he crouched at Ryan's side. "Ten seconds to go, if the fuses are still reliable."

Ryan nudged Doc. "Put your hands over your ears, Doc, and open your mouth."

"Why?"

"Save you from the bang. Do it."

The explosion came almost immediately, flat and dulled from being out in the open. Since the Armorer hadn't been able to use the confining force of the plas-ex, he'd been forced to use a lump the size of his fist. As the yellowish smoke cleared away Ryan wondered whether it might have been too much and brought the whole building down.

But J.B. had gotten it just right.

The doors had peeled back on their concealed hinges like wet cardboard. The reinforced concrete had been cracked just above the doors, bringing down the faded sign. But the main structure didn't seem to have been damaged.

"I confess myself somewhat at a loss," Doc said as he peered at the wrecked sec doors in confusion.

"Someone lost key," Jak explained, which seemed to satisfy the old man.

"Worth leaving a guard?" J.B. asked. "Bang like that'd be heard from here to the Lantic and back."

Ryan hesitated. Their party was so small that to reduce its size at all would be to greatly weaken it. And they hadn't seen any signs of recent humanoid life around the region.

"Stick together," he said, leading the way into the entrance hall of the cryonics center.

EVERYTHING WAS functioning perfectly.

It was an uncanny time capsule, sealed in 2001 and not disturbed until this moment. The lights were steady, pitched at a moderate level. The air-conditioning hummed quietly away, keeping the air clean, cool and circulated every forty-eight minutes, as per regulations for United States Government buildings.

There was almost no dust, and no trace of the green lichen that had seemed to stain everything in the area. They walked across to a desk marked Reception.

Krysty smiled. "Gaia! I swear I expect to see some nurse or doctor in a white coat come out to ask us what we want and would we mind leaving. It's just like being in an old vid."

Under a sheet of curling plastic was a staff rota for January 2001 and a red-typed notice giving the details of the final hasty evacuation. Filled with mistakes and showing all the signs of having been circulated at the shortest possible warning, it gave details of how all the automatic servo-systems should be switched away from Manual.

As soon as the state of ergency ends, the entire center will revert to all normal procedures.

"Never did," Ryan said.

"Let's go see if we can find some freezies," Krysty suggested.

The building was just about the best preserved that any of them had ever seen. Yet oddly, there was very little there to interest them. It was obvious that the cryonics complex had been fully staffed and functioning right up to the last moment, and that it had then been successfully evacuated. But it was such a sterile environment that nothing personal remained. It wasn't like a hospital with living patients, more like a totally disinfected laboratory.

The brittle pieces of paper tacked to boards didn't cast any light on what had happened or how people had been feeling. Someone was selling a '94 Chevy, and someone else had some rabbits for sale; there was a dance in the cryo-tech's quarters on the next Friday; the local branch of the Seventh-Day Adventists was holding a doughnuts-and-coffee morning to raise funds for some child with leukemia; a woman named Medina was selling her precious record collection and wouldn't refuse any reasonable offer.

"The trivia of living and dying," Doc commented. "They shouldn't have planned anything for tomorrow. Tomorrow was the yesterday you worried about.... No, I fear that I have that a tad incorrect." He shook his head sadly.

Ryan caught Krysty's eye and rubbed at his chin thoughtfully. Doc kept showing tiny signs of recovery, then he'd go plunging all the way back down into the abyss.

"Look," J.B. said, pointing to a sign that hung at the far end of one of the corridors. "Seen it before."

Ryan remembered it too—in the redoubt where they'd met Rick Ginsberg: Cryo. Medical Clearance 10 or B Equivalent Only Permitted.

"Down there," Ryan said.

"Hope the freezies don't go triple-fucking crazy like last," Jak muttered. "Dreamed bad. Real bad."

Ryan fervently hoped that as well. Remembering the nightmare scenes in the last cryo-bunkers made his mouth go as dry as neutron bones.

They continued onward until they encountered a sec barrier that would once have been manned by armed guards. Now only the silken whisper of a crumbling spiderweb stretched across the wide passage. Beyond it stood a pair of doors marked Air Lock—Do Not Enter.

"If there's any freezies left, lover, they'll be through there." Krysty's hand dropped automatically to the butt of her blaster.

The tension was so strong it could almost be tasted, prickling on the tongue. With the exception of Doc Tanner, all of them were wrestling with bad memories.

CHAPTER ELEVEN

NOTHING HAPPENED for several seconds after J.B. pressed the manual control on the air lock doors, and Ryan had a momentary, claustrophobic vision of being trapped between the ponderous, rubber-edged panels. Then there was the familiar hissing sound of equalizing pressure and the slight discomfort around the inner ears.

"Not another jump?" Doc queried with no more than mild curiosity.

"No," Krysty replied, patting him reassuringly on the arm. "Just going through the doors to see what's there."

"Who's there? What's there? When's where? Where's where? Men's wear. I swear." He stopped and looked at the puzzled faces of the others. "I do beg your pardon. Slight malfunction of the frontal lobes."

The second set of doors moved back silently, and they could all taste the chilled flatness of recirculated air.

"Anything, lover?" Ryan asked.

Krysty shook her head, her blazing hair swinging across her face. "Not a thing. Whatever lived down here once, lives here no longer."

"Cold." Jak shuddered.

"Think we'll find any freezies in here?" J.B. asked. "Complex was secure. Looks like they just switched it to auto and walked away."

The corridors were spotlessly clean and free from all dust. Doors lining both sides opened onto sparsely furnished offices. A long list of warnings and regulations was posted on a double pair of swing doors at the end of the corridor. Most were linked to the importance of keeping all germs at bay by wearing the right clinical uniforms.

"Not worth it," Krysty said quietly. "If any freezies leave with us, we'll be taking them into Deathlands. A few specks of dirt before then won't likely make a lot of difference."

A long way off, dulled by the thick walls, they could just hear the persistent sound of a security siren blaring the warning to guards long, long dead that there were unidentified and illegal intruders within the complex.

Noncorporeal Section. The sign was above yet another set of doors.

"What the dark night does that mean?" J.B. asked.

They all stared at it in silence. Finally Doc Tanner answered the Armorer's question.

"Without a body, Mr. Dix. A section for people who no longer have a body. A peculiar concept, I must admit."

"Just arms an' legs," Jak suggested, cackling with delight at the bizarre idea.

"Or heads," Doc said.

It *was* heads.

They walked into a huge control room, at least eight thousand square feet, that was packed with all kinds of sophisticated monitors. It made the control consoles for the gateways look like kiddie toys. But it wasn't the banks of comp-displays and flickering monitors that caught the eye first—it was what lay behind them, ranged along the back wall, each in its own Plexiglas capsule.

Heads.

At a rough count Ryan figured on close to a hundred: white, black, brown and yellow, and all the shades in between. All had been severed with a surgical neatness across the center of the throat, the lower section submerged in a viscous liquid. Wires and tubes trailed from each neck into a box of light green plastic, which in turn was connected to its own individual control console. Ryan assumed that the consoles would all be linked to the master boards.

There were old heads with strands of hair pasted thinly across leathery scalps; young faces, with teeth that gleamed in secret, wolfish grins; men with clipped military mustaches; women whose hair was bound up in thin nets to keep it from the preserving liquids.

"Gaia," Krysty breathed. "This has to be the...the ultimate nightmare."

"They dead?" Jak asked.

"Depends on what you mean by death," Ryan replied. He was so disappointed that he could almost taste it. This wasn't what he'd imagined and hoped for.

"I knew of this kind of experimentation," Doc said, sounding more like himself. "To freeze the entire body wasn't proving that successful. We saw the failure rate last time. Microsurgery meant they could always graft a live neck back onto any convenient corpse."

"You joking me, Doc?" Krysty asked. "Old head on a new body?"

"Indeed, yes. Easier, I think. The head and brain are kept wired and nourished. My guess is that the capsules are filled with liquid nitrogen or some such."

"Sick fuckers," Jak hissed as he went to sit in a polished swivel chair at the main desk.

None of the others took any notice of him as they walked along the rows of severed skulls.

Each head bore a coded reference, a string of numbers and letters. Ryan wondered who they were. From what Rick had told them about freezies, they must all have been special. The U.S. government had frozen only people of ultraimportance, and most of them had been scientists—military scientists who had contracted some terminal illness and had been deep-frozen, like so many sides of mutton, to await the new Jerusalem, the age of enlightenment when their diseases could be cured by medical advances.

What nobody could have forecast was Deathlands, a world of brutality, where medicine was at roughly the same level as it had been in the early part of the nineteenth century. These frozen semicorpses didn't have much chance of being successfully revived.

Several of the suspended heads clearly showed signs of illness, and many were emaciated with dark shadows of pain smeared around the sunken eyes. Ryan spotted one or two that still bore scars of operations, the skin seamed and sutured.

He was aware of Krysty, standing at his side. "Poor bastards," she whispered. "Think there's some sort of life there?"

"You mean can they see and hear?"

"I mean . . . are they sentient, Ryan? Do they know what they are? Do they sense time passing?"

Doc joined them, in front of the head of a middle-aged white man, the pupils of his eyes just visible behind slitted eyes.

"What is time, young lady? It is a series of moments of reality, strung uneasily together to give an illusion of continuity. These . . . I came close to calling them people, do not feel that. There is neither day nor night for them, both sweet things. Life is endless . . . nothing." He shook his leonine head. "Who would wish to die? *They* would wish to die, my friends."

The lights flickered, and Jak cursed under his breath, drawing everyone's eyes to him. "Don't fucking look me," he growled. "Didn't mean press button."

"Which button?" Ryan walked quickly to where the albino boy sat looking at the dancing display in front of him, hands flat on the desk top.

"Big one. Blood one."

There was only one large red control on the console, which was set in its own clear plastic box with a flip-top lid to it. In embossed silver letters, it carried the message: Speed-Thaw! Max-Caution. Emergency Override Only! DO NOT ACTIVATE!

"You pressed that red button, Jak?" Ryan asked, realizing that it was really an unnecessary question. From the crazed lights and swelling sound of sirens, it was obvious what had happened.

"Yeah. Didn't read. Can stop?"

J.B., peering owlishly over Ryan's shoulder, shook his head. "Doesn't look like it. Seems them heads are going to start warming up real soon."

"The boy was always a hothead." Doc nudged Krysty in the ribs with a bony elbow. "Do you comprehend my jest, young lady?"

"Yeah, Doc," she replied, turning to look at the nearest row of wired skulls.

"A joke, you see. Hot heads. The heads will soon become warm now that the manual defreeze switch has been activated. Hot heads. You see..." His voice trailed away as he suddenly lost interest and went to sit down at one of the side desks.

"Starting," Krysty called.

"Sorry, Ryan," Jak muttered, shaking his head miserably. "Fucking triple-stupe."

Ryan patted him on the shoulder. "Don't figure that we'd have done much with nearly a hundred heads. Do 'em a favor pulling the plug like that. They didn't have a hope of a future."

"Nor do I," Doc said quietly.

"Gaia!" Krysty sighed. "You want a double-bad sight, then I got one over here."

Ryan, Jak and J.B. joined her, standing horror-struck in front of the small capsules, watching the result of Jak's fiddling with the control.

"Madness," the Armorer said, whistling soundlessly between his teeth.

There wasn't a thing that they could do other than just stand and watch the beginning of the end, the conclusion of a doomed fantasy that had begun a century ago.

Some of the containers were misted over with condensation, as the coolants drained away and the temperatures began to climb. Ryan glanced along the row, stone-faced at the variety of the circus horrors.

Some heads were vibrating with a demonic life, eyes opening and closing, lips parting and soft, pink tongues protruding; a thick colorless slime oozed from the staring eyes of a skull near Ryan; an elderly white woman next along clamped her jaws together with such power that her teeth were splintering into jagged, powdery stumps; there had been some kind of electrical short in one of the microcircuits of a middle-aged Hispanic man. His hair was standing on end and beginning to smolder. His skin blackened and burned, smoke coming from the depths of the mutely gabbling mouth.

"No point staying here," J.B. said as he turned away from the dying puppet-skulls.

"Might as well leave the whole place, Ryan agreed. "We get moving, and we'll be back through the forest and into the redoubt again before dark. I could use another hot, clean shower right now."

"Gets my vote, lover. Looks like this whole place could go through its own roof."

There was the acrid stink of overloaded wiring, and the air was beginning to get heavy and thick with smoke. Sparks flew out of several of the capsules, and at least a half dozen had already cracked open with the heat. Over everything else, Ryan could almost taste the too-familiar stench of roasting flesh.

"Barbecue time down on the old Panhandle Ranch," Doc cried, starting off with a whippoorwill whoop. But he inhaled some of the smoke and it sent him into a nasty coughing fit.

"There's another door that way." Krysty pointed. "Might as well try it."

"Go ahead. Jak, take Doc. J.B., you get going. I'll cover the rear."

Though there was no overt threat, it was automatic with Ryan that anything they did should be done as efficiently as possible. The Trader used to say, "Get it right when it don't matter, and you'll get it right when it does."

More containers exploded as the manual override continued its destructive work.

As the plastic melted, some of the heads were actually tearing loose from the wiring. It was like being in the middle of an exploding charnel house. As Ryan brought up the back of the group, he had to dodge and step over several rolling, smoldering skulls, hair alight, eyes melting in long-dead sockets, teeth clacking in frenzied paroxysms of what might have been rage and disappointment.

Once they were through the next set of hissing double doors, the air was immediately cool and clean again. Another short stretch of sterile corridor ended in yet another pair of half-glassed doors. To the left was a sign with a red arrow and the single word: Exit.

"That way?" Krysty asked.

Ryan looked at the doors ahead, leading to yet another part of the cryo-complex. As far as they knew, there was only one other such institution in the whole of the Deathlands and that was a good fifteen hundred miles away, near the Grandee River.

A gentle voice spoke from the hidden speakers in the walls. "Warning to all cryo-personnel. There is no cause for alarm, but senso-detectors indicate the possibility of fire. Do not panic. Go to the nearest evac-point and await orders. Repeat. Do not panic."

"Better get out," J.B. said. "Whole place could go up."

Ryan shook his head. "Not yet. Place like this is in sealed units. Have sprinklers and all kinds of safety shit."

The woman's calm voice switched on once more, but this time the hundred-year-old tape was defective.

"Warning ... all ... There ... no ... for ... but ... indicate ... possibility ... fire ... not ... Go ... nearest ... and ... orders ... Do ... panic."

"Things breaking up, lover," Krysty warned, glancing anxiously at Ryan.

"Still want to... Let's just take one look through those next doors. Nothing there, and we'll get out."

"Warning ... There ... for ... indicate ... fire ... Go ... and ... panic."

There was a moment of hesitation, broken by Ryan, who strode quickly toward the next doors. But Jak was faster, reaching them just ahead of him, the others at their heels.

"Warning... for... Go... panic."

They hurried through the first doors, and then past the second set, the boy in the lead. Doc stumbled and nearly fell, but J.B. hauled him quickly to his feet.

They came to a large lounge, with padded seats and framed unexceptional landscapes on the walls. There was only one door to it, and Jak ran ahead, pausing in the doorway. He looked back at the others with a grin.

"Heads?" Ryan called.

"Yeah, but this time got bodies with 'em!"

CHAPTER TWELVE

"MY LOVE IS LIKE a goblet of purest crystal, studded with rich jewels. Chalcedony and onyx. Amethyst and fiery opal. There are times that this goblet brims over with the richness of our love for each other. And now...it is shattered into a million daggered shards upon the stones."

Doc sat in a black leather chair in one corner of the room, eyes closed, fingers to his temples, muttering to himself.

The other four friends ignored him, preoccupied with what they'd found—three deep-frozen bodies, pale and bloodless, with dozens of tubes and wires running to and from every part of them. Liquids were circulating slowly, some without color, most tinted shades of red.

The clear coffins that held the bodies were slightly frosted and ice-cold to the touch. But it was possible to make out something of each of the three freezies inside.

"It's a child here," Krysty said. "Little girl. Can't be more'n three years old. Why did they freeze her?"

"Old man this," Jak called from the far end of the row.

"Middle-aged black woman," J.B. announced. "Handsome looking."

Ryan sat down at the single long control console. The capsules were numbered 1, 2 and 3. There were sections on the console labeled with those numbers. On an impulse he pressed the main key for 1, the glistening pod that contained the child.

The screen lit up, glowing an unearthly green. The others went to stand behind Ryan and watch what was happening. Even Doc stirred himself from his almost catatonic lethargy to join the group.

There were forty or so lines in the display, each offering a different menu of information. One said simply: Bio. Ryan operated the flickering cursor to bring it to the right place, then pressed the Go key.

They all read as the information scrolled upward, Jak's lips moving as he whispered the more difficult words under his breath. It was very short.

Hope Future, girl child abandoned in New York's Museum of Modern Art on April 7, 1998, newborn and in coma. Has massive and inoperable brain damage under existing parameters of medical knowledge. As part of cryo-campaign of late nineties she was treated in hope that one day she might be awakened to full and happy life. Her name, Hope Future, was selected after a nationwide TV and video competition.

That was all. Ryan pressed the Off switch and sat back with a sigh.

Doc broke the silence. "If I might paraphrase that great Englishman, Sir Winston Churchill, some future . . . some hope."

"Going to thaw her out?" Krysty asked.

"Three-year-old brat? The heat scrambled your brains, Krysty? Leave her. Maybe one day she really can be a future's hope. But not with us."

"The others?" J.B. asked. "One's kind of old and sick."

He was eighty-seven years old and had been frozen at the point of death from a cerebral tumor. He had won a Nobel Prize for atomic physics and had been an expert on remote-control missile detonators. So the comp-screen proudly announced.

The decision to leave the physicist on ice was unanimous, though Doc mumbled something about thawing him out and cutting his throat.

"The lady?"

Ryan's fingers moved over the keys to try to find an answer to Krysty's query.

"Least she's not too old. And she doesn't look too ill," J.B. said, waiting for the screen to display the information.

Wyeth, Mildred Winonia. Doctor of Medicine. Degrees earned and honorary see full printout. Born December 17, 1964. Parents black activists. Father, minister, killed in KKK (qv) firebombing in 1965. Mother marched in late fifties and sixties: *see also* Connor, Eugene ("Bull"); Kennedy, John Fitzgerald; Kennedy, Robert Francis; King, Martin Luther; Montgomery, Alabama; Selma, Alabama; Young, Andrew Jackson, Jr. Height, five feet four inches. Weight 136 pounds. Eyes brown. No distinguishing marks or scars.

Doc abruptly lost interest again and wandered off to peer into the cryo-containers.

Unmarried. Next of kin, mother. Leading U.S. authority on cryogenics, specializing in cryo-surgery. Frozen December 28, 2000 after complications arising from minor exploratory abdominal surgery. Details available under Medical History.

"Sounds quite a lady," Krysty commented. "Be interesting to try to defrost her."

"Probably kill her," Ryan replied. He watched as the screen continued to outline details of Mildred Wyeth's long-ago life, including where she'd lived and been educated, and titles of scientific papers she'd written. But there was one item that attracted the interest of all four of the watching companions.

Was chairperson of pistol club in hometown of Lincoln, Nebraska. Represented United States in

Olympic Games of 1996 in free-shooting competition. Won silver medal.

J.B. ticked off the points on his fingers. "Woman.
Looks healthy. Bright. Doctor. Real one, not like Doc.
And she can handle a blaster. What are we waiting for,
Ryan? Let's get her thawed out from the rad-blasted
coffin."

Ryan couldn't see a single reason to argue with the
Armorer. "Yeah. Let's do it."

THE FRIENDS REMEMBERED from their previous experience that the ritual of thawing out a freezie could
take a long time.

All of their combined skills were needed to master
the consoles. Fortunately, the basic process, once
properly initiated, was run by the all-knowing comp-
controls. But they had to try to monitor the display
panels showing vital functions. For nearly two hours,
every dial and meter remained blankly, stubbornly
unchanged.

Doc had fallen asleep, head on his hands, snoring
gently.

They could tell that things were happening. The
flow of liquids became swifter, and the pod began to
fill slowly with a swirling gas that obscured Dr.
Mildred Wyeth.

"Look." Krysty pointed to the monitor labeled Vital Function 3. A small blip had been traveling
soundlessly along a central line, but now there was a

tiny hiccup in the blip's movement and the faintest beeping sound from the speakers.

Doc looked up blearily. "We have lift-off," he said, and fell straight back asleep again.

Gradually the other monitor screens clicked into reluctant life. Drainage levels of certain fluids rose, while others dropped. The at first imperceptible heartbeat became audible. But the misting grew thicker, until it was impossible to see into the capsule that held the late Mildred Wyeth.

Jak went out after a half hour to check the rest of the complex, and found that the automatic fire controls had put out the blaze. "All heads dead," he told them, grinning happily.

It took more than three hours before all the vital signs steadied.

"Soon," Ryan predicted.

The fog of vapors within the pod gradually cleared, and they gathered around, waiting for the automatic lock to spring open and release the woman. Now they could see the rise and fall of her chest beneath the thin cotton of the shroud.

"Soon," Krysty agreed.

"Think she'll be a triple-stupe?" J.B. asked.

Ryan shook his head. "Way it looks from what we've seen, the dice don't roll for us. Soon as the capsule opens we'd best get blasters cocked and ready."

The liquids bubbled and seethed, with a hollow, draining sound, loud enough to jerk Doc from the welcoming arms of Lethe into a sudden, startled wakefulness.

"What, what? I agree with everything that the last speaker said." He looked around, rubbing his eyes. "Sorry, gentlemen. My apologies. Must have closed my eyes for a moment. Pray carry on with your experiment. I shall be with you shortly." He laid his head back down on his arms and immediately began to snore.

Ryan looked at the old man, the thought crossing his mind that the day might be coming fast when they and Doc would have to part company. As long as he still kept a reasonable hold on reality then it was fair enough to let him keep riding with them. But this current madness seemed more deeply rooted than ever before. And you couldn't carry crazed passengers with you through Deathlands.

"Things moving," Jak called from beside the pod. "Think moved."

The fingers, with pale long nails, were twitching, opening and closing as though they gripped some invisible weapons. The eyes blinked open, staring blind and blank at the misted interior of the cryo-pod. The mouth moved in a nervous tic, the tip of the pink tongue flicking out over wrinkled, dry lips. Ryan noticed that like Doc, the woman had excellent, strong white teeth. A rarity now, in Deathlands.

"Come on, Mildred," Krysty whispered, her hand resting gently on the exterior of the capsule. "It's getting warmer," she added, looking at the others.

The blips on the screens were moving faster, like dancing emeralds. The beeping sounds were louder and closer together.

"Heart and breathing quicker," J.B. observed, his tone revealing his worry. "Could be too quick."

"Can we open it up faster?" Ryan asked, looking back at the main control consoles.

"There's a clock counting down on her numbered pod," Krysty pointed. "Down to three minutes and eighteen seconds."

"Bleeps going mutie-shit," Jak observed. "Explode any minute."

The four watchers slowly moved back from the pod, all holding blasters, ready to protect themselves against . . . whatever.

"Two minutes dead," J.B. said.

They heard the synchronized snap of heavy sec locks opening, the noise again stirring Doc from his slumbers. He sat up, peering curiously across the room. "Nearly cooked to a turn, is it? Then let the thanksgiving commence."

"Forty seconds," Krysty counted. "Pulse and respiration are steadying."

At thirty seconds they heard the hiss of stabilizing air and the lid began to move slowly open. They smelled the strange odor they all recalled from the last freezie center, a bitter scent carrying the taint of an ancient, chemical death.

"Like knifing gut of up-belly gator," Jak said, wrinkling his nose and turning away in disgust at the fetid stench.

"Take your word for it," Ryan told him.

The digital printout clicked its way through the last ten seconds, freezing to a stop on 00.00.

The lid was now fully open, tendrils of dank mist trailing over the edges of the container. Dr. Mildred Wyeth lay there, eyes open, breathing steadily. She showed none of the signs of madness they'd seen on other thawing freezies.

The room was flooded with a sudden stillness as the five companions stared at the woman from the far-off, almost mythic past. And she, reclining, looked back at them.

"Hi," Ryan said.

Brown eyes turned to him. The woman's tongue moistened her lips, but she didn't speak.

"Hi," Ryan repeated.

Mildred Wyeth cleared her throat. "Hi, yourself," she said huskily. "If you're a cryo-ressus team, then I'm the goddamned Queen of Sheba!"

CHAPTER THIRTEEN

"NOW YOU KNOW. You know who we are, and you know what's been happening in the hundred years or so since you went under."

Ryan leaned back against the pile of blankets, looking around the circle of friends, in case anyone had anything to add. Only Krysty offered to speak.

"That's about five years per minute, Mildred. But I don't think Ryan left much out."

"You got any questions?" J.B. asked.

They were holed up for the night in what had been some kind of staff lounge for the doctors and nurses. They'd found blankets in the closets and plenty of sofas. With the sec doors, it was a reasonably safe place to pass the dark hours.

One of Mildred's first requests had been for some clothes, "So's I can get out of this damned shroud."

She now wore a nurse's white blouse tucked into men's dark blue pants. They had also found white sneakers that fitted her and a heavy wool sweater in case they encountered colder weather.

Now she sat across from the others, almost as if she'd come along to be interviewed for a job. Despite the fact that she'd just been brought back to consciousness after a century of nothingness, Mildred Wyeth didn't seem at all fazed by the experience. And there was no sign, Ryan was delighted to see, of any kind of mental disturbance from the unfreezing.

Not yet, he thought to himself cautiously.

"Do I have any questions, J.B.? Let me see." The hoarseness was easing, though she had a beaker of distilled water at her side, from which she sipped constantly. "I guess that if I really set my mind to it I could come up with at least seven-and-a-half-thousand questions." The gentle smile disappeared. "What the heck do you think, mister? What a damn fool question that is!"

"Sorry, but—"

"Oh, forgive me for speaking while you're interrupting, mister. I've been lying in that icebox for a hundred years. You give me a fifteen-minute synopsis of what's been happening, and then ask if I *might* have a question!"

"Being frozen sure didn't do anything to improve your temper, lady," Doc said testily.

"What?"

"Perhaps it made you a mite deaf into the bargain, did it?"

"You damned old goat! Talk to me like that and I'll knock you on your skinny ass!"

Ryan, Krysty, J.B. and Jak watched in absolute amazement. Doc had shown no interest in the newly thawed Dr. Wyeth, totally ignoring her, which was yet another worrying symptom of the old man's withdrawal into catatonia. Now, out of the blue, he had launched into the woman—who seemed better than able to look after herself in any full and frank exchange of views.

"You and whose army, ma'am?" Doc bellowed, drawing himself up to his full skinny height.

"Go piss up a rope, asshole," Mildred snapped, also standing. But her muscles were weakened by the long immobility, and she tottered and nearly fell over.

Doc laughed. "It'll take some time before you can back up all the big talk. You're as feeble as an hour-old colt, ma'am."

"I believe that your name is Theophilus Tanner, is it not?" Mildred asked with a deceptive quietness.

"Such is my name, Dr. Wyeth," Doc replied with a courteous bow.

"Well, Theophilus Tanner," the woman began. Suddenly she raised her voice to a piercing, eldritch screech of insensate rage. "Fuck you!"

Krysty was sitting next to Ryan, and she leaned across to him, whispering, "Doesn't seem much wrong with Mildred Wyeth, lover."

"Long as you keep to the windward side of her temper." Ryan grinned.

THE MOVEMENT WOKE Ryan, and his finger automatically slid onto the trigger of his SIG-Sauer.

"Don't shoot, Ryan."

"Mildred?"

Most of the lights had been disconnected by J.B. so that they could sleep in something close to darkness. Ryan, on one of the long sofas, could just make out the silhouette of the woman looming over him.

"Sorry to wake you."

"Sure."

"Mind if I sit down here a spell? Legs aren't that strong yet."

Ryan sat up, gesturing to her. "Sure. Pull up a corner."

"Thanks. Got to talk some. You're leader of this group."

It wasn't a question, but Ryan nodded anyway. "Yeah. I am."

"And this Deathlands is simply the good old U.S. of A. but reverted to a kind of primitive way of life. Like Pol Pot and the Khmer Rouge. Back to Year Zero and all that crap."

Ryan didn't know what she was talking about, but it sounded like a kind of sense, which was reassuring. He nodded again.

"And you and the others are like . . . like . . . I guess like a sort of Magnificent Seven."

"There's only five of us now. Six with you. Not seven."

She laughed. "I guess I've got so much to learn that . . . No. What I'm trying to get to, Ryan, is that the Deathlands is full of baddies. Black hats. And you are the goodies, the white hats?"

He shook his head this time. "No, Mildred. In Deathlands there isn't much of good or bad. Generally it's just a lot of people, doing the best they can." He was aware that the phrase had a familiar ring to it, but he couldn't just remember where he'd heard it before.

"A place of mean streets. But you and the others walk down them and you aren't mean. Something like that, Ryan?"

This time the question was clearly there. "Yeah. Sounds about right, Mildred."

"Then I might be lucky about being thawed out by you and not by some of the others, I guess." This time she seemed to be almost talking to herself. "Thanks, Ryan. Thanks for unlocking Sleeping Beauty from her ivory tower."

"Sure."

Mildred stood up on wobbly legs, smiling down at him, her teeth showing white in the dimness. "Some charming prince, Ryan. Sorry I woke you. Good night, now. Sleep tight."

"And you."

BY MORNING Mildred had recovered still more of her strength. Jak had scouted around and discovered some sealed packs of food-tabs. Though they tasted much like a compressed mixture of mud and chaff, they provided all the essential proteins and vitamins to get a person through a day.

"Nourishing, they may be," Doc said, "but delicious they are not."

Mildred grinned at him. "Just for once, Doc, you and I are in agreement."

"Then I hope that it will not be the last time, Dr. Wyeth," he replied gallantly.

"And my name is Mildred, if that isn't too familiar for you."

Doc half bowed. "Mildred it shall be."

Krysty caught Ryan's eye and winked at him. The change in Doc was astounding. The arrival of this freezie, with her opinionated manner, had been just what the old man needed to nudge him from the madness of the triple jump.

After the meal the companions headed out. When they reached the doors that opened onto the tropical jungles of Minnesota, Ryan eased cautiously through, then beckoned the others to follow him into the humid sweltering air.

Mildred was third out, and she paused, looking around in amazement. Then she turned angrily and accusingly to Ryan.

"Some damned joke, isn't it?" she snapped.

"What?" Only part his attention was on her. Most was focused on searching for potential threats from the alien landscape.

"Funny, Ryan. If that's your real name. This institute was in Minnesota, near Duluth. I don't know what's going on here, but I know fucking well, if you'll pardon my French, that this is *not* Minnesota. It could be Hawaii, but Duluth it ain't, Jack!"

"This is the Shelley Cryonic Institute, Mildred," Krysty said. "Sign says so, right there."

"Nuking blew the world apart," Ryan reminded her. "There was a botanical complex here. The hot spots must have changed the weather and scattered some freak mutie seeds. That's our guess."

"Well, I'll shove my vibro through a flying doughnut! When they brought me in here it was bleak midwinter."

"Snow on snow." Doc earned himself a nod of appreciation from the woman.

"Near twenty feet, if I remember right. By God! But this is so wonderful! I always wondered what would happen if... Now I know, and I'm fine. Freezing really works."

J. B. Dix hawked and spit in the lush turf. "Not often, lady," he said, laconic as ever. "We tried thawing out lots, and you and one other guy were the only ones who made it."

"How come you froze?" Jak asked. "Look fucking good me."

"Thanks, son."

Jak opened his mouth, closed it again, opened it and, to the amazement of the others, said nothing.

Mildred watched this performance with some surprise. "What's the matter, son?"

"Please, don't call 'son' or 'kid' or nothing like that."

"Sure thing, Jak. Sorry. You asked me why I was frozen. I went into Bethesda for a routine checkup and biopsy, suspecting an ovarian cyst. Surgeon didn't think it was serious."

"But they found it was . . ." Krysty struggled a moment for the word she wanted. "Malignant? Was that what they found?"

Mildred shook her head. Her black hair was shaped into dozens of tiny, tight plaits, and they glinted in the watery sunlight. "No. Never got that far. I had this totally freak reaction to the anesthesia and the preop, and I went into convulsions. Really far out, like I was up there on the ceiling of the operating room watching my body down below. I went into a coma for a time. All the vital signs were failing. Because I was important in the cryo field, they wanted to keep me if they could, and coptered me up here. Snow was everywhere. I remember that. I could see and hear, but I couldn't move a damned thing. Then they started the cryo-processing, and the rest, as they say, is silence."

"And now you find yourself here, in this wicked, ravaged world," Doc concluded. "Believe me, dear lady, you have my entire sympathy for your grievous predicament."

In his careful introduction, Ryan had touched on the backgrounds of himself and the other members of the group, so Mildred understood the reason behind Doc's kind words. She nodded and smiled at him.

"Thanks. I guess, like you, there'll be times I find all this madness easy to cope with. Other times it'll be harder." She paused, looking out over the rich vegetation and the slow-flowing river. When she spoke again, her voice crackled with emotion. "Knowing that everyone you ever loved ... has gone—not just gone, but long, long gone—that's not easy. Ma must have passed away at least eighty years ago. My nieces ... all dead."

"You were not married?" Doc asked gently.

"No, no. Work came first for this child, and fighting for rights. My people's rights and the rights of women. You folk can't realize what a shit-world it was, back then."

"Times it's like that here, Mildred," Krysty told her.

"Ma told me that life wasn't just a bowl of damned cherries," Mildred continued, "and, by God, she was surely right."

A dragonfly darted from the trees beyond the water, fully eighteen inches in length, shining with a dazzling, iridescent purple sheen. It hovered for a few moments near the group, then moved away, its wings a shimmering blur.

The freezie watched it in silence, before shaking her head in disbelief. "And now you'll tell me that it isn't just the trees and flowers that have gone extra-freaky! That was one of the most beautiful things I've ever seen in my life. Are there more of those around the Deathlands?"

Ryan answered. "Beauty and horror. Most species, including humans, have mutated over the past century. You'll see something of both sides of the jack around here, Mildred."

"I can't wait." She looked at the five friends in turn. "Seems to me I've got a fair range here, from what you told me about yourselves. A redheaded medium, an albino street punk, a two-hundred-year-old fart, a gun freak and a one-eyed killer." She laughed. "Ma always used to moan that I made some odd friends. Boy, oh, boy. If she could see me now!"

Her amusement was infectious and they all began to laugh.

CHAPTER FOURTEEN

To THE NORTHEAST of the rambling complex, the surrounding hills seemed to rise higher. It was the obvious procedure in a strange place to try to get a good vantage point to see the lay of the land.

Jak led, picking his way through the twining undergrowth, disturbing flocks of brilliant butterflies, which rose about him as thick as a curtain. There didn't seem to be much animal life in the region. Once a startled deer broke from a thicket, its knobbed antlers trailing ragged fronds of yellow ferns. A coyote could be heard calling, far away, the mournful echo bouncing back. Once J.B. heard rustling in the thick foliage and just glimpsed what he swore was a diamondback rattler. But its body was as thick as a man's thigh.

"If we're really in Minnesota, and I still find it kind of hard to believe, then the way we're heading should bring us up toward the Great Lakes. The western tip of Superior is my guess." Mildred paused and wiped streams of perspiration from her forehead. "Worse than a Harlem summer."

Ryan couldn't remember whether he'd ever been up close to what had once been called the Great Lakes.

He'd seen them on maps from predark days, and heard the talk of traders and traveling men that there were still great inland seas. Some were said to be so polluted that if a man fell in the water the acids would strip sinew from bones within seconds.

They paused in a clearing and sat down for a five-minute rest. There were more insects around, and Krysty had heard the distant ominous humming of what might have been another swarm of killer bees. But all that threatened them was a large hornet, its body bloated and striped, its barbed sting dripping a thick poisonous ichor as it flew close by. Jak drew one of his throwing-knives, but the giant insect seemed to perceive the hostile gesture and buzzed away.

"Screen back there made out you were good with a blaster," J.B. said, industriously polishing the smeared lenses of his glasses.

"It did?"

"Ninety-six Olympics you got a silver medal in free shooting."

Mildred nodded slowly. "Wasn't worth the gilt coating."

"How's that?" Ryan asked. "Thought the Olympics were something special."

"That altius, fortius shit! What was more important was just who had the best drug specialist. Blockers, uppers, slowers, biggers and fasters."

"You took drugs?" Jak asked.

"Sure. Everyone did. In pistol shooting you need to squeeze between heartbeats. So you take blockers to slow the pulse. Then you need covers to conceal what you've taken. Most teams had up to thirty outside specialists helping."

"If everyone took drugs, then everyone was the same," Doc said slowly. "So if everyone stopped taking drugs, then everyone would still be the same. So why..."

"Why take drugs, Doc? Because how d'you know the bastard in the butts next along hasn't taken anything? You trust the Russians? Or the Japanese? Or the Brits? Or the Germans? Hell, nobody trusted anyone."

"Should have been Games four years later, shouldn't there?" Krysty asked.

Mildred lay flat on her back, hands clasped behind her head. "Right, lady. But my medal was kind of devalued. Half the Eastern bloc didn't show. Most of the Third World countries joined in a boycott. Only about a dozen left in my event."

"What kind of blaster did you use?" J.B. asked.

"Ah, I had some lovely pistols. I never cared much for the latest guns. I bought a beautiful .22 made just before the Second World War. Udo Anschutz. The Record Match, Model 210. Also had a couple of Schultz & Larsens that I picked up from a dealer in New Orleans. I tried a Walther OSP and a Model 80 Beretta. In the end I had Ruger make me up a special. Cost an arm and a leg, but it was just like part of my wrist."

Ryan and J.B. listened, fascinated. Though the Armorer was probably the greatest living expert on firearms, Ryan, too, was always interested in different blasters.

"You fire anything bigger than a two-two?" J.B. asked.

"Of course. I figure here you need something that'll man-stop with a single hit. I saw that you both carry big handguns."

They both nodded. "What other kind of blasters did you favor, Mildred?" Ryan asked.

"Lots. It was my hobby. I went through the usual range of Smith & Wessons, Colts, Blackhawks, Walthers... Oh, my club bought me a real nice Hammerli Match pistol, last year." Her face changed as she realized what she'd just said. "Guess I don't mean that. I mean the year before the pool of blackness opened at my feet and I dived into it. Ready for the big sleep."

"Have to get you a blaster, soon as we can," Krysty suggested.

"Wonder what happened to my guns?" Mildred mused. "Burned up in the big bang, I guess. I had a Le Mat like Doc here. Big pinfire, ten shot. Had a Remington rifle cane, not like that swordstick, Doc. Percussion cap. Still worked. You know, I used it once, for real."

"When?" J.B. asked, fascinated by Mildred's recital of her weapon collection.

"Son of a bitch mugger, just a hundred yards off Beacon Hill in Boston. Came at me with a pissant little zip gun. Thought he was Rambo. I put one through his pissant little cock with the Remington and taught him different."

They all laughed. Ryan looked wonderingly at the black woman, hardly able to believe their luck in finding a freezie like her. Mentally stable, seeming in great physical shape and also a good hand with a blaster. *And* a doctor, he reminded himself.

J.B. stood up, stretching. "I can't tell you what it's like to talk to someone like you, Mildred. Truly."

She grinned and got to her feet, helping herself with a hand against the trunk of a gigantic eucalyptus. "I bet you say that to all the girls."

The Armorer adjusted his fedora and wiped sweat away from his forehead. "It's true, though. Someone from before the long winters and who knows a lot about blasters. I could listen to you for days."

"Talk's cheap," Doc muttered tetchily.

"How's that?" she snapped, turning on him, eyes narrowing to pinpoints of anger.

"I remarked, merely, that talk was very cheap, Dr. Wyeth. But the price of action can sometimes be more realistic."

"Realistic! Are you implying that I'm making this up? That I can't really shoot?"

"No, no no. I read the screen on you, as we all did. I'm sure that it was once true. But that was many years ago."

"And besides, Doc, the bitch is dead! Is that what you mean? That I couldn't do it now? Ryan, give me that pistol of yours. I'm getting tired of this old guy's flapping tongue and that hornet's endless buzzing. Can't do much about the one, but I can sure as shit stop the other."

Ryan handed over the SIG-Sauer, watching the woman carefully. He noticed that J.B. had eased his own pistol, just in case. Looking out for "just in case" was a good way of staying alive.

"Thanks." She looked at Doc. "You figure I don't know guns? This is the SIG-Sauer, P-226. Fifteen rounds of 9 mm ammo. Barrel length is just under four and a half inches. Overall length is seven and three-quarter inches. Weighs in at a fingernail under twenty-six ounces. What else? Yeah. Push-button mag release. This built-in baffle silencer's a later addition, coming in not that long before I was . . . ill." The hesitation was almost imperceptible.

"Talk," Doc whispered.

The humming of the darting mutie insect was loud enough to almost drown out his word. But not quite.

"All right to fire one off, Ryan?" Mildred asked.

"Sure," he replied, impressed that she'd thought to ask first.

The woman tested the pistol for weight and balance, smiling approvingly. Her eyes followed the huge insect as it lunged and thrusted menacingly, feinting in toward the watchers, then cutting away, its hum increasing to a raging whine. Ryan's guess put it at close to a foot long, but it was moving very fast and erratically. If Mildred Wyeth really thought she could hit it, in midair, then she had a lot of confidence and nerve.

With the silencer, the sound of the SIG-Sauer was little louder than an elderly clergyman's clearing his throat. Mildred had braced her right wrist with her left for extra steadiness, shooting, Ryan was pleased to see, without squinting an eye shut. He was a lot better than average shot himself, but he was aware that his monocular vision prevented him from ever being outstanding.

On the evidence of that single, squeezed shot, Mildred was outstanding. The mutie insect disintegrated in a rainbow burst of shattered pulp as it was obliterated by the 9 mm full-metal-jacket round. There was virtually nothing left of its corpse to fall lightly to the dense foliage around them.

"Nice shot," Krysty said.

"Terrific shot," J. B. amplified admiringly. Ryan nodded his agreement. Jak gaped, slack-jawed.

"Could have been luck," Doc grunted, but his eyes were twinkling and he couldn't check a foolish grin from establishing itself across his face. "But," he added hastily, "I guess it wasn't luck. Just damnably good shooting. My congratulations, ma'am."

"Old hand and eye haven't lost much of their coordination." Mildred handed the warm gun back to

Ryan. "It pulls a half inch or so left over fifty yards. If you like, I could fix it for you."

Ryan shook his head in amused disbelief. Now they were six again.

CHAPTER FIFTEEN

THE FRIENDS CONTINUED northeast, stopping every hour or so to try to draw breath in the fetid heat of the jungle. Twice they crossed flowing water. On the second occasion Jak tripped over a web of tangling vines and tumbled into the river. Ryan was there first, crawling onto a fallen tree to peer for the vanished boy.

The silt was so thick that he feared for a dozen heartbeats that Jak might have been sucked under and trapped in the mud and weeds. Then his eye was caught by a tremor of movement, deep in the turgid stream. A flash of white, like a fish moving belly-up or like waving strands of albino hair.

Hanging on with his left hand to a moss-slick stump, Ryan swung himself over and down, his right hand reaching into the warm waters. He fumbled for a moment, then found the tangled skein of hair. He clutched at it, knotting Jak's hair in his fist and heaving up with all of his strength. Then J.B. was at his side, pulling on Ryan's belt to save the man from being drawn in after the teenager.

Krysty was also on the log, helping the Armorer to tug Jak from the river's sucking embrace. She tucked him under her arm and carried him to the bank. J.B.

heaved Ryan to safety, and the two men also made it back to solid earth.

Jak lay on his back, arms limp, one leg folded under him. His eyes were closed and brown water trickled from his open mouth. His hair was matted and filthy, framing his white face.

"We going to stand around and watch the boy die?" Mildred snapped.

"I was—" Krysty began, but the older woman elbowed her aside.

"Cemeteries are full with folks who got there because of other folk's good intentions. Lad's swallowed most of the river. Give me room."

Mildred hoisted her pants and dropped astride the unconscious boy, digging fists hard under his rib cage and pushing. Jak expelled more of the river and jerked spasmodically, his left leg kicking out. Mildred nodded to herself. "That's it, son," she said. "Let's fight for it." She bent lower and applied her mouth to Jak's bloodless lips, breathing into his body, then easing away again. She lifted his arms from the ground and then lowered them, repeating the process several times.

"Will our snow-headed chum be all right, Doctor?" Doc asked cautiously.

Jak gave the answer himself, suddenly coughing and spitting out a mixture of brackish water and vomit. Mildred had anticipated the reaction and dodged sideways.

"This is the moment I hate most. Been puked over when I summered as a lifeguard, premed school. Sit up, Jak."

The boy coughed and spluttered again, and she helped him with an arm behind the shoulders. His eyes were open, glowing like chips of molten ruby in the caverns of washed ivory.

"Better?"

"Yeah. What fuck happened? Tree grabbed me. In water. Thought farm bought."

"Ryan pulled you out," Mildred replied, standing and brushing moss and dead leaves off her blouse. "You should thank him."

"And Mildred brought you back to us," Ryan insisted, trying to wring water out of his clothes. He dislodged a black leech from his wrist and stared at the blurred streak of diluted blood where it had been happily feeding.

"Thanks, Mildred. Thanks, Ryan."

The woman grinned and patted him hard on the back, making him cough again. "Think nothing of it. Just take two tablets and call me in the morning if you don't feel better. You do have Blue Cross coverage, I take it?"

Jak shook his head, bewildered.

"No? Then I might just have to throw you back in the river."

IT WAS the middle of the afternoon, and they'd been climbing steadily for the past couple of hours. The vegetation was beginning to show the first signs of thinning out, and the overwhelming heat was easing a little.

Krysty was taking her turn with Ryan's panga, which had by now lost its keenest edge. They had just beaten their way through a towering cluster of waxen, orange and scarlet flowers, whose twisted trumpet shape defeated even Krysty's knowledge of botany.

"Listen," she said, holding up the panga, the steel dripping emerald sap.

Ryan was next in line. "What is it, lover? Trouble ahead?"

She shook her head. "Two things. Heard them both, round about the same time. One of them is a kind of drumming."

"Drumming?" Mildred asked. "You mean the war brought some kind of weird natives along with the jungle?"

Krysty didn't smile. "Don't know, but it's definitely some kind of rhythmic drums. Could be three miles or more ahead. Over the ridge that we're heading for."

"You said two things," Ryan pressed. "What's the other one?" He noticed that her hair was suddenly curling in closer against her neck and shoulders, a sure sign that she "felt" some kind of trouble threatening them.

"Don't know. Mixed-up sort of signal, like some animal, or lots of animals. But it's overlaid with a lot of fear."

"How do you receive that kind of signal?" Mildred asked interestedly. "Do you see it in some way?"

Krysty looked at her, blinking as though she didn't recognize her. "Oh, sorry. Miles away. How do I feel threats? Don't know. Mebbe if I knew I couldn't do it. Mother Sonja taught it me back in my home ville of Harmony. No. No, *taught* isn't the right word. She showed me how to use something that was already within me. Can't tell you more than that, Mildred. Sorry."

"Orange alert," Ryan said. "Move a little slower. I'll take point, Krysty." He saw the argument surfacing angrily in her eyes and defused it quickly. "It's my turn, lover. That's all."

He took the panga and began to slice through the undergrowth, leading them slowly toward higher ground.

Fifteen minutes later they became aware of movements in the jungle around them. First it was small animals, swinging high and invisible in the top branches, chattering and squealing excitedly as they went. Then it was bigger creatures, lumbering along narrow, twisting paths, parallel to the track that Ryan had found.

Birds, many of them just brightly colored blurs, hummed between the low branches, squawking madly as they flew south. An animal resembling a panther, but lower to the ground and with light gold stripes across its flanks, came straight at Ryan. He drew a bead on it with the blaster, holding his fire until the last moment. The creature cut aside, breaking through a scented bush. Its eyes had been blankly staring and its muzzle laced with white foam.

"Could it be a blaze?" Doc suggested. "I have seen this sort of terror down in the southwest, many years ago. Every living thing for fifty miles was racing for its very life."

"Wind's blowing toward us," Jak said. "Can't smell smoke."

J.B. took off his hat and smelled the air. "Yeah. No fire. Something else, though. Mebbe worse."

Ryan looked around them. There was an enormous tree about two hundred yards dead ahead, with multiple trunks that twined around one another. The leaves were dark olive green, shiny in the late-afternoon sun.

"Make for that," he ordered, pointing. "Give us some shelter and a fire defense from whatever it is that's coming this way."

At that moment he distinctly felt the earth tremble beneath his feet as if some massive underground monster surged deep below him.

"Fireblast! What the..."

The others felt it, though less strongly. Mildred jumped sideways and clutched at Doc's arm. Ryan noticed that the old man didn't make any attempt to remove it.

"This is a dreadful place, this Deathlands!" she gasped. "Maybe you ought to have left me frozen back there."

For several minutes the jungle had been filled with pounding, racing life. But the tropical vegetation was so thick that it wasn't possible to do more than glimpse what was happening.

A large brindled wolf, dangling a mewing cub from its jaws, appeared on the path, stopping as it saw the six humans blocking its escape. It snarled through bloodied teeth.

"Chill it," J.B. warned.

"No," Krysty said. "Let it pass. It's already terrified. Why chill it?"

They all edged back into the bushes and luxuriant shrubs, opening up the track. After a moment's hesitation the wolf moved toward them and padded quickly along, glancing over its shoulder as though it sensed something rushing behind it.

"A frightful fiend doth close behind him tread," Doc said quietly as the animal vanished.

"Listen," Krysty warned, standing stock-still, the silvered Heckler & Koch pistol gripped in her right hand.

"What?" J.B. probed.

"Can't hear a sound, lover," Ryan said.

"That's the point, isn't it, Krysty?" Mildred asked. "It's totally silent. So what put the fear of the Almighty into those creatures? What comes on silent feet?"

"Get to the tree," Ryan commanded, feeling a prickle at his nape.

The light wind had dropped, and the sweltering heat had returned. They seemed to stand at the center of a dome of overpowering stillness.

They'd closed half the distance between themselves and what Ryan could now see was a ponderous mangrove tree when he glimpsed something in front of them, across an area of more open ground that was dotted with light yellow flowering bushes.

His first thought was that a dam had burst somewhere up the slope ahead of them. It looked as if a stream of water, shimmering and gleaming, had forked around the massive trunk of the tree.

But his second thought was the right one.

"Ants! Mutie ants!" he yelled, glancing around for the safest escape route.

Behind them lay the jungle and any number of fleeing, terrified creatures. The flanks were cut off by impenetrable walls of jungle. Which left one possibility.

"Come on!" he shouted, springing toward the unknowable insect army.

CHAPTER SIXTEEN

THE STREAM OF ANTS was only the advance guard, which numbered in tens of thousands, rather than in tens of millions, but still enough to make the race for the shelter of the mangrove one of the most desperate of Ryan Cawdor's life.

Each ant was more than a foot long, with a carapace of fiery copper. The mandibles were huge, disproportionate even to the insect's grotesquely mutated size. Longer than a man's finger, they clicked together in a deafening warning as the ants picked up the approach of the six companions. Those at the front reared up on hind legs, their heads turning from side to side.

As Ryan led the charge, the very front row retreated a few yards, then regrouped in a solid phalanx of glittering death.

To hesitate was to die.

For the first dozen steps, Ryan tried to dodge the ants, but they were packed too closely for him to find any clear ground between them. The crunching of delicate skeletons beneath boot heels almost drowned out the clicking. Ryan kept moving, powering himself toward the tree, which was now only twenty yards distant. He didn't dare turn to see if the others were making it. A stumble would put a person on the last train to the coast.

He could now see something of the main body of the killer army beyond the mangrove. Not an inch of ground was free of the iridescent horde that swept toward him.

Weighing up the chances as he ran, Ryan had already spotted several low branches within easy reach. He became aware of Jak sprinting past, white hair streaming behind him like a snowy banner. The boy made the tree a torn fragment of time ahead of Ryan, diving for a branch and swinging himself onto it with a prehensile agility.

When Ryan was perched four feet from the carpet of ants, he was finally able to look around for the others. He saw Krysty running like someone dancing on hot coals, trying to pick her way between the mutie insects. J.B. was level with her, running flat-footed, deliberately crushing as many ants as he could.

Mildred and Tanner shared last spot in the desperate race.

"Go!" Jak yelled.

Ryan reached a hand down to Krysty and heaved her up beside him. J.B. made it on a lower branch to the left of the mangrove, standing up and looking down at the tide of insects, hand trembling over the butt of his pistol as though he wanted to spray lead into the limitless swell of the ants. But he recognized the utter futility of the thought.

"Doc!" Krysty cried, seeing the old man stumble and nearly fall, ants snapping at his knee boots. Mildred snatched his elbow, keeping him on his feet and bringing him close enough to the giant mangrove for J.B. to haul him up in a flailing tangle of arms and legs.

The woman screamed as one of the mutie insects managed to nip her just above the left ankle. It clung to her flesh as she staggered the last few steps to the tree. Krysty and Ryan both stretched out hands and pulled her off the ground.

"Jeez!" Mildred yelled. "Get that mother off of me."

Ryan swung a fist at the huge ant that pincered her leg in its sawing mandibles. Its thin neck snapped and the body fell away, legs twitching, to be immediately swallowed in the sea of its voracious fellows. But the head remained in place, feelers vibrating, huge eyes swiveling in their sockets. Blood was flowing freely through the thin material of Mildred's pants, soaking her sneaker.

"It's still biting me," she cried, her face contorted with pain.

Cautiously avoiding the snapping mandibles, Ryan squeezed the ant's head between finger and thumb. Its skull was as large as a rat's, and it was all he could do to keep a grip on it. He pulled it away from Mildred's leg, until the claws came free. The severed head wriggled in his grasp, trying to snap at him, until he dropped it to the ground. Ryan was unable to restrain a shudder of deepest revulsion.

"Best get higher!" J.B. shouted. "Bastards are trying t'figure a way of climbing up here after us."

Fighting to control his breathing, Ryan looked down. The clicking had stopped, and the army of killer ants was moving in a sinister, restless silence. It was like being suspended above a sea of molten lava, endlessly shifting, surging around the trunk of the tree.

The Armorer was right. Already a few of the nearer insects were on hind legs, exploring the smooth bark of the mangrove with their feelers.

"You okay, Mildred?" Ryan asked.

"Yeah, I'll make it. The bite burns, like it injected acid. Probably did."

"Thanks, ma'am," Doc called from his perch. "Never thought I might, mayhap, end my days as live food for ants."

Krysty had been peering above them, into the dark, leafy bows. The roots that twined beneath them all seemed to finally come together in a single main trunk. "That way," she said. "Got to find a place they can't come at us in numbers. Get up there and spread out."

Ryan looked where she pointed and nodded his agreement. "Yeah. Everyone? Jak, go first."

"Climbing on each other's backs," J.B. said. The place was so quiet now that he hardly needed to raise his voice for the others to hear.

The ants were forming a brazen pyramid, scrambling over one another's bodies, gaining height.

Within a few seconds their leaders would be into the lower branches of the tree.

Jak was up and away, barely using his hands as he scampered into the upper branches. "Here! Fuckers can't get other way."

Ryan motioned for J.B. to go second, helping Mildred and Doc as he went. Krysty went next, leaving Ryan alone on the low, angled part of the bole of the tree. As he readied himself to move, Ryan saw the first of the questing ants appear, its feelers tasting the air. He drew the panga, waiting a moment until the whole of the creature's body was in sight.

"So long," he grunted, the broad metal blade slicing easily through the center of the ant's swollen belly. A foul-stinking liquid squirted out, a few drops pattering on the skin of his wrist. Feeling it beginning to burn his flesh, Ryan quickly wiped it off with his sleeve.

Almost instantly a dozen more of the mutie insects came chittering over the side of the branch, scuttling toward him.

"Move, lover!" Krysty called from thirty feet above him.

"Yeah. Guess I'd better."

"THIS IS what I believe is called a Texarkana stand-off," Doc said. "We can stop them getting at us, but I fear that they can make it confoundedly difficult for us to remove ourselves."

Darkness was creeping over the land, drawing a cloak of night across the jungle. The drumming that Krysty had heard earlier had ceased. Clouds had come up and the setting sun, away behind them, was only visible as a crimson glow at the edge of the bowl of mountains.

"Could be the last hurrah for us," Mildred said quietly. They kept their voices down once they discovered that any noise they made seemed to provoke the ants to ferocious activity.

As long as the friends watched the main trunk of the mangrove immediately below them, the mutie insects had no way of reaching them. It wasn't hard to hold them off with the panga if they came crawling up.

It would be a little harder in the dark.

The traveling army of giant ants seemed content to wait.

The dying embers of the day shone over their orange-red bodies, making it seem that the very land was smoldering. After Ryan had killed a hundred or more, they'd suddenly ceased their efforts to climb the mangrove. Once or twice a lone soldier had attempted an attack, but its headless corpse had fallen to the earth.

J.B. had methodically checked their options, climbing to the soaring, swaying peak of the tree, to try to find out whether they might be able to scramble away into the nearby branches. But the closest was more than twenty feet away and was so slender that to jump would mean a fifty-foot fall into the carpet of ants.

He and Ryan had discussed the possibility of using some of their newfound supply of grens to try to dissipate the patient army of gigantic insects. Even a couple of burners might only kill a few thousand ants. Frags and implodes wouldn't even scratch the surface of the limitless forces, which surrounded the tree as far as the eye could see in every direction.

"Outwait them" was J.B.'s best offer.

Ryan didn't have anything much better. "If they're still here through tomorrow, then we have to reckon they'll stay here forever. Or for long enough."

"But they'll starve," Krysty said.

Mildred knocked that one down. "Army of ants like this could survive days. If they just use a small part of their force to scavenge around for food for the others, they can outwait us. We have those food-tabs, but in heat like this we're sweating about a pint of water an hour."

"How long could we survive?" Doc asked. "Until tomorrow night?"

She nodded. "Probably. But we'll be in poor shape by then."

Ryan sniffed. "So, the only chance is to try and run through them. If we can keep going, and not fall, our speed could get us through and out the other side. Unless anyone's got a better idea, we can try it at dawn. Mebbe drop a gren or two to give us a head start on them."

"Why dawn?"

Ryan looked at Jak. "Can't risk it in the dark. False step, twisted ankle... and goodbye was all she wrote. Wait longer and we just get more tired. Dawn's the best moment."

Nobody agreed with him out loud. But then again, nobody disagreed either.

BOTH KRYSTY AND JAK had excellent night vision, but the darkness in the jungle was so intense that neither could even see the ground. The blackness was so smothering that it wasn't even possible to see an outstretched hand.

The ants stayed quiet. Ryan organized everyone into a double sentry watch, keeping the guard in pairs to make sure there was no sleeping. If a dozen or more of the creatures below succeeded in sneaking up the tree under the cover of night, the venom of their bites could be enough to prevent any worthwhile defense.

Ryan and Krysty took the four hours that ran from early morning to the first pallid hint of the false dawn.

"Sure I heard drums again, around midnight," Krysty whispered.

"Same direction?"

"Think so. Northerly."

"If we make it out of this, we can go take a look."

She touched Ryan gently on the arm. "Just in case we don't, tomorrow," she began.

But he reached for Krysty's face, finding her lips, and laid his hand across her mouth. "No need, lover.

We both know what we feel about each other. Doesn't take words. If we get chilled in the morning, then it'll likely be quick. But I don't reckon on going. Not yet. Got too much living to do, lover.''

She held his hand and breathed a kiss into his palm. ''Fair enough. We'll make it together. Like you say... we both got a lot of living still to do.''

The layers of the night peeled back with an imperceptible slowness and subtlety. Ryan suddenly realized that he had caught a faint spark of fire from Krysty's long red hair.

''Dawn's coming,'' he announced.

CHAPTER SEVENTEEN

"My daddy was a Baptist minister, in a town outside of Montgomery, Alabama, until the Klan burned down his church and him inside it. He taught me how to pray, and this time I guess someone must have been listening in."

Mildred sat on the lowest branch of the mangrove, feet dangling over the bare earth. The heels of her sneakers rubbed against the main bole of the massive tree, which was scarred and torn by the serrated mandibles of the ants.

The army had gone, vanishing silently in the black middle of the night. It left nothing of itself behind, other than a swath of utter desolation, fully eighty paces wide and stretching in two directions as far as Ryan could see—toward the mountains, now visible as rounded silhouettes against the opalescent pink light, and back toward the river and the distant redoubt.

The trees remained, though some of the smaller ones had been stripped of leaves. Every flower and shrub had been devoured down to the ground, and every blade of lush grass had disappeared. The earth itself had been trampled flat, from the pounding of tens of millions of feet.

Ryan had wakened J.B., Jak, Doc and Mildred, showing with a wave of the hand that they'd been saved from testing themselves against the mutie ants.

"Where've they gone?" the Armorer wondered, rubbing his fingers over the scarred bark of the mangrove. "Looks like they thought about trying to cut this bastard tree down. Then gave up on it."

Mildred nodded. "Guess their scouts told them there was better eating ahead. If they'd really wanted us, they'd have stayed and cut through ten solid feet of wood as easy as a razor through an artery."

"I would hazard a guess that they could scent the river behind us," Doc suggested. "I also suggest that we might profitably begin to move ourselves. The migrations of killer ants are a total mystery to scientists. There isn't a guarantee that the little chaps won't return the same way in a couple of hours."

Moments later they were on the ground, following the trail of the army of ants. "It's like going from Atlanta to the sea," Doc commented. "Not a living thing left."

Away to the left, through the stripped, ravaged land, they glimpsed a river, perhaps the same one that had nearly taken Jak. At this point the ants' beaten track meandered away to the west.

"Didn't run fast," Jak said, pointing to something that gleamed white in the shadows.

"Wolf cub?" J.B. queried.

They stood in a silent half circle around the neat pile of polished bones. The ants had done their job with a total, finite efficiency, leaving nothing but the skeleton. Not a trace of sinew or ligament remained on the bones, but a few scrubby bunches of coarse, brindled hair lay on the ground. The eye sockets were empty and the long jaw was scoured clean.

"Not a wolf," Krysty said, stooping. "Not wild, anyway."

"How come you...? Oh, yeah." Ryan looked at what Krysty held out to him.

It was a narrow collar of plaited silver wire with a flat medallion on its end. Something was scratched on it.

"What's it say?" Mildred asked. "A name?"

"Odin," Doc replied.

"What fuck's an Odin?" Jak asked, turning the silver disk so that it caught the morning rays of sunlight.

"It's the name of one of the old Viking gods. Some people claim that it was the Vikings who first discovered the United States of America. Leif Eriksson, son of Erik the Red, called it 'Vinland,'some say. Odin was the leader of their gods, who was in charge of death and war, among other things."

"I saw part of an old vid once, Doc," Ryan said. "Long ships with oars on each side, and a man with only one eye. That's why I recall it. Swords and axes. How come there's a mess of bones out here called by the name of one of their gods?"

"Vikings here?" Krysty asked.

Mildred threw her head back and laughed, long and loud. "Hardly! No. Odin's the kind of jerk-off name that people gave their guard dogs back when I was...you know. Probably someone in a village or city somewhere came across the medallion. Liked it and tied it around the neck of his pet dog."

"Mebbe," Ryan replied. "Don't get many dogs kept as pets in Deathlands. Food, but not often as pets. And you have to remember there aren't cities anymore. Big villes and small villes. Not many big villes, either."

"God of death, you said, Doc." J.B. stirred the tumbled bones with the toe of his boot. "That's all he got."

THE AIR WAS GROWING cooler and fresher as the companions climbed toward the brink of the hill. They encountered more trails, some of which seemed to show the marks of human feet. But it had obviously rained within the previous sixty hours or so, and the spoor was indistinct.

"Look," Mildred said, pointing high above them, in the pale purple sky.

A bright crescent of flame arced from east to west, setting off a crackling chem storm of lightning as it passed.

"Nuke debris," J.B. explained.

"Sweet Lord! You tell me the world damned near blew apart a hundred years ago and there's *still* pieces of techno-shit falling from the heavens? If I could just go back—"

"One small step for the Totality Concept, one billion-dollar hunk of scrap iron for mankind," Doc muttered.

"Looks like some fog up ahead," Ryan called, easing the strap of the Heckler & Koch over his shoulder. "Must be where the edges of the hot air and the cold air marry together."

The top of the hill was about a half mile away. The thick jungle had gradually faded into low scrub, and the temperature had dropped to somewhere in the low sixties. Mildred had pulled on the hooded sweater. The ant bite she'd sustained had been swollen early in the morning, puffy and inflamed around its edges. But she'd pressed on, saying she figured it was best to try to walk the poison out.

"It looks like the mist tumbling in over the hills around San Francisco Bay," she said, shaking her head nostalgically. "I swear to God that it was one of the most beautiful sights in the whole ever-loving world."

The damp earth and compressed leaf mold had given way to small pebbles and bare rock. The trail had narrowed and become more distinct, zigzagging above them in a steady climb. The last hundred feet or so had now disappeared in the clinging bank of low cloud.

"Heard the drums again, lover," Krysty whispered at one of the sharp bends in the path.

"Sure?"

"Sure."

"SLOW DOWN, JAK!" Ryan called, feeling his voice muffled in fog the moment it left his lips. The skin on his cheeks felt cold and tight, and his coat was covered in a layer of fine drops of water. On an impulse he tasted it, finding the slightest hint of salt.

"I'm top," the boy replied from somewhere ahead and above them.

"I fear that the bellows to this organ of mine are becoming a trifle short of pressure," Doc said, doubling over in a coughing fit, hands on his knees.

"He means he's run out of breath," Mildred translated, picking up the ebony cane the old man had dropped and handing it back to him.

"You certainly have a way with words, ma'am. Short and simple."

She didn't rise to his baiting.

"Looks like the ridge, here," J.B. said, moving a few cautious feet along the spine of the hill, testing the path beneath his boots.

"Hear drums?" Jak asked suddenly, looking first to Krysty, as he knew that she had the best hearing in the group.

"Last night, in the tree, and this morning," she confirmed. "Down there. I can also feel water. Like an ocean. Could be one of those big lakes you mentioned, Mildred."

"Lake Superior? Could be. Would account more for this blasted fog."

J.B. joined Ryan. "Drums like they hear could mean Indians. Could be more of this stinking wet forest down there. Figure we go on or turn back now? Could be near the redoubt before full dark."

Ryan thought about what the Trader used to say: "Most men, faced with going on or turning back, will likely go forward. Nobody likes turning back. All you have to do is think clear which option is best." Ryan sometimes wondered if Trader's words had always been true. Certainly, in Deathlands, most men would strike ahead.

"It'll be closing on dusk when we're down in that jungle, J.B., and we don't know where those bastard mutie ants went. I say we go on, but slow and careful. You?"

"On? Hell, I knew that all along, Ryan. Just wanted to check you thought the same."

"DRUMS AGAIN, louder this time," Krysty called over her shoulder.

"And trees," Jak added, dancing light-footed ahead on point. "Spiky, not soft."

They were conifers, sparse at first, looming from the mist like stunted guards wrapped in cloaks of dark green. Then there were more of them, packed in closer to the edges of the winding trail.

By now they could all hear the rhythmic beating of drums.

"Kind of chilly for Indian savages," Doc said.

"Crap!" Mildred spit.

"How's that, madam?"

"Saying Indians don't come from cold regions. I guess I could name you a dozen tribes or more that do."

"Go on," Doc challenged, stopping on the path and bringing the whole group to a halt.

"Micmac, Penobscot, Algonquin, Huron, Ojibway, Mohawk, Yakima, Okanagan, Tlingit, Chinook, Beaver, Tanana, Cree, Bannock, Crow, Shoshone, Cheyenne. How many's that?"

"Around fifteen or so," J.B. said, grinning. "Better'n a dozen."

"If you like I could go on with another fifty, Doc. My minor was North American Indian Sociology, groupings and distribution."

"Humph!" Doc snorted and turned on his heel, setting off again down the trail at a fast lick.

The trees grew thicker, filling the damp air with the scent of balsam, and the mist became thinner.

"Think there's water close by," Krysty said, putting her head back and sniffing.

The steady beat of the drums was very loud. The path was leveling off as they came onto a flat wider trail among the trees.

"Meat cooking," Jak said.

Moments later they all caught the flavor of roasting, overlaid with the tang of smoldering pine logs.

"I'm not sure that noise is Indians," Mildred guessed. "More like African. Or...I don't know. It's not really like anything I ever heard."

There was the sudden sharp barking of a dog, followed by a shout and a blow. The barking stopped.

"Got to be a ville. Sounds less than a coupla hundred yards off," J.B. said, unholstering his Steyr AUG.

The wind gusted, and like a magician's trick, the curtain of fog vanished. They could see that they were close to the edge of the forest, and off in the distance they could make out the glittering expanse of a vast body of water. But between trees and lake was a largish ville: huts and fires, cows and hogs, men, women and children.

For several seconds none of the six friends spoke. It was Mildred Wyeth who broke the silence.

"Well, pardon my French, but you can fuck me sideways if they aren't Vikings!"

CHAPTER EIGHTEEN

JORUND THORALDSON, the baron of Markland, stood five inches over six feet and weighed nearly three hundred pounds. Not a lot of it was soft fat. His eyes were as blue as melting sea ice, and the hair that hung over his broad shoulders was white blond. Not quite as stark a hue as Jak Lauren's hair, but not far off it. His voice was a hearty rasping bellow that carried the flavor of oak-aged beer and salted herrings. He wore a shaggy woolen coat and leather pants, which were tucked into knee-length suede boots. A long, two-handed sword was sheathed on his left hip, and he carried a .38 Colt on his right.

"Greetings, outlanders!" he called, striding into the main hut of the ville, where Ryan and the others had been taken.

There had seemed no great threat as they hid at the fringe of the forest, watching. Then a skinny mongrel had scented them, its furious yapping bringing a dozen men to investigate.

It was a hair-trigger decision. Five or six of the villagers were carrying blasters, but they looked like old cap and ball pistols with a couple of ancient automatics. If Ryan had given the word, the villagers would have been down and dying in the damp grass.

"Hold it," he'd said.

And that looked like the correct decision.

The men, all of whom had long or plaited blond hair, had surrounded them and asked their business. Ryan had explained they were travelers from the other side of the hill, beyond the tropical jungle. Their wag had broken down and then they'd run into the army of ants that had driven them up the mountain, and down into the ville.

They were greeted with no hostility, nor was there any clear evidence of friendship. Just a calm acceptance of what they said and the suggestion that they should all come to the ville's meeting house to explain themselves in front of the Vikings' karl, Baron Jorund Thoraldson.

The last half mile or so of the friends' trek had been colder, and Mildred Wyeth had pulled the hood up higher, covering her head and shadowing her face. Krysty's red hair was tightly curled and dulled by the mist. Jak's white hair hung limp like curdled milk over his shoulders.

No one had made an attempt to try to take away their blasters as they walked toward the largest of the wood-roofed huts.

Ryan, as ever, had kept his eye skating all around him.

The ville contained forty dwellings, but no sign of any sort of mechanization, which wasn't unusual in isolated villes throughout the Deathlands. There were no wags in sight and the packed, moist earth around the huts didn't bear any tracks of vehicles. The smell of cooking was much stronger, but the drumming had ceased—had ceased at the moment the raw-eyed cur had begun its yapping.

The feature of the ville that had caught the friends' eyes were the boats—or were they ships? Ryan had never been that sure of the difference between the two.

Each craft was forty to fifty feet in length, narrow with high sides and ports for a number of long oars. The elongated prow ended in a carved head of what Ryan recognized was supposed to be a kind of fire-breathing monster or dragon.

Most of the men of the ville wore some kind of dagger or short sword at their sides, and several had axes with hafts two feet long. A number of helmets hung over the entrances to the huts, looking as if they were made from varied combinations of iron and leather. The one common factor of the helmets was that all of them were horned.

But now the baron was speaking.

"Outlanders here in Markland! By Baldur's eyes! This is a strange day. There have not been outlanders here in more than a score of years. Fishermen, cast up on our shores in a violent storm when I was a stripling of a dozen summers."

"What happened to them?" Ryan asked.

"The outlander fishermen?" Jorund gave a great bellow of laughter, echoed by many of the thirty men who had crowded into the hut. Not a single woman, Ryan noticed. "By Freya's dugs, my one-eyed friend, if my memory serves me well, I think they went to sleep with their fish."

"A man swims badly when his knees are broken, outlander!" someone yelled, earning a look of angry reproach from the baron.

"Egil Skallagson! Hold your tongue, or I swear I'll feed it to the midden curs. These men are our guests."

Krysty took a step forward. "And the women, Baron? Are we not welcome in your ville?"

Jorund ignored her and spoke to Ryan. "In this ville the nonmen do not speak out like that. Not without our permission. Will you chastise the firehead thrall for her forwardness?"

"She is not a thrall." Whatever that was, thought Ryan. "Where we come from the women are equals of the men and can speak how and when they wish."

There was some laughter at that, as though he'd said that where he came from it was usual to drink through your arse and piss through your ears—laughter tinged with a profound disbelief. The baron didn't even smile.

"Here in Markland, you follow the old ways of Markland, or it will go hard with all of you. Your women will be as our women—a willing thrall at the cooking and a pliant receptacle when we wish to spend our passion. Is that one also a woman? Beneath the hood?"

Ryan's heart sank. He had only known Mildred for a couple of days, but he already knew enough to guess she wasn't going to sweet-mouth Baron Jorund of Markland.

He was right.

Mildred didn't remove her hood, but her voice was loud. Loud and angry.

"Try to spend your passion in my 'receptacle,' bro, and you'll be picking slices of your cock out of the middle of the lake."

Ryan felt the chill of the butt of his pistol, knowing that J.B., Krysty and Jak would be doing the same.

The tall Viking looked at Mildred, wrinkling his blue eyes as though trying to penetrate the darkness beneath her hood. There was a total and quite overwhelming silence in the hut. Outside they heard the laughter of a young woman and a child crying for comfort.

"The ways of an outlander—" he spoke with a measured slowness "—are not our ways. But we have our own rules, and any outlander while he is with us in Markland shall observe them. Or the price will be high."

In his life Ryan had heard a lot of threats and more than a few promises, and he'd learned to tell the difference. This was a promise.

Mildred turned slowly to look toward Ryan, holding his gaze for twenty beats of the heart. Then, even more slowly, she turned back to face the baron and dropped a deep curtsy. "I apologize for my forward tongue. I shall endeavor to keep it guarded while I am in the presence of . . . of men.''

A strong, white-toothed smile split the face of Baron Jorund Thoraldson, and he slapped his thigh. ''Well said, woman. Well and wisely said.''

''Will we feed the outlanders?''

The voice came from a slightly built young man who stood at the front of the crowd, his hand ostentatiously on the silver hilt of his sword. His right shoulder was noticeably higher than the left.

''Feed them, Odo Crookback? Why should we not? Do we forget all hospitality because an outlander is such a scarce sight?''

''Forgive me, Karl Thoraldson, but can we know a little more of them? Their names?''

''True ale from a cracked vessel, Odo. We shall know their names. Speak, One-Eye.''

''My name is Ryan Cawdor, and I am the uncle of the baron of Front Royal ville in the Shens. This is Krysty Wroth and Mildred Wyeth. J. B. Dix here, Doc Tanner and . . .''

He was suddenly conscious that this was what everyone was waiting for. There was a breath of tension that hadn't been present before.

''And this is Jak Lauren.''

Thoraldson nodded slowly. ''Jak Lauren. It doesn't sound like the name of one of the people here.''

''Come swamps south,'' the teenager muttered, shaking his head, the long mane of snowy hair whipping around his narrow shoulders.

"Not a Norseman?"

"Don't know. What's horseman?"

The blooming smile on the face of the Viking leader began to wither and fade. "Norseman. A man from the north."

"Said south," Jak repeated.

"Yes, yes. But your hair... Every man here in this ville has yellow hair. But no man has hair as pure and white as yours. It's a miracle to behold."

"You talked of a wag breaking down." The insistent voice was that of the local called Odo Crookback. "We do not have any such vehicle, but we know of them from old times. Tell us more."

"Surely. We were traders. The wag had a failure of the engine. We got stranded. None of us had ever been up this way before. Found a hot, stinking jungle, then these ants came and we got kind of driven up the mountain. Over the top into the fog and down again. And here we are."

Jorund looked at Ryan, then turned his eyes to each member of the party. He lingered longest on Krysty, whose sentient hair was beginning to relax and uncurl, revealing its full flaming beauty.

"Ants? Big killers? We hardly ever go up and over the crest of the mountain. On the other side lies many-faced, sharp-toothed, swift and silent, long-sleeping death."

"The ants sure killed a dog on the far side," J.B. said.

"Odin!" shouted a young man at the front of the crowd.

The Armorer looked at him. "That was the name on a kind of medal around its neck. Your dog, was it, son?"

"What color was he?"

"Mostly white."

"Odin wasn't white, so it cannot have been him you saw, outlander."

"Bones, son. Ants left nothing but bones, and they were sure white. Few bits of fur left were brindled."

"Oh, no..." the lad cried, falling to his knees and burying his face in his hands. "Then that's why he didn't come back last night. He was..." His weeping swallowed up his words.

Baron Thoraldson banged a fist on the long oak table in front of him. "By the runes of Baelthorn! Is this your son, Sigurd Harefoot?"

The boy looked up, his face wet with tears. "I'm sorry, Father. Sorry, Karl Thoraldson. Forgive me for my weakness."

"Weakness! Milksop wench! You whining bitch! Your dog dies and you howl as if your honor was lost. You were warned not to take the name of Father Odin for a cur. Look what ill fortune you've brought on yourself."

The boy stood straight, wiping away the signs of his weeping. "Forgive me."

"Nay. You behave in such a feeble, womanish way in front of outlanders. And even in front of their own women! What must they think of the warriors of Markland? Until you can learn the true ways of manhood, you had best spend some time with the maids, doing their work until the end of the Cuckoo month. And you will not ride or sail or walk with men until that time is spent. Go."

"He keeps up this antiwomen shit, lover, and I'm going to help Mildred on her suggestion about some thin-slicing." Krysty's whisper only reached Ryan's ears.

When the totally dejected boy had left the hut, the baron brought their first meeting toward its ending.

"I will tell you this, outlanders. In the history of this ville, strangers have often had a short shrift. We keep to our own. But in the past year or more there has been much visiting with the gray-haired widow-maker. The waters have not always been clean. Men have wasted to the bone, and we are falling short of numbers who can hold a blaster or a sword. You and the one with the eyeglasses and the slow-headed boy could join us if you pass the testings."

"And what of me?" Doc asked.

The Viking looked at him and shook his head slowly and sorrowfully. "I know not what fire still smolders in your belly, old man, but you have seen too many winters to be a warrior."

Doc was about to bark back, when he caught Ryan's warning glance and closed his mouth again.

The baron walked to Doc and patted him on the shoulder. "But lament not. Old men may sit by the fire and spin tales of their courage and pass on their wisdom to the young men. And the maids will bound to do their bidding at all times.''

Doc looked at Mildred's shadowed face. ''Then it might not be so bad. I can get our maids to leap about some.''

Ryan was next to the black woman, and he was the only one who heard her mutter. ''Fuck you, Tanner, you asshole!''

Jorund stared at Ryan, who realized with a sense of some shock that the man's talk of their joining his warriors wasn't just casual, friendly conversation. This was a serious invitation. But like a lot of invitations in isolated villes, it came hedged around with barbs.

''Thanks for the offer, Baron,'' he replied, trying to pick his words with some care. ''You mind if we get a chance to talk this over some?''

The Norseman nodded. ''You may have this night. At dawning you will tell us whether you will stay here as our brothers. Or... whether you will choose not.''

Once again, Ryan knew the difference between a threat and promise. This one was both.

The fire in the hut blazed up as one of the men kicked some logs into its center. It was very hot, and Mildred reached up a casual hand and pulled down the hood of her sweater, for the first time revealing her face to the Vikings.

The world fell in.

CHAPTER NINETEEN

"THE RAVEN OF DEATH!" shrieked one of the men at the back of the crowd, his voice ragged with stark terror.

There was pushing and jostling near the door, and at least half of the warriors of Markland fought their way outside. Even the baron took three steps back, half drawing his sword as though he feared that Mildred might physically attack him.

Instantly, magically, guns appeared in the hands of Ryan and his party. The only person in the large hut who seemed unconcerned was Mildred Wyeth.

She looked calmly around at the fearful confusion, shaking her head slowly. "I've made some spectacular entrances in my time, but this has to be the best. What—"

"Her skin..." Jorund Thoraldson hissed, licking his lips nervously. "Her skin is as black as jet. She is the spirit of death, the widow-maker herself, and you have brought her among us!" He pointed accusingly at Ryan.

More and more of the leading men of the ville were sidling out of the hut, stumbling over one another in their eagerness to get away.

"Have none of you ever seen a person with black skin before?" Ryan shouted. "It's not a thing to be frightened of."

"Of course it is, outlander fool! I have lived through more than thirty summers and I've never seen anyone with black skin. Except for those who are bitten by the jungle snakes or those whose corpses rise swollen from the depths of the water." The baron was shaking with nerves.

"No. Have none of you ever left this ville and traveled through the Deathlands?"

Jorund shook his head. "No. Markland has always been here. It was here before the long winters and it is still here. It will always be here. No man leaves, and what happens beyond the water or beyond the hot forest is nothing to us."

"You must trade with other villes along the coast here," J.B. said.

"No. It would be unclean and would damn us. There is a ville, forty sea-miles off to the east. There have been fights over the years, and they get stronger as we grow more weak. One day..." He suddenly recalled the origin of all this. "But the black witch must go. Nay, she must die."

"Be a lot of blood spilled if you try that," Krysty warned.

"We are many." He glanced around and saw that only a handful of his men remained behind. "Stay, you dogs! Come back!"

It was a delicate, balanced moment. Ryan knew they had overwhelming firepower on their side, but it would be a desperate gamble to try to take on an entire ville. It wasn't the initial firefight that was the problem. It was getting safe away afterward without being sniped off.

"Better not try it," Ryan said. "We got blasters that can take out a dozen of you just like *that*." He snapped his fingers loudly.

One by one, the blond warriors came sheepishly back into the meeting hut, most of them trying hard to avoid looking directly at Mildred Wyeth, who still stood among the friends, arms folded, a faint smile on her lips.

"No man's face is black," Jorund protested, "And no woman's. It is not natural. *Not* natural!"

The young man with the hunched back pushed to the front of the others, his slim sword drawn in his right hand. "Waste not breath, Karl Jorund! Empty words from the outlanders! Legends tell of black witches...Valkyries from the pits of darkness. This is why there have been deaths. Sickness. Two-headed babies whose guts spilled from them."

Mildred glanced over to Ryan. "Sounds like radiation malformations. It would be interesting to try to find out why."

"She mutters a curse!" Odo Crookback yelped. "Fork-tongue, red-teeth, blood-eyed, black-skinned cursing. Burn her. Offer her to the gods. What do you say, my brothers?"

There was a roar of angry agreement, with every man waving either a sword or a pistol. Ryan's finger tightened on the trigger of the SIG-Sauer, but he held his fire. "I tell you that a dark skin is normal all over Deathlands. I have met many such men and women. All colors of skin. You will not harm her." He made sure that his gun pointed at the stomach of the baron of Markland.

"Burn them all!" Odo shrieked, brandishing his sword at Ryan.

The suggestion brought the threat of slaughter even closer.

Ryan squeezed the trigger once, putting a bullet into the earth precisely between the hunchback's feet, splattering him with earth. He jumped a yard in the air, then nearly fell into the fire.

"Be a lot of death," Ryan said into the seething stillness.

Jorund Thoraldson took a deep, slow breath. "I see you are skilled with your blaster, outlander. But you will not make a change in our laws. There cannot be a nonman with black skin in Markland. It has never been. It will never be."

"I would venture to suggest to you that your statement is not correct, Mr. Thoraldson," Doc said. "I have great knowledge—almost personal, you could say—of the times before the long winters. I assure you that a person with a black skin was as common as a person with blond hair. Probably more common. It just happens that Markland has survived in its own little Aryan way.''

''What do you say, old man?''

''I say that—unless my supposition is flawed—there must once have been blacks here in this vicinity. But after the great nuclear war that devastated our land and destroyed the American way of life, there must have been strife. Fights between villes. Between social groups within a particular ville. I believe that here the blond man ruled and the black man has vanished.''

''Nothing changes,'' Mildred said bitterly.

''No. We have always been Norse here in Markland. Through my memory and that of my father and that of his father and—''

Doc held up an imperious hand to quiet the baron. ''Crap! He said and he said and he said.... All of that's like history written by the winners. We're talking here, my friend, about events from a century gone. None of us, even I, can conceive properly of the horrors of those first few charnel-house years.'' He shrugged. ''But all of this is of scant interest. Your rules will be as entrenched as a redneck sheriff in rural Georgia way back when. I suggest, Ryan, that we simply make our excuses and leave this place.''

''Sounds good,'' Mildred agreed, glancing at Ryan. ''We go?''

It was the young hunchback who shouted the first objection. ''An old man, a black witch and a one-eyed outlander make the decisions here, do they, Jorund Thoraldson?''

There was a chorus of yelled approval, and some of the Vikings began to shuffle forward, their initial fear of Mildred forgotten.

"She must burn, outlander. And you and the others will remain here. One way or another, that is how it will be."

Ryan caught J.B.'s eye and nodded imperceptibly. It had gone past talking; now it was down to shooting first. His finger caressed the narrow trigger of the pistol. Like Trader said, it was always best to get in the first bullet.

"What of trial by combat?"

Mildred's voice rang out through the hut, loud and clear, making Ryan hesitate before opening fire with the P-226.

"You were ordered to keep silent," Jorund said, but his voice lacked confidence.

"She speaks sooth," called out a stout, older man, who Ryan recognized as the father of the disgraced youth.

"And will you champion the black slut, Sigurd?" Odo mocked.

"It must be one of her own. Outlander—" he looked at Ryan "—it is true that our laws in Markland make it possible for the... for her... to have someone to defend her right to live. Will you take up that challenge for her?"

"Yeah."

Mildred shook her head. "Just let me borrow that pretty little handgun of yours, Ryan, and I'll give the yellow-haired son of a bitch one through the fore-head.''

''Wait. See what kind of rules they come up with. Might not just be who can get nearest to the center of the target. Killing's like a lot of things, Mildred. It's a craft that you have to learn.''

The baron of the ville smiled. ''Not blasters. Our champion selects the weapon and the grounds for the challenge.

''Don't take fucking chances!'' Jak spit disgust-edly.

Ryan waited. Over the years he'd come across an occasional duel, generally over a woman. Or drugs. There'd been two stupes up near the northwest coast, logging country, who sat on adjacent, identical branches, eighty feet up a ponderosa pine. Each started sawing on the other's branch at the same point and finished sawing through at the same moment.

Both hit the ground at the same moment.

There'd been a skinny little kid in some pesthole gaudy house near a desert hot spot, someplace. He'd been challenged by a big bounty hunter to fight, and the kid picked pool balls from the length of a table. The big man laughed at that. The kid wiped him away with his first shot—an eight ball between the eyes, with a vicious snap of the wrist. Ryan could still see the look of shock in the dead man's eyes as he went down.

''I'm the champion of the ville of Markland, and Sharptooth here is my chosen weapon. We shall fight on the shore of the water. To the death, outlander. Aye.''

Somehow, Ryan had guessed that it would be the slightly built Odo Crookback who would stand against them. Despite his physical disability the young man was light on his feet, the narrow sword in his hand dancing and darting in the crimson glow of the pine fire.

''Swords? We don't have a sword, Jorund.''

Baron Thoraldson smiled. ''We shall be happy to give one to you to fight against our champion. If you lose, then you will be dead. And she will also die on the stake.''

''Sure.''

Mildred watched him, biting her lip. ''This is a shit-bad scene, Ryan. Why not just shoot them and run for it? We'd have a better chance than trying to sword-fight against the little weasel-prick.''

''J.B. knows that if I go down, or look like I'm going down, he'll open up with the automatic rifle. That's when we move.''

''But that guy looks like he could be real good with a sword.''

''Yeah. But I have to go—'' He stopped abruptly when he felt a hand on his shoulder.

''Theophilus Algernon Tanner, master of foil, epée and saber, at your service, Ryan,'' Doc announced, waving his ebony cane. ''I'll fight him.''

CHAPTER TWENTY

THERE WAS a brief but bitter argument among the Vikings when Ryan announced that Doc Tanner would be the champion for the life of Mildred Wyeth.

The baron led his men to the far end of the longhouse for a degree of privacy. But Ryan and the rest couldn't fail to hear the raised voices or see the clenched fists. It was noticeable that Odo Crookback took no part in the discussion. He sat alone on a scarred table, swinging his feet and tapping the point of his sword against the earth floor. He whistled tunelessly to himself and smiled every now and then at the group of outlanders.

Jorund came back, the rest of the Norsemen clustered behind him. "We think that the old man should not fight in this matter."

Doc smiled. "I happen to disagree, and I think that the old man *should* fight in this matter."

The baron sighed. "Well, enough. I cannot and will not stop you. But Odo is the best swordsman in this steading. He will cut the old one to pieces. There will be no quarter given."

Again Doc answered him. "And no quarter will be asked for."

"You'll borrow a sword, old man?"

"No. I shall use this." He drew the slim blade of steel from its ebony lining, gripping it by the silver lion's-head hilt.

Thoraldson nodded. "Then let us to it."

THE WOMEN AND CHILDREN were sent into the huts, and stray animals were safely penned. The bounds of the fight were quickly set. A rough square was marked out on the beach that sloped gently down to the edge of the water. The perimeters were gouged in the shingled sand, about twenty paces along each side, and a large, dying fire claimed the center. Doc was placed in one corner and Odo stood, light and easy, in the opposite corner, so that the burning logs lay between them.

Each man was allowed a second to assist him in his preparations. Odo had Sigurd Harefoot and Doc asked Ryan to stand with him.

"You sure you want to do this, Doc?" Ryan asked. "I don't want to screw up your confidence, but—"

"I fenced at Harvard and during my brief but pleasant sojourn at Oxford University. I was quite skilled, though I do say so myself."

"This won't be a game, Doc."

"I know it. There are times—too many—when my mind wanders from my control. But that doesn't mean that I am always a gull and a fool." He smiled, showing his peculiarly perfect teeth. "I rarely have the chance to pull my weight in this company, Ryan. Allow me this moment, will you?''

''Sure.''

''And if it goes badly, you must not interfere on my part. Promise me that.''

''Course, Doc. I promise.''

But it was a promise that Ryan hadn't the least intention of keeping.

Doc discarded his frock coat, choosing to fight in his shirt. His pants were tucked into his cracked knee boots.

Jak appeared for a moment in the corner of the fighting area. ''Get bastard face low sun, Doc. Blind fucker.''

''Thank you, dear boy, thank you. I shall endeavor to retain that advice as best I can during the coming duello.''

Ryan beckoned Thoraldson to come over. ''Any rules in this, Baron?''

''None, outlander. Except that no man shall break the bounds of the fight. Down is down, and down shall be dead.''

''Sure. Hear that, Doc? No rules. Anything goes. Right?''

There was a quick, nervous smile from the old man. He took several deep breaths, bending and flexing his knees, the joints creaking alarmingly in the quiet of the afternoon.

''Ready?'' Baron Jorund shouted.

''Ready,'' Doc replied.

"May Odin aid my arm and speed Sharptooth to the belly of the graybeard outlander," Odo called in a reedy, mocking voice.

As the two men began to shuffle forward, Doc replied to the Viking's taunting. "And may this blade, Bloodsucker, drain your life, you disjointed lump of humanity."

"I'll sever every joint in your body for that, you stinking heap of tripe!" the advancing Norseman screamed.

There was a light wind from out of the east that raised small ripples on the limitless expanse of leaden water. Ryan stood close to the edge of the lake and noticed that his tiny rad counter was showing amber, warning of some middle-power hot spot that was fairly close by. But the start of the fight distracted Ryan from the thought.

Doc began to shuffle sideways, keeping a careful eye on the Viking on the far side of the fire. As Odo went left, Doc matched him, feeling for a footing, testing the ground. His sword hung loose from his hand, almost as if he'd forgotten he was holding it.

"Go for him, Doc!" J.B. called.

Far above them some gigantic mutie bird flew across the sun, giving a piercing, mournful screaming cry, its shadow sweeping the earth far below.

At Ryan's side, Mildred shuddered. "Like one of the Dark Riders," she whispered.

Ryan didn't know what she meant and was too involved in watching Doc to worry about asking her. His hand still rested on the butt of his pistol.

After a couple of minutes there had been no contact at all between the two men. Ryan noticed that Odo shuffled a little, dragging his left leg, the same side as his dropped shoulder. Doc was moving slowly, breathing easily.

"Must I chase you all the way to Valhalla, old man?" Odo called.

"You hobble like some bottled spider. If you prefer it, I shall stand here and wait for you, my friend."

With spots of hectic color standing out on his pale cheekbones, the Norseman rushed around the blazing logs to where Doc now stood his ground.

"Ready?" Ryan asked quietly.

"Yeah," J.B. replied. Jak simply nodded his agreement.

There was the unmistakable sound of sword blades clashing. A burst of sparks tumbled into the air between the two men.

Doc easily parried the first clumsy lunge of the Viking, twisting his wrist so that the thicker blade of Odo slid away from him.

"Try again, young man," Doc taunted, grinning wolfishly at the hunchback.

Odo gripped the hilt of his sword as though it were a tool, shuffling around Doc, feinting at groin and throat. The older, taller man held the rapier as if it were a delicate musical instrument and ignored most of the false attacks.

"Fight like a warrior, grayhead!" yelled one of the circle of watching men.

Doc ignored the shout, wisely fighting his own way, letting the younger man come to him, occasionally flicking away a tentative lunge with an almost contemptuous ease.

"Is this your best, Baron?" Ryan called, knowing that it would help Doc if Odo could be kept angry and off balance.

"The man whose wound heals first relishes the jest most, One-Eye," Jorund countered.

Odo tried again, feinting for the head, then closing in, dropping his point to try to hack at Doc's legs. It put the older man under pressure and drove him back toward the fire.

"Hold him!" Jak called, a note of worry riding his voice.

For a moment the combatants stood toe to toe, straining against each other, the metallic grating of sword against sword. As Ryan had feared, the young Norseman was stronger, fitter and more used to fighting with steel.

Slowly Doc gave ground, unable to move away quickly because of the blazing logs at his back, unable to disengage his swordstick without giving Odo a clear opening to thrust at him from close range.

The beach under their feet had harder patches of packed pebbles, interspersed with much softer areas of grayish sand. As he retreated, Doc's boot heels slithered into a soft patch and he lost his balance. He fell backward and sprawled defenseless in the sand.

"Farewell, champion," Odo yelled.

The SIG-Sauer was out of its holster, and Ryan's finger whitened on the trigger. Everyone's eyes were fixed to the frozen tableau.

As Odo braced himself for the thrust that he intended would spit the old man through the chest, Doc's outstretched hand grasped a handful of the white dust that lay around the edges of the fire, and he heaved it into the young man's face. Odo shrieked and staggered backward, his free hand rubbing furiously at his eyes.

"Screw him, Doc!" Mildred shouted, her voice rising into the startled stillness.

Doc made it to his feet and advanced remorselessly on the blinded man.

"Foul fighting!" someone called.

"No rules," Ryan retorted. "You said no rules."

Odo waved his blade in a whirling mill of frantic defense, trying to hold Doc at bay. But the older man didn't rush in. He took his time, occasionally lifting his own rapier to flick at the other man's sword. There was only Crookback's labored, harsh breathing, and the clang of steel on steel.

Tears streamed down Odo's face, caking it with gray streaks from the ash. His retreat was taking him down the gently sloping beach, toward the edge of the lake.

Doc, his mouth set in a grim line of deadly intent, pursued him. He began to use his swordstick with increasing aggression, thrusting and making the Viking struggle to parry the blows.

"Lunge, riposte and lunge and riposte," Doc recited, as if he were at some Victorian fencing school.

Both men were knee-deep in the water.

"Now, Doc," Ryan breathed.

It was almost as if the old man heard his whispered words. With an easy cut of the wrist he caught Odo's flailing blade on his, turning it away. Half turning so that his shoulder dropped, Doc swung his rapier up and to the right, ripping the Norseman's steel from his hand.

There was a soft sigh from Odo's watching companions. Ryan holstered his pistol.

Odo Crookback stood and waited for his end, arms spread. His sword seemed to hang high in the air, the red sun bouncing bloodily off the steel. It finally fell with a surprisingly small splash, twenty yards away from the two men.

"Strike, outlander," he said to Doc. "Hard and clean."

"Yes."

Doc thrust his left leg forward, right arm and wrist extended. The point entered the body of the Viking a hand's span above his belt and a couple of inches to the left of his breastbone. It slid between the guarding ribs, slicing through the outer muscles of the heart, cutting open the lungs. The power of the blow brought

Doc up close against the doomed man, the point of his weapon standing out under the shoulder blade by a good six inches of blood-slick steel.

Odo lurched away, ripping himself clear of the rapier. His fists punched at the sky and he screamed the single word "Odin!" and toppled sideways, falling in a flurry of foam, landing facedown.

"Looks like Mildred stays alive, Baron," Ryan said.

Jorund Thoraldson looked at him, his face betraying no emotion whatsoever. "The gods will it so. You must be hungered. We shall feed you. Come."

CHAPTER TWENTY-ONE

RYAN AND HIS COMPANIONS were given a hut that had belonged to a family that had died recently. Harald Verillision, who had been the brewer of ale in the ville of Markland, his wife and both sons had fallen sick of a wasting illness after they'd returned from an expedition to fetch mountain spring water some miles along the coast.

The young woman who brought food to the outlanders told them about it in whispers, looking over her shoulder to make sure nobody overheard her.

"Great buboes grew in their armpits and between their legs. Blisters sprang up around their cracked lips. The nails dropped from their finger ends, and their teeth fell from their bleeding gums."

Mildred glanced across at Ryan, as though she were about to say something. But she chose to keep her own counsel.

"I've been in Markland all my life...." The girl laughed. "Stupid. Everyone in the steading has been here all their lives. Nobody ever leaves, and hardly anyone ever comes."

As she spoke she was fingering the neck of her dress, scratching at a small red spot at the side of her throat.

When she pulled down the woven material, the girl revealed the top of an iron collar, locked in place.

"What's that?" J.B. asked, pointing. "Some kinda punishment?"

The young woman looked puzzled. "My thrall ring? Is that what you mean, outlander?"

"Yeah. The iron collar."

"All thralls wear it."

"What's thrall?" Jak asked.

She turned to the boy, then glanced hastily away, making a strange sign with her fingers, almost as if she were averting some sort of evil.

"Thrall, my dear young man," Doc replied, "is simply an old word for slave. The Vikings built their social order upon thralls."

"You're a slave?" Krysty probed, unable to hide her shock at the idea. "There aren't slaves anymore."

"Tell that to barons like Teague," Ryan said, "and plenty more. Plenty of frontier plague pits have folks no better'n slaves."

"How many of you are thralls, child?" Mildred asked.

The girl repeated the same sign with her fingers, averting her eyes again. "Some."

"Who decides?" Ryan asked.

"What?"

"Who's a slave...thrall, and who isn't? Who makes the rules?"

She laughed, shaking her head. "Outlanders are double-stupes! A thrall is thrall-born. A freeman is free-born. How could it be any different way?"

Ryan nodded. "Yeah. I see that was sort of stupid. Thanks. And thanks for bringing us the meal. Looks good."

"Eat in fine heart and may Freya bless your dining," the girl replied. She curtsied and left the hut, taking care not to look at either Jak or Mildred.

"These people are scared shitless by you, Mildred," J.B said.

"White folks in Montgomery used to feel the same about my parents."

"She looked triple-stupe me," Jak said, sitting himself at the dusty table and pulling a wooden bowl in front of him.

Ryan joined the boy. "You're right, Jak. But it's different to the way they look at Mildred here. She terrifies them, because I guess they've never seen anyone black before. But it's almost like the opposite with you. Your hair's pure white, and that sort of impresses them."

The food was excellent.

Ryan thought the meat was rabbit, but Krysty assured him it was hare, roasted over a fire with sprigs of thyme pushed beneath the skin to give it a marvelous tangy flavor. It was served with a sauce of sugared cranberries. There was also a shoulder of mutton cooked with leeks, mushrooms and sweet potatoes.

A dark caldron of iron held a simmering stew of herrings and some other, unidentifiable fish in a vegetable stock; a wooden platter was piled high with sun-ripened apples, sweet and delicious and crisp to the teeth; there was a tankard of foaming ale and beakers made from horns, and some bubbling, fresh milk. Two loaves of flatbread with salted butter completed the repast.

"That ale smells wonderful," Doc said, breathing in its odor with a beatific smile.

"Run a radiation counter over it before you touch it," Mildred suggested.

"How's that?" J.B. said, his hand hovering over the earthenware jug.

"You heard that slave girl."

Ryan punched his right fist into his left palm, angry at himself for having missed it. "Yeah! Course. The guy who lived in this hut and all his family died. He was the brewer."

"And the symptoms sounded a lot like radiation poisoning of some kind," Mildred added. "If I had to make a guess I'd say that something's happened up the coast."

"Hot spot?" Jak asked, helping himself to a generous ladling of the fish stew, slopping some on the table in his eagerness.

"You mean somewhere that there's a higher than usual leakage count? Yeah. Could be. But it has to be something kind of recent or the whole of this village would have been snuffed by now."

"How about the rest of the food?" Krysty asked. "If it's in the water, then mebbe the fish could have absorbed some of it."

Mildred nodded. "But it's hardly likely a few small meals can hurt. You'd need repeated low dosages over months for any significant health risk."

"If you'll forgive me," Doc said, "I don't think I'll sample that beer, even so. But the hare can surely tempt me."

After some hesitation, they all sat around the table and tucked into the meal. Within twenty minutes almost everything was gone.

No one touched the ale.

JORUND THORALDSON, with a half a dozen of the senior men of the ville, appeared shortly after the companions had finished eating.

"You are relishing the food that . . . ?" He noticed the empty dishes. "I see that you have. Yet our best ale is not to your liking?"

Ryan stood and faced the baron. "We come from a ville where alcohol is forbidden by our religion. But the milk was good and the food was marvelous. Thanks for it."

"Now we should talk of the future, Ryan Cawdor. Of you and your friends. And the women."

"Talk away, Baron."

"The women can leave."

"How's that?" Krysty asked. Her temper often flared close to the surface. She stood and turned to stare at the huge figure of the Viking leader, her green eyes flashing with anger.

"Now, now. Markland has its rules, its laws that go back to the beginning of history. You are all here, and outlanders must pay our price of living here. We have agreed to let the black live, have we not?"

Ryan rubbed his chin and sighed. "One way of looking at it, Baron. Course, another way would be to say that our man beat your man. Left him chilled, facedown in the water. That's a different way of looking at it."

One of the other Norsemen whispered something to his karl, and Jorund nodded. "Sooth. We should not fall to bickering over this. The women must leave this hut to live with the other unmarried women in their longhouse at the center of Markland. There they can help the other women at their duties."

"Like sewing and cooking? That kind of stuff, Baron?" Krysty asked with a venomous sweetness.

"If you don't guard your tongue, you flame-haired slut, then you'll find yourself at the stone, paying the blood price for—"

"Jorund!" one of his men said with an urgent, alarmed snap to his voice. "Take care of what you say to them."

The huge Viking turned his head slowly, like some great wounded beast, seeking the speaker. Jorund's pale eyes were veiled with his own anger, and Ryan noticed specks of white froth at the corners of his lips.

The eruption of blinding anger was an impressive and frightening sight.

"Egil?" The word was drawn out and splintered, like corn between two massive stones.

"Yes, Karl?"

"The words I heard through a berserker's mist came from you."

"Yes. You were..."

Thoraldson nodded. "I know, friend. My ears heard the words I was uttering, but my mouth could do naught to check them."

Ryan was, as ever, at Krysty's elbow. He leaned toward her, lips scarcely moving, his breath not stirring a tendril of her long scarlet hair. "Better do it."

She nodded. "How long?"

"Day. Two at most. There's some double-bad things in this ville."

The baron of Markland caught their whispered conversation, and he turned to Ryan. "My anger took me from myself for a moment. I fear that I came near to... What do you say?"

"Krysty and Mildred will do what you say. They'll go and live in the house with the other women of your ville. But they are not, and never will be, *your* women. Or anyone else's women. They are our companions, free and equal in every way."

"Right on, boss," Mildred said, grinning at Krysty.

Jorund Thoraldson stroked his long blond mustache and looked down for a moment at his feet while he considered Ryan's words. "You will not leave

Markland until we say you may. Nor the women. But it shall be as you say. Now, they can go with the thrall. She can show them where they will live. You stay here.''

"The tests?'' suggested one of the Vikings, a wall-eyed man with a jagged scar across his face.

"Tests?'' J.B. said.

Jorund smiled what looked to be a genuine, happy smile. "Aye. We have seen how your oldest man can butcher one of our best swords. We wait eagerly to see how you three fare as warriors.''

"What are these tests?'' Ryan asked.

"Halfway between nothing and a small thing, outlander,'' Jorund replied. "Since you are to be with us, we must know your mettle.'' He waved a dismissive hand. "Do not worry.''

"I don't. But it would help some to know what kind of things you're going to throw at us.''

"Trials for a warrior.''

That was all he'd say. The Norsemen left the hut. Almost immediately the girl with the iron slave collar came and led Krysty and Mildred away, leaving the men behind to wonder what the next dawning would bring.

CHAPTER TWENTY-TWO

"ARISE, GENTLEMEN." Doc stood silhouetted in the doorway of the hut. "There is a gray mist upon the sea's face, and there is a gray mist breaking."

Ryan stretched like a big cat, his muscles almost cracking as he extended his arms and legs. The mattress beneath him, which was filled with sweet-smelling summer grass, rustled softly. The air was cool and he breathed in deeply, aware of how much he'd missed having Krysty to warm his back. He'd slept fully dressed, only kicking off the steel-toed combat boots. His rifle rested at his side and his SIG-Sauer was beneath his pillow.

"Slave girl's coming," Doc said, "staggering under a great platter of food and a flagon of milk."

J.B. yawned and sat up, rubbing at his eyes. His first move, as always, was to reach for his glasses and slip them on. The second move, as always, was to check that his blasters were at hand.

"Feel hungry. Wouldn't mind another of those rabbits from last night."

"Hares, my dear friend."

"How's that, Doc?"

"They were hares, not rabbits."

Jak threw off his heavy woolen blanket and was on his feet in a single, fluid movement. He ran his fingers through his dazzling mane of hair, hair that was so white that it seemed to burn with its own incandescent flame.

The thrall, Margaret, appeared in the doorway. Doc stepped aside, and she walked into the hut, laying the food on the table.

"Oatmeal and buttermilk," she announced, "with dried fish and some more of the mutton. Apples, bread and honey. Will it be enough?"

"Enough for these condemned men to make a hearty breakfast," Doc replied. "Thanks."

"Are Krysty and Mildred all right?" Ryan asked. "Nobody tried to harm them?"

The girl shook her head. "Nay, masters. It would mean a swift death if anyone went against the word of Karl Thoraldson." She dropped her voice. "Besides, they say the redhead is a Valkyrie warrior and the jet-woman is a witch demon from the dark world of fire and shadow."

"These tests we gotta do," J.B. said, smearing clear honey on a torn crust of warm, fresh-baked bread.

"Aye?"

"What are they?"

"Something and nothing. All young men of the steading must be tried by the older men, to show them worthy as warriors of Markland."

"Yeah. But what—"

J.B. was interrupted by a loud shout from somewhere beyond the center of the ville. Margaret's eyes opened wide and she hefted her skirts, scampering out of their hut.

"Something and nothing." Doc smirked. "I trust that none of you will drag our honor low in the eyes of these people, after I have played my part with such skill."

He picked up his ebony swordstick and waved it in the air with a triumphant flourish.

"Why don't you go piss up a rope, Doc?" Ryan said. "I know the baron said you didn't have to do these tests, seeing as how your skill with the sword was undoubted. But we still got to do them. So let us eat our breakfast in peace, will you?"

TO RYAN'S DISAPPOINTMENT the women of Markland had all been sent away, forbidden by ancient law to watch the ordeals of the warriors.

Jorund Thoraldson was waiting for the outlanders near the perpetually burning fire on the shingled strand below the ville. He was dressed in a long cloak of rich purple, trimmed with silver. Many of the other Norsemen were dressed in what were clearly their finest cloaks.

"Greetings, outlanders!" the baron boomed. "Once the fog has burned away we shall have a fine day of it."

"Hi, Baron," Ryan called. "Will all this take very long?"

"No, though the tests and ordeals for our young men often take several days. Weeks, even. For there are the tests of hunting alone where they must range the hills for many miles, armed only with a spear, a bow and single arrow."

"Apaches had the same kind of thing," Doc said quietly. "The old macho routine. We send out the boy and he returns a man. Horsefeathers!"

"And there is usually the test for their ability to handle a boat."

"Swimming?" J.B. asked.

"No."

"No?"

"If it is Odin's will that the waters return you safe to shore, then so be it," Egil Skallagson said solemnly.

"And if you tumble into the waters, then to be able to swim will only make your suffering the longer," Sigurd Harefoot added.

When Ryan had been involved with the whalers on the bleak New England coast, he'd sometimes heard them express similar sentiments.

"So what must we do?"

"Skill with arms and skill at grappling," Jorund replied.

"Grappling? You mean like wrestling?" J.B. asked. "Who against?"

"Some of the best of our warriors. But it is not to the death. It is only a testing with ax, spear and blaster."

The biggest surprise for Ryan and the others was the poor standard of performance from the men of the ville. While he watched their efforts to shine against the strangers, Ryan kept reminding himself of what Mildred had said about rad sickness. There was no doubt at all that there was something rotten in the steading of Markland.

"We begin with the throwing of the spear," Jorund announced.

The baron had selected eight of his own warriors to stand up for the honor of their people. Most were in their early to mid-twenties, but three of them looked less than well, with scabs around their lips and, in a couple of cases, open sores amid their thinning hair. One had an eye covered by a creeping leprous growth, and another had the nails missing from the weeping tips of his fingers.

But some were still tall and strong and filled with their own pomp.

The spears were about seven feet long and made from ash. The points were iron, embedded in the tip of the wood. The target was a man-size sheaf of bound grass, which had been set about thirty paces down the beach from a line that the baron drew with his own sword.

The spear was too heavy for Jak, and despite his agility and fighter's eye, he managed only to heave it the distance, where it flattened out and slid into the shingle. Every one of the Vikings succeeded in hitting the target. J.B. hit it two throws out of five.

Ryan shook his head when it was his turn. "No. Too simple. Thought this was supposed to be a real test."

"Bold words, outlander," sneered one of the young men, his lips peeling back off jaggedly broken teeth in a savage grin.

"Well said, Erik Stonebiter," one of the watchers called.

"Stonebiter?" Ryan questioned.

"When I was a *skraeling*—a child—I saw our karl throw his knife into the air and catch it between his teeth. I had no blade, so I tried the trick with a large stone. And I caught it. Sadly it snapped off most of my fine teeth."

The tale, clearly often told, brought bellows of laughter from all the listeners. Jak was one of them, still smarting at his own failure with the ash-spear. "Catch knife teeth! Who?"

"My father, Jak Snowhead. It was something he did when heavy in drink. Once he missed and it pierced his cheek. After that he ceased doing it."

"I'll do it," Jak said.

"No," Ryan called, knowing something of the albino teenager's stubborn pride. Knowing, too, that it would on occasion push him way beyond the bounds of good sense.

"Easy," Jak insisted, filling his hand with one of the throwing-knives with the leaf-shaped blades that he kept concealed among his clothing. The point and edges were honed to a whispering sharpness.

"Show us," Erik Stonebiter said. "Show us, young outlander."

"Jak, you'll..." But Ryan closed his mouth when the boy stared at him with his blazing ruby eyes.

"Watch," the lad hissed.

The sun couldn't break through the roiling banks of fog that hung over the lake, but there was still light enough to dance off the glittering blade as Jak sent it spinning high into the air.

The young Viking had time to begin speaking. "No. Not so high. Only a turn or two and..."

Then it was falling from its frozen zenith, revolving more slowly.

Jak's eyes were fixed on it, like a rabbit before a cobra. His lean body was tense and poised, his mouth slightly open.

"Merciful heavens!" Doc whispered just behind Ryan.

As the blade landed, Jak lowered his head in a sharp dipping movement, going down to his knees in the sand. Everyone saw it—the knife, held by its bone hilt, visible between Jak's teeth.

"Dark night," J.B. said with an almost reverential awe. "That is about the damnedest thing that I ever saw."

There was a moment of silence, then the morning was riven by the cheers and whoops of the Norsemen. Jorund Thoraldson himself clapped the white-headed boy across his scrawny shoulders. "By the sockets of

Baldur! That was something for the harpers to sing of during the winter nights.''

"Snow-head, steel-dart, high-flung, bird-threatened, bone-caught," one of the watchers chanted, using the old Viking poetic form of a kenning.

"Lip-cut," Ryan finished, pointing to a small pearl of blood that perched in the corner of the boy's mouth.

When the hubbub had ceased, the baron turned once more to Ryan. "Now, Outlander One-Eye. There is some business not completed. The throwing of a spear, I think."

"Sure. Move that target back another ten paces. No. Fifteen paces. Yeah. Better."

"You'd never reach that with a spear," a young Norseman told him.

But Ryan was thinking again of the harpooners of New England and the skill with which they threw the long irons.

"Show me your best man first," he replied. "I'll match or beat him."

There was muttering among the warriors, and finally a barrel-chested fellow was pushed forward. His shirt stretched tight over his shoulders and seemed to have been deliberately made two sizes too small for his bulk.

"Bjarni Earthmover!" Erik Stonebiter shouted. "Throw your best for Markland and for Odin, brother. Shame us not."

The butt end of Bjarni's spear was studded with iron, and an intricate pattern of woven leather thongs crisscrossed its length. He smiled at Ryan, who nodded and stood politely out of his way.

With a studied slowness Bjarni measured out his run, eyeing the distant target. He then looked up at the sky, his lips moving as he offered a prayer to one of the Norse gods.

The spear seemed to whistle in the air. Ryan saw the effort put into the throw and guessed that the distance of about 130 feet was close to his limit. The point thudded home right at the very bottom of the sheaf of straw, to a cheer from the watching men.

"Not bad," Ryan admitted loudly. "It would have certainly clipped the man's toenails for him."

The stout warrior looked at Ryan as though he were about to say something, but he hesitated, then gestured to him to take his best shot.

Ryan hefted his own spear, finding the point of balance, then checked his run-up, making sure there were none of the soft patches that had so nearly brought Doc to disaster. He glanced along the beach, wondering for the first time whether he'd been overconfident about this. The sheaf seemed a very long way off, barely visible in the fog.

"Want it brought near again, outlander?" Bjarni asked with a sly grin.

"No."

Arm back, straight, to give the fullest possible power to the weapon; eye on the target, measuring and estimating; the run, not too far, and then the explosive burst of energy. Ryan felt his muscles strain for the final whip of the wrist that would yield extra yardage on the cast. The butt of the spear grazed the side of his head as he released it.

"Thor's hammer!" Bjarni gasped, his head cocked back to watch the flight of the metal-tipped staff.

For a moment Ryan thought that he might actually have overthrown the target. Then the iron point dipped and the spear thunked home about nine inches from the top of the sheaf, roughly in the center. Had it been a man, the spear would have hit dead center through his chest.

"Ace on the line, partner," J.B. said approvingly.

The next event was mock sword-fighting, using blunted weapons. The three outlanders managed to acquit themselves fairly well. Jak was outstanding, with his sinuous agility, strength of hand and quickness of eye. Both J.B. and Ryan took numbing blows from the more skillful and experienced Norsemen, though both men held back a little. If the fights had been for real, they both knew that the results would have been different.

Jak won the ax-throwing with almost laughable ease. The target was the top of a large beer keg that looked as if it had been around the ville for a hundred years. Rough circles had been painted on the keg, and it was set up twenty paces down the beach.

Ryan noticed that the fog was showing no signs of clearing. In fact, as the morning wore on, it seemed to be growing thicker, swirling in off the water and encircling the huts like some huge, amorphous beast that was scenting its prey.

As he looked around, waiting his turn to throw, he saw that Krysty and Mildred had left the other women and moved closer to watch the contest. Krysty, dimly seen in the veiling mist, made the unmistakable hand signal to him that warned of some imminent danger. But Ryan couldn't get close enough to talk to her, and the cloud of fog thickened and took her from his sight.

He managed to pass on the warning to J.B., Jak and Doc, but it wasn't much use without a little more specific information. All of them were on their guard anyway.

The Armorer put his three casts with the short-hafted ax within the inner rings. Ryan did the same with two of his, though his third throw slipped in his hand and it barely chipped the top edge of the target.

"Might have trimmed his hair, outlander." Bjarni Earthmover smirked.

Ryan only smiled in reply.

"Blasters," Jorund Thoraldson called. "This, I think, is where the outlanders will be able to reveal a trick or two for us, for their weapons are not like any that we have ever seen in Markland."

"The long guns are like those carried by the sea-born traders, four summers ago, Karl, who were—"

The young Viking was stopped in midsentence by the shout of anger from the baron. "You wish to join the green son of Sigurd Harefoot?"

"No," the man muttered, eyes to the ground.

"Then hold your mouth closed!" Jorund controlled himself with a considerable effort. "We go among the sand dunes, that way, through this thrice-cursed fog. I fear we cannot have any long shooting, so you won't be able to show how cunning your blasters are. It will be closeness and accuracy."

Ryan wondered, as he walked among the Norsemen, what had happened to those sea-born traders who's visited the ville. Baron Thoraldson wasn't telling the whole truth.

Then again, barons very rarely did tell the whole truth.

THEY WERE about three hundred yards from the nearest point of the ville, completely hidden by the mist. It muffled sounds, so that the occasional dog barking, or woman calling, was barely heard.

"This is wasted time," Egil Skallagson protested. "The widow's scarf is wound too tight around the meeting place of land and water."

"I can see well enough to shoot an apple from your head," Ryan said to Bjarni Earthmover, who had walked along with him and was still teasing him about the ax-throw that had so nearly missed.

The Viking responded by pulling a small pippin from the pocket of his homespun breeches and offering it to him.

"Here, outlander. But is your skill with the blaster to be measured against spear or ax? If the former, then shoot away. If the latter...I'd as lief fight at broadsword against the oldling there." He pointed at Doc.

Jorund shook his head at the suggestion. "This cursed fog is too thick for *skraeling* tricks, Bjarni. I think we should return to the steading. These four outlanders have all shown they are sturdy warriors and worthy of joining us."

"Let him fire," Erik Stonebiter called. "I would see it."

There was a chorus of approval from the group of men, with not a single voice raised to support their leader.

"We should return," Jorund insisted.

Suddenly Ryan had a familiar feeling, the prickling of the short hairs at the back of his neck. He felt as though someone were standing behind him, but if he turned, that someone would turn with him so that he would never quite catch him.

"I can blast the apple after noon," he offered. "Or tomorrow."

Bjarni slapped him on the shoulders, nearly felling him in the sand. "Come, outlander! No man cuts himself a haunch of mutton then fails to devour it. Keep to your promise. Here's the apple."

There was no way out. Jorund recognized it and so did Ryan.

The fat Norseman walked forward and stood with his back to the water, close to the edge, facing Ryan. The others stood in a loose circle around them. Very carefully, Bjarni placed the golden apple on top of his blond hair.

"Shoot away!" he shouted, making the fruit wobble from side to side.

"Stand still," Ryan called. He unholstered the SIG-Sauer and steadied it. The Viking was only fifteen paces away, but the roiling banks of fog made it a slightly more difficult shot than usual. Ryan never had a moment's doubt that he could pull it off.

"Ryan."

"What, Jak?" He lowered the pistol, knowing that the teenager wouldn't have spoken unless he had a good reason.

"Heard something."

"What?"

The boy shook his head, the white hair dew-frosted and lank. "Not sure. Someone."

Erik grinned. "Probably some kitchen thrall sneaking off for a quick swiving with a stable thrall. They come out here, and get a sound thrashing if they're caught. And a branding if they do it again."

The moment of tension eased, and Ryan again lifted his handgun, extending his right arm and sighting along the barrel at the small circle of the apple. The fog behind Bjarni was white and translucent, making the target easier to see.

"Ready?" he called.

"Blast away," Bjarni replied.

The crack of a gun rent the air and the stout Norseman staggered back into the lake, the apple falling from his head, a mask of crimson spreading from the bullet hole above his left eye.

CHAPTER TWENTY-THREE

"NOT ME!" Ryan yelled as he threw himself flat in the sand, his eye raking the fog for some sign of where the attackers were hiding.

A ragged volley of shots barked out of the mist, and two more of the Norsemen fell, wounded. The volley dispelled the microsecond suspicion that Ryan had shot Bjarni, who was already rolling belly-up, his blood pinking the lake around him.

The apple bobbed merrily in the ripples at the side of the corpse.

"Eight, maybe ten. Cap and ball!" J.B. yelled. He was lying a dozen yards away from Ryan.

"Ready, warriors? We will charge them!" the baron shouted, from where he crouched with most of his men, a short distance to the right.

"They'll fucking chill you!" Ryan bellowed, angry at the stupidity that the Norsemen were showing. They'd been coldcocked from the dunes behind them, under the cover of the fog. To try to attack the unseen enemy was suicide.

"We must stop them, outlander, or they'll get to the steading."

That was a fair point. The thought of Krysty and Mildred being caught helpless and unawares was a goad toward some swift action. Then again, Ryan knew that his lover already suspected trouble and would certainly have heard the crackle of gunfire, even through the wall of mist.

"Then we move back," Ryan called. "Together, and follow the waterline."

"We do not run, outlander!" someone shouted.

"Then stay and die, you triple-stupe bastard! Me and my friends'll go and try to save your women, kids and homes."

There was another burst of shooting, most of it aimed at Ryan's voice. Three rounds came close enough to kick sand over him.

"Eight," J.B. said quietly. "Five got single-shot muskets. Homemades. Rest are old pistols."

Behind them, in the direction of Markland, they all heard more shooting; the scream of a woman or a young child; a barking dog, suddenly silenced. It was enough to prompt the leader of the Vikings into more sensible action.

"To the steading, brothers! Follow me close and slay any who stands against us."

Ryan, followed by Jak, J.B. and Doc, scrambled from the sand and moved at a fast jog along the beach. A couple of wild shots pursued them, but they didn't even hear the buzzing of the bullets. Ahead of them, there were the more distinct sounds of a bitter fight.

"Ryan found himself alongside Erik. "Who are they?"

"Enemy."

It was always unnecessary to state the obvious—Ryan had already guessed that the attackers weren't likely to be friendly. But they were nearly at the edge of the ville and there wasn't time for any further conversation.

One of the huts, roof ablaze, loomed from the mist to the left. Ryan caught a glimpse of a tall figure that carried a struggling, kicking pig, but it vanished into the center of the ville.

"Split up! Man for man!" Jorund Thoraldson shouted. "Slay them all."

Ryan had his pistol drawn and paused a moment to try to get his bearings. As he moved on, close to the longhouse, he tripped over something. It was the body of a young woman, her skirt hiked around her thighs as though the return of the Vikings had saved her from rape.

But it hadn't saved her life.

As he stooped over her body, Ryan could taste the scent of fresh-spilled blood, sweet and a little sickly. Once savored, it was a smell that was never forgotten.

Someone had slit the woman's throat so savagely that the edge of the blade had scored a bright silver gouge from the iron thrall collar that circled her neck. As Ryan moved the corpse, he saw that the death had been a double one. A very young baby, covered with blood, lay beneath her.

A shot was fired close by, and the odor of puddled blood was smothered for a moment by the tang of black powder. Ryan didn't know if the ball had been aimed at him.

"Odin!" The Viking war cry was followed by the sound of metal cleaving through bone and solid flesh, and immediately on its heels came a gurgling, choking scream of pain and fear.

"Fireblast!" Ryan muttered. It was the sort of muddled brawl that he hated. A man could be struck down and butchered in the fog and confusion and never even see the hand that slew him. For a few moments he stood and waited, his back against the mud and wattle walls of the building. Smoke, gunpowder and the scent of blood filled his nostrils.

Ryan remembered that Trader said that a man who waited in a firefight would likely be chilled. The man who moved carefully would likely do the chilling.

"Time to move," Ryan said to himself.

He saw the first of the attackers as he dodged across the open space between two of the huts. One of the older Norsemen was hard-pressed, defending himself with an ax against the short, stabbing spear of his enemy, who was a skinny mutie dressed in a dancing assembly of rags and tatters.

The mutie looked about six feet tall and had long hair that clung to a yellowed skull in greasy clumps. Its right arm was only slightly longer than normal, but its left hand protruded from near the shoulder on a tiny, paddlelike arm. As the fighter whirled about, Ryan glimpsed at least two more residual hands poking feebly through the mutie's clothes. One leg was inches shorter than the other and seemed to fork at the ankle into a bizarre, cloven foot.

Ryan saw all of that in the first couple of seconds. He also saw that the Viking was tiring fast against the demonic energy of his attacker.

Shifting a touch to his right, Ryan leveled the pistol and put a 9 mm round through the mutie's head. The silencer muffled the sound, and the Norseman looked around in amazement as his opponent's skull exploded in his face like a stamped melon.

He spotted Ryan holding the pistol, and waved his ax in acknowledgment of his help.

The next four or five minutes were a maelstrom of fog and death, screams and blood-slippery earth, hacked limbs and occasional gunfire.

The attackers, mostly men, with a few women, were among the most severely mutated that Ryan had ever seen in Deathlands. The faces were grotesquely distorted, with eyes or noses missing, noses where there should have been ears, a single eye, low on the cheek, near the twisted corner of a misplaced jaw. Arms, legs, hands and feet were present in varying numbers and proportions. One capering man had a length of leather bound across the top of his head. It had come loose in the fighting and flapped to and fro, revealing a hole in his skull as large as a man's fist.

Because of the patchy mist it was impossible to make out the number of the attackers. Ryan's fighting instinct told him there were more than a dozen in the group that had circled around and come straight at the heart of the ville. And he accepted J.B.'s informed guess of eight in the other party that had ambushed them down at the beach.

The Norsemen had overwhelming numbers on their side, but the muties had the surprise of their shock attack on theirs. Several huts had been set on fire, and Ryan himself had seen the hacked bodies of nine or ten of the Norse women and children. And several of the Viking warriors were either down or dead.

But the arrival of the outlanders, with their superior weaponry, quickly tipped the balance in favor of the Markland people. Ryan heard the unmistakable boom of Doc's Le Mat, finding, moments later, the dying figure of a mutie with half its belly blown away by the huge scattergun round.

He saw J. B., crouched like a gunfighter in an old vid, blasting from the hip at a trio of haggard women armed with cleavers. His Steyr handgun put all three down in the dirt in as many seconds.

In combat like this, Jak Lauren was absolutely supreme, the best that Ryan had ever seen or ever expected to see. Wherever Ryan moved in the chaos of the ville, Jak's dancing, wild-haired dervish figure was there, a short-bladed knife in each hand, blood streaked to the elbows, like a maniac butcher on the run from the nearest abattoir. Crimson dappled his pale face and dripped from the steel points of his blades. Where he stepped, men and women died.

Ryan paid his own entry charge to parade the killing-floor.

A totally bald, skeletal figure came lurching out of the fog toward him, holding a burning torch of resined wood. In the other hand it held a single-edged ax with a long handle. The mutie was naked apart from a belt of broad leather with an enormous brass buckle. A woman's severed head hung from the belt, its face dangling against the creature's groin.

It saw Ryan and began to swing the ax. Its mouth opened, and its cry of rage and menace was absurdly thin and piping, like a trapped bird's.

But the bloodied steel was coldly real.

Ryan fired once as the axman charged him, but by one of life's viciously freakish accidents, the whirling blade of the ax caught the bullet and sent it howling into the fog-bound sky. The impact made the ax ring, and the mutie paused, fighting to keep hold of it. Had the creature carried on, Ryan would have been in serious difficulties. As it was he snatched the microsecond to snap off another round.

The bullet hit the blond head hung at its belt, smashing it apart. The jagged splinters of bone tore into the mutie's naked abdomen and crotch, shredding its genitals to scarlet rags of torn flesh.

The scream of agony and despair rose so high that it became inaudible to Ryan, though every dog in the ville began to howl in terror at the same moment.

Ultimately it would have been a killing shot, but Ryan figured it might take too long. He quickly put a

third round through the center of the mutely screaming mouth. The skull bounced once with the impact
and then was still.

It turned out to be the last death of the raid on
Markland.

JORUND SHOWED his generalship in the aftermath of
the attack. There were fires to be extinguished; live-
stock to be retrieved; Viking wounded to be tended
and their dead to be readied for burial; the corpses of
the muties to be dragged away by the heels, hauled into
shallow pits by teams of thralls.

And the mutie wounded were to be dealt with.

"Egil, take four of our wisest men and place a circle patrol about the steading. I think the enemy will
not return, but . . ." He shook his head and looked
around, seeing the devastation of Markland.

A tiny, wizened woman pushed her way through the
crowd of watchers, stopping, eyes bird-bright, in front
of the karl. Behind her Ryan could see Krysty and
Mildred, both smoke-stained but looking unharmed.

"The bad that has come is from the outlanders and
the black woman," the stooped crone croaked, "yet
the good is from the outlanders and the white boy."

Sigurd Harefoot clapped his hands in approval.
"Well said, wisewoman. Without the blasters of the
outlanders the evil ones could have harried us toward
destruction."

She shook her head and waved a warning hand at
the Norseman, a sapphire ring flashing on her wrin-

kled first finger. "More than the tools of Odin, Sigurd Harefoot. I tell you that it is the balance brought by the outlanders. The wrong of the black and the right of the white. Cherish the one and remove the other. Or the steading is doomed."

Ryan looked at her, holding her veiled eyes, steady, until she broke and turned away. "Anyone harms any one of us, the shit breaks the air lock. Y'all better remember that." He glanced at Jorund.

"You are with us, One-Eye, and we have agreed the women can live here, with the others. The evil ones have attacked us before, from up the coast. They have not come in the day behind the cloak of the fog before. But we turned them, and they have paid a heavy blood price."

As he finished speaking, Jorund stared at the wisewoman, who spit on the ground in front of him and turned away. She threw her last words over her hunched shoulder. "The day will come when you will search your heart for a way to change what has happened. And Freya herself will not aid you. Nor will any man, Jorund Thoraldson, Karl of Markland."

CHAPTER TWENTY-FOUR

BJARNI EARTHMOVER and two of the other warriors were ready to begin the journey to Valhalla, and the three wounded mutie prisoners were to accompany them.

One of the boats, fallen into some disrepair, was to be used for the funeral ceremony. Ryan and his companions passed the afternoon in their hut, resting, eating and cleaning and reloading their weapons. Erik Stonebiter had come by and explained what was to happen and to invite them, on behalf of the karl, to join the ritual of death.

"It will all take place as the fire-sun touches our sister earth, and the water and night close the eyes of the world."

Now, dusk had come.

Other than the men who stood watch around the perimeter of the ville, everyone was there, including the women and children, free-born as well as thralls. Krysty and Mildred, like the rest of the nonmen, had their heads covered with shawls of dyed wool, a mark of respect for the passing of Bjarni and the others.

Ryan guessed that the slaves and the women and children who'd been butchered would be buried somewhere quietly. This funeral was only for the warriors of Markland.

Ryan led Doc, J.B. and Jak out into the calm gentle evening. The main fire of the steading had been built up and blazed so brightly that no one could stand within twenty feet of it. A number of smaller fires had been lit, some on the beach, some on a low headland where the trees grew close to the shingle.

Jorund beckoned the four to stand near him. "This will not take long. We do not grieve much over one of our brothers fallen in battle."

It crossed Ryan's mind to ask whether being shot through the temple while carrying an apple on your head really counted as falling in battle, but he decided to keep silent.

"What about the prisoners?" J.B. asked. "You question them?"

"You mean did we torture them, outlander? Of course we did. But we spared them life."

"But did you discover why they were attacking you?" Doc pressed, wiping a dab of mud from the ferrule of his ebony cane. "Did you find out if they planned to attack again?"

The baron looked puzzled. "Talk to the evil ones? How?"

Ryan sighed. "Course. Muties like them...they won't likely talk much of anything close to what you speak."

"No."

"So, what happens to them?" Ryan asked.

"There." Jorund pointed toward the headland.

At first, Ryan thought that three large men stood there, but the shapes were too big to be people, and he could make out something odd. The outlines were fuzzy, as if the men were built from branches and sheaves of grass.

"What are they?" he asked.

It was Doc who replied. "I believe they are called wicker men, my dear Ryan."

"What?"

Jorund nodded. "The old one answers truly. I have heard them called that. Wicker men. Straw men. Basket men. All the same."

"But I don't get it."

"You will get it soon enough," Doc replied. "Then you will quite possibly wish that you had not. It is damned barbaric."

THE PRISONERS WERE to die before the funeral began so that their souls could accompany Bjarni and the other Vikings on their last dark journey.

They were led out, naked and bound tightly. As they stumbled past Ryan he noticed that the thongs around their wrists and ankles were thick strips of rawhide that had been soaked.

He glanced at Doc. "Why have they wet the cords on them?"

"Fire doesn't burn water, my dear fellow," Doc replied grimly.

The bodies of the muties showed clear evidence that they had been tortured, but not in the fiendish way that Ryan and the others had witnessed in the *rancheria* of the Apaches. This seemed to have been more in the nature of a prolonged and brutal beating.

There was a woman and two men, one much older than the other. As with the rest of the attackers, the three were severely deformed. The woman had at least five pendulous breasts, and her nose was a ragged hole above a gaping, slobbering mouth. The younger man was unbelievably skinny, his ribs sticking through pale bruised flesh. He was clearly a deaf-mute, the sides of his shaved skull not showing a trace of ears. The oldest of the trio had only one eye, and his legs were unnaturally short for his body.

As well as bearing the marks of fists, boots and whips, each captive was wounded. The woman limped, and could stand only because a warrior supported her on each side. The deep cut from a sword had severed a hamstring. The old man had a gunshot in his right shoulder, and the third mutie had two deep stab marks under his ribs.

The people of the ville moved in behind the prisoners, walking in relative silence toward the low bluff. As they drew near it, Ryan caught the smell of lamp oil. And then he guessed what the wicker men were for and why the ropes were sodden with water.

"Fireblast," he whispered.

The wisewoman was there, carrying a small brass bowl with holes drilled into it in an ornate pattern. It held some scented herbs that were smoldering and giving off a light blue smoke. The setting sun flooded her malevolent little face as she capered around the tethered prisoners.

"Freya take thee and may thy passing be slow and hard," she croaked.

"Night comes fast," Egil said to the karl. "We must dispatch them."

"Aye." Thoraldson made a gesture with his right hand for the prisoners to be taken the last few yards to the three wicker men.

Then both Jak and J. B. Dix realized what was going down.

"Why not slit throats?" the albino boy asked.

"Because this makes a finer sight for everyone, Jak," J.B. replied.

Once they caught the sickly taint of the oil that drenched the three enormous straw figures, the muties also realized their fate and began to struggle. They were subdued with such speed and efficiency that Ryan wondered to himself how often this ritual had been performed in Markland.

Each wicker man stood about twelve feet high and was only a crude representation of a human being. The stout legs and the main trunk were made from thick twigs and slender branches, which formed a tight cage for the prisoner.

The bound muties were shoved into the wicker bodies, and more branches were hastily tied and woven into place to prevent their escape.

"We have to watch this through?" J.B. whispered to Ryan.

"Yeah. Don't like it any more'n you, but I guess we stay till it's done." He looked to the west. "Sun's down, so it won't be long."

"Figure more of the muties'll be back? These could have been a recce outfit."

"Depends on the size of their ville. They were a triple-poor lot. Poor armed. If we set our minds to it, I guess we could clear out the nest for these people."

The Armorer nodded. "Want to?"

Ryan glanced sideways at him, ignoring the old woman, who was now kneeling before the three wicker men and droning an incantation. "Guess not. You?" J.B. shook his head. Ryan sighed. "Stay down. Wait and watch. Try and get word with Krysty and Mildred tomorrow."

He was interrupted by Jak's exclamation of disgust. "Fucking triple-hard. Kill 'em, yeah. But kill them fast."

Three iron-collared women had been assigned the task of lighting the wicker men. At the karl's signal they touched their smoking torches to the lowest branches. The oil caught quickly, and yellow flames licked eagerly at the dry grass that covered the framework.

The screams began immediately.

The oil was crudely processed and gave off vast quantities of choking smoke, which quickly handed a kind of mercy to the condemned muties. There was little wind, and the column of boiling darkness rose straight into the evening air, like an accusing finger.

The wicker men were transfigured into giant men of fire.

Most of the Vikings watched the hideous passing of their captives with a stoic silence, the flames staining their cheeks a bloody scarlet. Within a bare minute the piercing screams had ceased.

"Suffocated," Doc pronounced. "The best that one could hope for the poor wretches. Murderous they might have been, but that is a damnably wicked passing."

Jorund realized that the ritual of revenge was too quickly done, and he lifted his sword, shouting to his people. "So they perish, and their soured spirits shall tread the path of tears for our brother, Bjarni, and for the other warriors. Let us now go to them!"

Ryan trailed along with the Norsemen, hoping to be able to get close to Krysty for a word, to sound her out about making a run from the archaic ville within the next forty-eight hours. But the press of moving men stopped them.

THE LONG SHIP WAS PUSHED out into the still waters of the lake, with Bjarni and his companions laid out on its deck. Ryan saw for the first time that the corpses of three of the young women—thralls—were also lying on the doomed vessel.

Erik Stonebiter was next to him, watching the ceremony. "The girls? How did they get chilled?" Ryan asked.

"Strangled by three women, free-born, to accompany their masters on the road to Asgard."

Ryan didn't say anything. One of the first lessons he'd learned in life was that there was a time for speech and a time for silence. Knowing the difference was real important.

The warriors chanted a paean of death to the lost men, as the ship floated away, its sail furled on the high mast, the dragon's head on the bow nodding at the wavelets. Ryan couldn't catch many of the words, but it sounded like it was all about honor, valor and brotherhood.

He caught the odor of lamp oil again. At first he thought it was still filling his nostrils from the fiery slaughter of the muties, but he soon realized that the woodwork of the long ship was also soaked with it.

Jorund threw the first flaming torch. The fire caught immediately, tongues of smoky red and orange dancing along the deck and creeping up the mast, lapping their way toward the snarl-toothed figurehead.

The next senior warrior threw his torch, followed by Egil Skallagson and Sigurd Harefoot, then all the others. The lights whirled through the dusk, then flames exploded in roaring streaks. In less than a minute, the ship was ablaze from end to end, the smoke beginning to obscure the small group of corpses.

"It's the way for a warrior to leave this life for the next," Erik said with an almost religious awe.

"What's the next life like?" J.B. asked interestedly.

"You carouse with a multitude of available women," the young man replied.

J.B. turned to Ryan and lowered his voice. "Sounds like living forever in a frontier pesthole gaudy house."

"Yeah. Look. Boat's near burned down to the water already."

"With the evil offered through the wicker men, there will be no need of further gifts," Erik told them.

"Gifts?" Doc asked. "What kind of gifts, young fellow?"

The Viking turned to face him, his mouth working uncertainly. "Gifts? I had not meant that. It is that our warriors need company on their sky-road, once taken and never retraced. The sluts and evil ones are enough, and they will keep off more dark days."

There was a roar of noise from the throng of watching Norsemen. Fire hissed as the lake swallowed the flaming remains of the long ship. The fierce dragon's head was the last part to be consumed and disappear beneath the water.

The sun had gone, the last sliver of scarlet vanishing over the hills. Darkness had come to the ville of Markland.

Ryan led the other friends back to their hut, feeling tired from the fight, the killing and the brutality of the executions. And he still hadn't been able to snatch a private moment with Krysty.

The night would call for a lot of thinking and talking with the others.

And the development of some kind of plan.

CHAPTER TWENTY-FIVE

THE SUN ROSE into a sky of brilliant blue, with only a handful of scattered, purple chem clouds to mar its perfection.

Ryan, J.B., Doc and Jak had talked quietly until late in the night, trying to formulate some sort of plan. There'd been general agreement among them that Markland surely wasn't the kind of ville in which to pass the rest of your life.

The conclusion was simple, and Doc voiced it best. "A rad-sick, brutalized, antiwomen, primitive and lost community. To visit here is like visiting the dark side of the Middle Ages on a bad day."

"So we get out." Ryan's words weren't any kind of question.

"Today," Jak agreed.

"Tonight," J.B. offered.

Ryan hadn't been so certain. And now, as he stood with one hand on the crudely carved door frame, looking out across the great lake, he felt his worries were justified.

The setting of the ville made it difficult to break clear and run. The bowl of wooded hills were a maze of twining paths, and the Norsemen would know and hunt along all of them. Once the crest of the ridge was reached, there was the perilous descent into the hothouse tropical world that hid the redoubt.

Some of the Vikings were obviously sickly, but there were enough healthy warriors to make escape hazardous. Though Mildred looked as if she could wrestle a grizzly, she obviously wasn't anywhere near fit yet, after the long freezing. And stamina over rough backcountry had never exactly been Doc Tanner's strongest suit.

J.B.'s idea to creep away at night was the best, but since the muties' sneak attack, Jorund had announced that there would be extra roving guard patrols after dark.

They'd even talked about trying the lake. In addition to the dragon-head long ships, the ville possessed smaller boats. But there was little prospect of getting far in those without the faster ships catching them.

On the far side of the steading, beyond the big central fire, Ryan glimpsed Krysty's dazzling hair. Mildred was only a step away, as she'd been ever since they arrived at the Norse ville.

Ryan glanced around furtively, then beckoned to the women. There was no doubt that they had seen him, but they kept walking at an angle, cutting around the side of the longhouse, ignoring him. Nobody noticed them. The ville went about its business: men worked on one of the boats and a hunting party readied itself to go out into the woods; women carried water and wood and began the preparation of the evening meal.

Ryan looked back into the hut at his three friends, who were finishing off a jug of buttermilk. "Women are off some place. I'm going to meet them if I can. Stay here."

"Would it not be possible for the rest of us to accompany you, Ryan? A stroll through the pine trees would be most beneficial in purging my mind of the unpleasant scenes of yesterday. I would be most obliged, Ryan."

"Sorry, Doc. If anyone comes, try and cover for me. Don't straight out lie. Kinda hint I'm inside resting. Be back soon as I can."

He left the rifle inside, carrying only the pistol at his hip and the sheathed panga.

It was a fabulous day, one of the finest that he could ever remember. The air was free from the taint of dust and death that still lingered, century-old over so much of Deathlands. The gentle wind that came sighing in off the lake stirred the topmost branches of the big pine trees as he walked among them.

Krysty and Mildred could only have taken one trail, which meandered gently toward a razorback ridge, some fifteen hundred feet above him.

The ville shrank beneath him, like a picture he'd once seen in a scorched and tattered mag. It had had the remnants of a bright yellow cover, he recalled, and had contained photographs of different places taken from a hot-air balloon. That was what Markland looked like from a turning of the trail, across a flower-spotted meadow.

There should be a guard somewhere along this track. Ryan wondered whether Krysty and Mildred would have cut away from the path before they encountered him, and if they did, what kind of a marker would they have left him?

He'd met men with better woodcraft than he possessed. But not many. Krysty would know he'd be coming slow and cautious, on the lookout for her sign.

It was easy.

A small branch had been snapped off a little more than head high, broken in two and laid at the edge of the path. It pointed away into the gloom under the branches. Perhaps one man in ten thousand would have spotted it for a deliberate sign.

There was only way the women would have gone—onward and up. Once Ryan was off the well-trodden track, the marks became easier to follow. Pushing between the pines had snapped off small twigs, and in the moist places Ryan could see clear impressions of their feet.

Shortly after entering the forest, he heard the sound of someone whistling behind him, and guessed that it must be the guard.

After another ten minutes or so, he glimpsed two figures ahead of him, both wearing dark clothes. Only Mildred's white sneakers showed up in the shaded gloom. Ryan pushed on faster, and almost immediately he saw Krysty turn around. He knew she couldn't possibly have heard him. But she'd "felt" his closeness.

The women stopped and waited for him.

"Hi, lover. How goes the thrilling life of the warrior?"

"Beats standing neck-deep in a cesspool, I guess. How about on the female side?"

Mildred answered him, her eyes flashing angrily. "It's not funny, Ryan. This place is like Boston in the 1800s. A woman's position is not just in the kitchen, or under her husband. She's a very poor third after the dogs and cattle!"

"Keep your voice down," Krysty warned. "Trees muffle sound, but the sentry's not that far away from us."

Ryan looked around. As far as the eye could see there was just the limitless expanse of trees, blurring eventually into a solid darkness. The forest would be an easy place to get lost.

"Best get the talking done. Don't want a hunting party coming after us."

"We think we should get out. Soon. Sooner. Soonest. Preferably yesterday."

He looked at the black woman, whose brown eyes were fixed to his face. Ryan sensed the great strength of character that Mildred possessed.

"I kind of agree. But it's not that easy."

"Krysty said the same. I don't see it. We have overwhelming firepower."

"Look around, Mildred. What's the good of having a rifle that'll rip off fifty rounds in a coupla seconds in this kind of terrain? Come on. One guy with a decent black-powder musket and a good eye could take us all out."

"So what've you men decided, Ryan? Do tell me and Krysty. I'm sure it would be nice to be told what we have to do. And how long we have to keep carrying firewood and washing greasy pots. *Do* tell us, Ryan. Please."

He looked at her without speaking for several seconds. "Don't fuck with me, Mildred."

"Sorry. Bit O.T.T., was it? That means 'over the top,' Ryan. Point taken. But we'd still like to know what you plan."

Ryan hunkered down, his back against a tree, relaxing on the soft carpet of pine needles. He listened to the distant song of a bird, enjoying the calmness. Mildred and Krysty sat down close by.

"We talked it through last night," he said. "Yeah, we all feel like we have to get out. But in a ville like this, isolated, the locals have the edge. I figure we stick it another day or so. Then we break close to midnight. Try and pick a clear time. Go fast and hard as we can for the ridge and into that swampy jungle. Hold up there and watch for pursuit. If it comes, we can try for an ambush. That's the plan." He looked at them. "Well?"

"Two days?" Mildred said.

"No longer, lover? There's something about this place I truly don't care for."

"And there's the radiation sickness," Mildred added. "We've seen a dozen or more of the folk— mainly kids—with too many symptoms."

"Yeah. We've noticed some of the men don't look well. Sores around the mouth and nails missing from fingers. That kind of stuff."

"So we wait for you to give us the word?" Krysty asked.

"Yeah."

"Best get on back."

Ryan led the way, ducking and weaving among the trees until they struck the main trail toward the ville. They kept together, passing a couple of narrower side tracks, one of which snaked away toward a steep outcrop of granite.

Krysty suddenly grabbed at Ryan's sleeve. "Someone's coming."

"Up or down? Front or behind? How many?" His questions machine-gunned out.

"Up. Front. Four or so."

Ryan hesitated, glancing to the woods on both sides of them. Here the trees weren't quite so densely packed, and there was a risk of their being spotted, even if they went some distance undercover.

"Back to that last cutoff. Quick."

Neither Krysty nor Mildred stopped to argue. They followed him up the hillside for a hundred yards, then onto the side trail. It snaked to the left and right, working its way up the steeper part of the mountain, zigzagging like a broke-back cottonmouth.

Ryan stopped and held up a hand for silence. He bent to try to peer through the pines to the main trail, but the foliage was too dense. However, they could all hear the sound of men's voices, raised in bellowing laughter. The noise grew momentarily louder and Ryan reached for his pistol. But then it faded again as the Norsemen continued up the main track.

"Carry on, lover?" he asked.

Krysty shook her head, the flaming red hair starbursting around her shoulders. "This path . . . there's something up here that . . ." Her green eyes were clouded and puzzled. "Don't know. Don't like it. We got time to take us a look?"

Ryan glanced at his wrist chron. "Tight." But he saw the concern on her face. "Let's go a ways and look. Watch the time."

Mildred was beginning to pant with the exertion of the climb. "Wouldn't think I used to hike the High Sierras, would you? Spent three weeks up in Glacier Park one summer. Grinnell Glacier—what little was left of it—went there and back in a morning. Most beautiful place on God's earth up there. Now I'm bushed in five minutes."

"Wait here. Me and Krysty'll go up and take a look. Be back inside twenty. You be okay on your own, Mildred?"

"I'm bushed, Ryan, not totally senile. Maybe Krysty should leave me her shooter."

"No." Ryan shook his head, smiling at the look of disappointment on her face. "We'll get you a blaster as soon as we can. But we aren't directly threatened. Worst'll be they make you go back to the ville. Not killing time. Not yet.''

A MARMOT SCAMPERED across their path as they neared the top of the climb. It was the only wildlife they'd seen, though there were old deer tracks everywhere. The trees thinned out, and they could see the silvery water of the lake stretching below them.

"Quiet up here. Thought there'd have been more signs of fresh game," Krysty said.

"The boy, Erik Stonebiter, told us that hunting was getting harder. Their fathers talked of hills that teemed with deer and rivers that brimmed over with trout and salmon.''

"Could tie in with what Mildred suspects. Another good reason for moving on.''

Ryan glanced around them. "Path leads over there toward that flat rock. We got time for a look.''

Krysty hesitated. "Something bad, lover. Something up there.''

"Danger?''

"No. Not direct danger.''

"What?''

She reached out and touched him on the cheek with a long forefinger. "Better go and look.''

On the far side of the high rock was a kind of natural amphitheater, the turf trodden flat by hundreds of feet. Ryan and Krysty stood together, looking up at a block of granite that was about ten feet long and five feet wide. The pale stone was streaked with glittering seams of quartz, and its flanks were heavily carved in ornate, swirling, interlocking patterns. A heavy ring of black iron on a short chain was inset at each corner. Long, thick stains of something black or dark brown had run down the sides of the rock that were exposed to them. The clotted streaks were unmistakably old blood.

Neither Krysty nor Ryan said a word. They turned away from the sacrificial altar and retraced their steps to where Mildred waited for them.

CHAPTER TWENTY-SIX

THE THREE FRIENDS succeeded in slipping back into the ville without anyone having noticed their absence. Ryan passed the news of the hidden stone to J.B., Jak and Doc. "Had to be blood. Had to be some kind of sacrifice. I figure it as another reason to shake dust off this place."

Doc was most concerned at hearing about the slab of hewn granite out on the hillside above the lake. "I agree we should make haste to depart from here, gentlemen. Primitive societies have all manner of unsuspected totems, and human sacrifice would not appear to be out of character here. We saw the symbolic burning of the three prisoners."

"Tad more'n symbolic, Doc," J.B. said. "Looked like a real fire to me."

Doc tsked-tsked as though J.B. were a precocious student at a Harvard seminar. "The deaths were real. But the use of the human-shaped wicker figures turned them into symbols. I have noticed with some alarm that Jak here appears to be some kind of totem person to the villagers—I think because of his very white hair and pale skin. Several of the thralls make a detour to avoid walking through his shadow." He paused and looked toward the doorway of their hut. "Of greater concern is that they clearly regard our new freezie companion, Mildred, as the dark side of the same coin. If anything goes wrong I could imagine they might seek a scapegoat. And it might be Mildred."

It was one of the longest speeches Ryan had ever heard the old man make, and it was totally free of his usual slight confusion.

"You say that they think Jak's a sort of god and Mildred is . . ."

"A black demon. Yes. I think we should make our move before something else goes awry and we, the outlanders, are conveniently around to be blamed."

During that morning, two young children died in Markland.

THE SCREAMS BEGAN around noon, and came from one of the huts near the forest. Ryan and the others were sitting outside, enjoying the sunshine, when Erik Stonebiter walked by, his face drawn with tension.

"What's happening?" Jak called.

The Viking hesitated, but didn't look at the albino teenager. He talked past him toward the lake, his eyes flickering nervously. "It's the bloody flux again. The wisewoman said Odin and Freya would punish us for taking in the . . . your dark woman. Said ill would come from it."

"Who's ill?" J.B. asked. "Sounds like a woman screaming. Or a child."

"Two *skraelings*. Little ones. Sons of Ragnar Lothbrok, who was kin to the ale maker whose house this hut once was. The men often went off together with Ragnar's children. Harald would carry kegs of fresh spring water, and Ragnar would fish in the same river."

Ryan glanced at the Armorer. Two families rad-sick and this common link. If the friends had had more time and far more desire, it would have been interesting to go along the coast and visit this strange and dangerous place for themselves.

"What is wrong with them?" Doc asked.

"I said it was the flux. Their bowels run blood and they vomit up everything they're given to eat. Both children have lost teeth, and their skin is covered in a dreadful rash."

Ryan had seen enough examples of rad poisoning around flaring hot spots to recognize the unmistakable symptoms. "Can—"

His words were interrupted by a tremor in the ground. From far off came a deep rumbling sound, like a convoy of laden wags grinding below their feet. Dogs barked and the burning logs on the main village fire toppled noisily in a fountain of exploding sparks. Ryan looked beyond the beach and saw that the surface of the lake was covered in fine ripples, as though a bowl of soup had been shaken by a careless hand.

A black-backed gull that had been perching on top of the longhouse flew squawking into the air, circled the ville once then vanished toward the far west.

"What!" Jak exclaimed. "Fucking earthquake!"

"The hammer of Thor strikes at Earth Mother," Erik said. "It happens four or five times every year. A few months ago there was a bad trembling and some huts fell. This was small."

There was a brief aftershock, and then the earth was still again. The dogs stopped howling and Markland slipped quickly back to normal—except for the thin screams of the sick children.

Ryan recalled what he'd been about to say when the small quake had interrupted him. "Can we help the sick?" he asked.

"No. The wisewoman is with them and will do what can be done."

"Burn a few chicken feathers and rub some pig fat on them." Doc snorted contemptuously. "At least let Mildred see them. She's a qualified doctor, you know."

"Leave it, Doc," Ryan cautioned.

"But if we can do some good, Ryan, my dear fellow, then surely..."

"No. Mildred looks and then they die, like rad-sick kids most likely will. Who gets the blame, Doc?"

"Ah. Point taken."

"And she won't have much in the way of medicine," J.B. added.

Erik looked from face to face, carefully avoiding Jak's ruby eyes. "What is this Mildred? The black nonman?"

"You could call her that," Ryan said. "But it's best your wisewoman cares for the kids."

Something happened then to the volume and pitch of the screaming, but Ryan couldn't immediately identify what it was. Jak's hearing was sharp and he picked it up first. "One dead," he announced. "Other's sinking. Go soon."

Jorund Thoraldson came out of the hut where the sick children were being tended and looked quickly around his steading. He spotted Ryan and the others, and took a few steps in their direction. He hesitated, then continued on.

"The older boy has gone to the gods," he said, "and his brother treads fast upon his heels."

"I'm sorry," Ryan said.

"Will the young whitehead look at the living boy?" the karl asked. "He can touch him and bring his own blessing, as the chosen one. Will he help our sick *skraelings*?"

"What's say?" Jak asked.

"He wants you to go and cure the sick and raise the dead," Doc replied angrily. "Just a normal morning for a god."

"Doc!" Ryan warned. "Keep that mouth under control or, better still, keep it shut."

Erik Stonebiter turned away, staring across the lake, the water now placid and mirror calm after the brief quake.

"Things go ill here, outlander," he said to Ryan. "I am not one who will lay blame at your door. But I tell you this—'' he looked around to make sure nobody was close enough to overhear ''—I fear that there are others who will. Many who will.''

Seconds later the screaming died away in a drawn-out bubbling moan.

A NOON MEAL WASN'T BROUGHT to Ryan and his companions. They kept to their hut, making sure their weapons were primed and ready. Through the open door they saw that the ville was almost deserted. There had been an outburst of keening from the women shortly after the death of the second child. Since then the steading had been quiet. Everyone seemed to have retreated to their own homes.

''I'll go scout some food,'' J.B. said. His chron showed one-thirty in the afternoon.

''Why not?'' Ryan agreed. ''But we'll all go. Mebbe get to Krysty and Mildred. I don't like being separated from them. There's a real bad gut feeling about all this.''

''No,'' Jak said from the doorway. ''Baron and Krysty and freezie coming.''

Jorund had a couple of the elders of the ville with him. Krysty and Mildred walked at his heels, followed by half a dozen kitchen thralls, carrying bedding and cooking pots.

''Looks like they are about to be moved in with us,'' Doc observed. ''I wonder whether that is a good omen or not.''

Doc's supposition was correct, and his concern was also confirmed.

Jorund Thoraldson stood in their doorway, signaling everyone else to remain outside. His face was grim and he was perspiring heavily, though the afternoon was cool. "Your women must come to stay with you," he said. "It has been decided. The wisewoman has cast runes. The red thread and the rowan sprig tell a sad tale, outlanders."

"I was sorry to hear that two young children had died," Ryan said.

"It was a sorry day that ever you came to the steading of Markland," the baron replied.

"There was the sickness long before we came here," J.B. said, anger creeping into his usually calm voice.

Thoraldson shook his head. "I will not argue. It has been decided that you will remain here. None of you must leave this hut, but for the exercise of your bodily needs. Any attempt to depart from Markland will be looked upon as hard and treasonous."

"For how long?" Ryan asked.

"A day. Two, perhaps."

Ryan knew with total certainty that the tall Norseman was lying.

"Then what?" J.B. asked, taking off his glasses to polish them. He glanced at Ryan, showing his own disbelief.

"Then the wisewoman will cast the runes again. And it may be that the light will come again."

The baron turned away. Doc looked as if he were about to argue, but Ryan spotted him and quickly held a finger to his own lips. Doc shook his head in disgust.

Jorund Thoraldson paused, then turned back to them. "We give you back the black woman. It may be we shall have need of the white-haired boy. A small thing, only."

Then he was gone, calling out orders to the thralls, and gesturing Mildred and Krysty to join their friends.

Only when the six companions were left alone did they talk. And the talk was brief.

Ryan told the woman what the baron had said to them. "You know about that bloody altar up in the woods. We've all gotten the feeling that they regard Jak here as some kind of mysterious stranger-god, and that Mildred is evil on the hoof."

"Story of my life." She grinned.

Doc cleared his throat. "Are you suggesting, my dear Ryan, that these Viking throwbacks might somehow wish to sacrifice this lady to their pagan gods? And use young Jak here as their chosen instrument on earth? Is that it?"

"Yeah. In a cartridge case, that's it."

"So, we go?" J.B. asked.

"Yeah."

And that was the end of the discussion. The plan of escape took only a little longer.

THE VILLE WAS RINGED by sentries at night, guarding against another sneak attack from the muties. But the central area, near the beach, was left unguarded. The large fire was allowed to smolder during the hours of darkness. There was a quarter moon, mostly hidden behind banks of tattered cloud. Though none of the companions had much experience on water, they had all agreed that the ships offered their best chance. The plan was to push off and make their way eastward, keeping close to land to avoid becoming lost. They'd strike inland at the first hint of dawn and head for the high ridge to the south. With luck the friends would get over the top before any pursuit could get close.

Jak left the hut first, his white hair covered by a hacked piece of blanket. J.B. followed, ready to move in fast at any sign of trouble. Doc and Mildred were third and fourth, with Krysty at their heels. Ryan brought up the rear.

There was no point in their stealing one of the fifty-foot-long dragon-ships. It would have been utterly impossible for so few to handle one. But there were several smaller boats, narrow, with single oars, and lying low in the water.

The ville was asleep; not even a dog stirred. They reached the lower part of the beach safely, though Ryan winced at the noise their feet made on the shingle. They reached one of the small boats, its oars neatly stacked inside. Jak took up a position in the stern, alert for any threat, while the others climbed aboard. Ryan and J.B. were last and set their shoulders to the task of moving the craft off the grating pebbles.

Very slowly they began to float away from the Viking ville.

CHAPTER TWENTY-SEVEN

"GET YOUR ELBOW off my tit, Doc!"

"I'm sorry, ma'am, but this contrary piece of wood won't do what I want it to do."

"Hold her straight, Krysty."

"Gaia! You want to steer, lover, then you come and have a go."

Trying to propel the boat in the direction they wanted was proving even more difficult than Ryan could possibly have imagined. Once the boat floated a few yards out onto the lake, Ryan and J.B. had each taken an oar to paddle the craft farther from the steading.

As soon as the others took oars, the chaos began. The oars were long and heavy, and it was hard for Doc and Mildred to control them. Ryan had to hiss a biting warning about the amount of noise they were making—splashing, cursing and banging the clumsy oars against each other and against the sides of the vessel.

Another big problem was that the boat had no conventional tiller or rudder. Ryan followed Doc's tentative suggestion that the bracket near the stern was for a steering oar. Trailed over one side the blade of the oar could be angled to change the course of the vessel. But Ryan found the method clumsy and difficult. If he altered the pitch of the oar a fraction too much, the boat went careering off in the opposite direction.

Eventually Ryan managed to find an effective way of running the boat. Jak took the steering oar and tried to hold the craft just within sight of the shore. Ryan, J.B. and Krysty each took an oar, while Mildred and Doc shared a thwart and did their best to share the last of the oars.

It wasn't terrific, but it was the best they could do.

The night air was cool, and Ryan could see his breath misting in front of him. Behind the boat he could just make out the silvery line of the wake, cutting erratically over what had once been called Lake Superior. His sight was only a little better than average, and he'd long since lost the red glow of the fire at the center of the ville. Nor had he been able to make out anything of the land to their right.

In the darkness it was difficult to judge what kind of progress they were making. As they were on a lake there wouldn't be much of a current, but there was a fresh breeze blowing.

"Jak?" he called.

"Yeah?"

"How're we doing?"

"Moving."

"How far off from the land?"

"Hundred yards, mebbe two."

"No sign of anyone coming after us, or anyone on shore?"

"Nothing. Quiet as a hunting gator."

Ryan, trying to keep a steady stroke that the others would be able to match, was worried that they were moving too slowly. The dragon-ships, fully manned, would overhaul them within minutes, once they were within sight. It was important that they keep a watch behind them, and look out for the first lightening of the eastern sky ahead of them.

The sky finally began to grow less dark, but with an infinite slowness. Ryan noticed the silvery sparkle of water off the broad blade of the oar. Glancing to his right, he realized that he could now make out the low silhouette of the shore. And, rising above it, he was now able to see the pinkish tint of the higher ground.

"Still nobody after us?" he asked Jak, aware of how tired he felt after the long row.

"No. But light's come. Head in?"

"Stop rowing a minute," Ryan instructed, taking several slow, deep breaths.

Krysty slumped over her oar, her hair trailing across it. J.B. sat back on his thwart, fedora pushed off his forehead. "I'll stick to walking or wags in future, if you don't mind, Ryan," he said.

There was a narrow headland jutting into the lake about a quarter mile ahead, with what looked to be a sheltered bay beyond it. The trees came down close to the water, and behind them the hillside seemed to slope steeply upward.

"There," Ryan called, pointing.

He sighed and wiped sweat off his face, wondering whether he'd be better off in less clothing. His attention was drawn to the lapel of his shirt, where he'd pinned the tiny rad counter.

"Fireblast!" he whispered softly. "Look at that."

"What lover?"

"Look." He pointed to the diminutive disk, which was usually a neutral green color. Now it was glowing with a deep reddish-orange.

"Hot spot," J.B. said unnecessarily.

THEY BEACHED THE BOAT in a narrow inlet at the head of the bay, pulling it as far in under some overhanging trees as they could. Ryan was worried that it might still be visible to anyone sailing by. Knowing the difficulty of the terrain they had faced before, his guess was that they'd the biggest head start that they could get.

He hefted the Heckler & Koch over his shoulder and looked ahead. They were at the bottom end of a steep-sided valley, which had a stream running through the middle. It was nearly wide enough to be called a river, about nine feet across where they stood. As Ryan looked at the water a large salmon swam slowly and erratically past him, flopping over on its side, then straightening.

Jak was bending down a few yards away, hands cupped, ready to drink from the clear, sparkling water.

"No!"

Ryan's bellow of angry warning sent the dawn birds screeching from the pine trees; a flock of gulls rose in a screaming protest from the rocks at the end of the headland. The echoes rolled and boiled off the hills.

"What!" Jak spit, stumbling with shock, water spilling from his fingers.

"Come here," Ryan said. "Put a few drops of that water on my rad counter."

"What?"

"Do it."

The boy reached out a finger and allowed a single drop of the spring water to fall on the tiny button, which immediately went from the orange-red color to a dazzling, flaring scarlet.

"Holy shit!" Mildred breathed. "Do that mean what I think it do?"

Doc nodded. "It do."

Mildred was vehement. "We don't have a choice. We go farther along the coast or we go back toward the Viking village. We *cannot* stay here!"

"If we go upriver and over the mountain, we'll be there and gone fast," Krysty said. "We won't be exposed to the rad for that long."

Mildred turned to face Krysty, her hands on her hips. "You got any brains in that pretty head, lady? The count here at the edge of the lake's hot enough to fry a side of pork. What d'you think it'll be like higher up, where the radiation leak has to be stronger? While we're here jawing about it, the sickness is settling on us like fine ash from an erupting volcano.

Ryan nodded. "All right, all right! No point going farther. Must be close to the ville of those muties. Have to be back. Take the boat and keep close in to the shore. Hope to spot any pursuers before they're close enough to hit us."

"Then let's go," Mildred said.

Doc coughed. "One brief moment, if I may, Ryan?"

"What, Doc?"

"It seems likely there's been some slow seepage around here for some years. Witness the appalling mutations we witnessed in the attackers. But the illness that is now striking at the Viking people seems to me to indicate some new and drastic increase in the radiation potential. The water. The fish. My interest as a scientist prompts me to ask whether we might take a half hour and go a short way up the river to see what we shall see."

Ryan looked at the others. Mildred shook her head firmly. So did Jak. J.B. shrugged his shoulders.

Krysty looked behind her into the clean-smelling pine trees. "Half an hour can't hurt much. I'd like to know."

"Fine. We leave now. And we're back in the boat in precisely forty minutes. Anyone wants to stay here can. Mildred?"

She grinned. "I'm not letting that old goat boldly go where no scientist's gone before. But we don't touch or eat or drink anything."

IT TOOK LESS than fifteen minutes. A clear path meandered along the left-hand side of the river, which they followed. The water flowed through a gorge, and fresh scars along its flanks testified to recent earth falls. Mildred pointed them out to the others, commenting on the minor quake they'd all experienced.

"I assume that nuking during the war was so intense that it triggered movements of some of the less stable tectonic plates. You said that most of California had slid into the Pacific, Doc."

"Right."

"So, bearing in mind a lot of the nasties were buried underground, lead-lined vaults and all that so-called 'safety' bullshit, major tremors could open them up like a hot knife through butter."

"Mildred," Ryan said as he walked beside her on the trail, "I never read anything that told how rad sickness works. I mean, I know about what it does. The rash and puking and all that. But *how* does it do that? You can't see it or anything."

She paused. "Not my specialty, Ryan. But I guess I know a little. Gather around, students." Everyone stood closer. "You won't know much about negatively charged electrons, ions or free radical molecules, right? No, I thought not. Me neither. Radiation has alpha and beta particles and they have a charge of electricity. They screw up the electrons and molecules in the body. Send them ape-shit wild. I know that structural proteins, like collagen, get smashed around. The DNA... No, you wouldn't know that, either. The tiny cells can reproduce themselves perfectly in a healthy body. Radiation messes that up.''

"The cell blueprint is ruined?'' Doc asked. "Is that it?''

"Sure. And the cells that reproduce fastest are the ones that get hit first and hardest. Blood, of course. And skin and hair. So, you get leukemia and your skin starts falling off and goodbye hair. More serious mutations are slower to show, but just as deadly in the long run.''

"Thanks, Mildred. I just...well, it's all way beyond me.''

"Radiation kills, Ryan. That's all you need to know. A man who gets a bullet through the brain doesn't need to know all about high-energy physics or ballistics. Just that he's been shot and he's going to die.''

"Time's passing,'' J.B. warned. "Should we be turning around for the boat?''

"Looks like path opens around corner there.'' Jak pointed.

"There and no farther,'' Ryan pronounced. "Then it's fast back.''

"I just can't believe this place is so poisoned,'' Krysty said as they walked on. "Tall pines and the freshest stream you ever saw.''

"No birds,'' Jak said.

It was true. Other than the chuckling sound of the small river, the morning was silent. The only life at all was a glittering coppery cockroach that ambled across the trail in front of them. J.B. raised a boot to crush it, but Mildred warned him not to touch it.

"Creatures like that'll inherit the earth. Radiation hardly slows them."

They rounded the corner, and everyone stopped. There wasn't the least doubt that they'd found the source of the massive rad poisoning.

There had been, fairly recently, a huge slippage of earth, and half the hillside had opened up like giant jaws. The tumbled remnants of several concrete buildings clung perilously to the jagged edge of the sheer cliff, two hundred feet above them. But the quake had done more than damage the buildings. It had also torn open great burial pits beneath them, spilling their secret load from the metal-walled, sealed caskets.

The whole slope, hundreds of feet across, down to the river, was a tangled mass of rusting drums and split plastic vats. Whatever they might once have held was now an unbelievable cocktail of hideous substances, mingled together, all leached through to the water. Into the soil. Into the lake beyond and into the food chain for the entire area.

"My God!" Mildred whispered. "It's like opening the curtains on Armageddon. It's worse. Much, much..." She turned to Ryan, her dark eyes wide in shock. "Now, fast! Down the hill and as far away as possible from this devil's brew."

She led the way back toward the lake, stumbling in her eagerness. Ryan was at her heels, the others following closely behind.

"But what is it?" he shouted. "What could be in those drums?"

"Lord alone knows," she panted over her shoulder. "The killers were so many. Radioactive iodine. Carbon 14."

"Uranium?"

"Sure. Strontium 90, radium 226, tritium, radon 222. That's a gas."

"Plutonium, Mildred?" Doc called, jogging along third in line.

"Of course. Oh, I'm losing breath. Can't breathe deep in case... Carbon 14, cesium 134 and 137. Anything! It's all around us."

She wasn't that far from the jagged edge of panic, stumbling and nearly falling into the river at a point where the path doglegged left.

"Slow it, Mildred!" Ryan said. After all the self-control that the freezie had shown since they thawed her, it was a shock to see the state she was in now. The discovery of the ruined rad storage site had freaked her out.

She turned and gripped him by the arm, fingers tightening like a screw trap. "Ryan, that badge in your shirt doesn't show us how bad this might be. The rem count could be massive. Hopefully the worst of the leakage is gone, seeped away when the earth first cracked. But it is appalling.''

"Just take it careful. Break an ankle on this trail and it won't help."

"This was the great fear of my generation, you know."

"What?" Krysty asked, taking Mildred by the hand to help her over a steep patch of tumbled stone.

"Chernobyl."

"Your knob'll what?" Jak called, not quite hearing what she'd said.

"A place in Russia," she said, her breathing becoming steadier.

"Upon my soul, ma'am, but I remember that," Doc said. "And there were two more such accidents within a few years. Damnably similar. One was in... Pennsylvania, was it? Or Manitoba? And one in Europe. Near Lyons? Or Cardiff. I can't recall."

The beach opened before them, the expanse of the lake narrowed by the enclosing rocks of the headlands on either side.

Mildred had recovered, and climbed into the boat to sit on a thwart, hand pressed against her chest. "If ever I have a coronary," she said, "I'll have it now."

The others got in, and they pushed off, paddling quickly toward open water. Ryan noticed that the rad count had fallen back to red-orange. Still high, but below lethal.

As they rowed past the obscuring headland, they found themselves on top of two of the pursuing Viking dragon-ships.

CHAPTER TWENTY-EIGHT

THEIR ESCAPE had been discovered a little after dawn, and Jorund Thoraldson had immediately ordered out the long ships. He sent two vessels, under the command of Egil Skallagson, toward the west, while he led two more dragon-ships in an easterly direction.

"I had thought we would take you, outlanders," he said, once the small boat had been hauled alongside and the six companions were on the deck.

"And you were right," Ryan replied. "But there's something important we have to tell you about."

"No. Escape is treachery. The karl of Markland will not talk with traitors."

"You damned fool!" Doc exclaimed. "You and your people—every man jack of them—faces a slow and painful death within a matter of weeks unless you move your steading."

"Words, words, words. Like small pebbles rattling in a crab shell. I have said I will not talk. Perhaps when we return to Markland, before you all take the long road without turning, we might talk."

"The flying eagle for the one-eyed outlander," Sigurd said eagerly.

Jorund nodded. "For such treachery...perhaps. We shall see."

He gestured for the prisoners to be taken into the bow of his ship, where they were guarded by a couple of the younger warriors. There had been no attempt to search Ryan or any of the others, but their firearms had all been taken and placed in the stern. One of the guards was Erik Stonebiter.

"What's flying eagle?" Jak asked him.

"You would not wish to know."

"Tell us," the albino boy pressed.

"It is a way of slaying, only to be done by the karl himself. Because you have betrayed his wishes, he may kill your leader in that way."

"What fucking way?" Jak insisted. Ryan, sitting on the gently heaving deck beside the teenager, was beginning to wish he'd stop asking about the flying eagle.

The young Norseman blankly refused to face Jak and stared out across the lake, where the first tendrils of gray mist were already appearing. "It is a hard passing," he finally said.

Jorund had also spotted the threatening bank of fog and was urging his rowers on to greater efforts, beginning to beat out a rhythm with his sheathed sword on the bulwark of the vessel.

With Jak and the others still waiting, Erik Stonebiter eventually told them of the flying eagle. "If the karl wills it, urged by the wisewoman, then you may be bound crossways, wrists and ankles to a frame. The point of the knife will enter here." He touched himself under the short ribs, low on the right side of his chest. "It is thrust in and drawn deep, up to the top of the ribs' curve. Then down again and out on the opposite side. The shape is like that of an eagle, flying high against the sun."

J.B. had been particularly interested in the telling. "And that's it? Doesn't sound anything special to me."

"No. That is but the half of it. Once the chest is laid open, the karl steps in close and reaches within the cavity. He seizes the lungs in his fists and draws them slowly out. I have seen it. The lungs flutter and fill for many minutes."

"A hundred years sure hasn't made folks any sweeter," Mildred said quietly.

THE FOG CLOSED IN, thicker and more blinding than before. It surrounded the two dragon-ships in a cocoon of muffling damp. Jorund ordered the two vessels to make fast to each other to prevent their becoming separated and lost. The oars were shipped, and they drifted in silence. Lookouts were posted at stem and stern. Water lapped and chuckled against the wooden bows. The crew sat around, not talking, made uneasy by the shrouding mist.

Krysty huddled against Ryan for comfort and for warmth. "You figure we did right not to take them on in a firefight, lover?" she whispered.

He shrugged. "Moment like that, seeing them on top of us, you shoot or you don't. There's a good forty men, most with blasters, hid behind the wooden sides of their ships. With the rifles we could have done some serious chilling."

She smiled at him. "Sure. And so could they, huh? They had speed on the water, too. Rammed us. And that would have been the end of the book."

"That's the way I figured it, too." He wiped beads of moisture from her cold cheeks. "I hoped the baron might have listened about the rad leak."

"It'll chill everyone in the ville, won't it? Hot spot as red as that?"

"Sure. Mebbe we can get him to listen to us back at the ville. If the flying eagle don't get—"

"Doesn't," she corrected.

Ryan grinned and shook his head. "Sure. If the flying eagle *doesn't* get us first."

A light offshore wind was blowing the two Norse long ships farther out onto the lake. Jorund refused to allow the oars to be used to bring them back closer to the invisible land, worried that they might run upon saw-toothed rocks that would rip the belly out of the vessels.

J.B. suggested to Ryan that they might risk a break for their boat, which was being towed behind the dragon-ship. "Grab the blasters. Cut the line. Be gone, out of sight, in a minute or less."

It was tempting.

"Not a zero option situation," Ryan replied. "Some of us'd make it. Sure. But we'd leave a lot of blood behind us."

J.B. nodded. "Guess so."

As the afternoon wore on, Mildred was working herself into a righteous rage. "That blond hulk of total stupidity is sentencing every living thing in his village to certain, slow, painful death. And the pig-ignorant son of a bitch won't listen."

Ryan touched her on the arm. "Sure. But a man insists on putting the barrel of a Colt Magnum in his mouth and pulling the trigger, you'll likely get hurt if you try too hard to stop him."

"If we get to live long enough, we can try and get the word through someone like the young guy with the broken teeth," Krysty suggested.

Mildred sighed. "I suppose so. I wish we could have had a good bath real soon to try to wash off some of the surface radiation we must have picked up from that hell's caldron back there."

"Will the lake water not be severely contaminated as well?" Doc asked, his angular figure looming from the mist. He'd been standing and leaning on the side, peering into the afternoon gloom.

"I wouldn't want to drink much of it," Mildred agreed. "But it's barely tepid compared to that boiling river."

UNBELIEVABLY the fog was growing even thicker as the afternoon dragged by. When sitting on the cold wood of the bow, the friends could no longer see the ferocious head of the dragon with its blood-tipped teeth, only ten feet away. Ryan could just make out the boots of the lookout who perched there.

It had also become much colder.

Somewhere out in the murk a fish leaped, entering the water again with a slapping splash. Everyone on board jumped, startled.

Krysty stared out into the blank wall of fog, her eyes slightly closed, her head a little on one side. Ryan had been with her long enough to know something was happening.

"What?" he said, straining his own eyes. But it was impossible.

"I can hear...could be a big fish. Fog blurs the way I know things. But..." She stood up, like a questing hunter. "Gaia! Ryan, they're almost on top of—"

She was interrupted by a jolting crash as the first of the muties' boats rammed into them.

CHAPTER TWENTY-NINE

THE ROCKING, shifting deck and the clinging, choking fog made combat lethally surreal. Blasters were of little use when a target more than ten feet away couldn't be seen. The wood quickly became slick with blood, and bodies jostled, screamed and fell to the deck.

Ryan held his 9 mm SIG-Sauer pistol in his left hand, grabbed from the stern in that first moment of the attack, his panga in his right. He blasted and hacked at anything that came within range that wasn't either a friend or one of the Vikings. Despite being a captive of the Norsemen, he had no doubt whatsoever that to be taken prisoner by the gibbering muties would be far, far worse.

Like so many similar battles that Ryan had lived through, this one was a series of desperate moments, strung together in a jerking, chaotic succession of half memories.

There was no doubt from the first seconds that the attackers had come from the same ville as the muties who had sneaked into Markland. They poured over the side of the Viking dragon-ship, one or two with primitive firearms, most of them hefting a weird variety of edged weapons.

The Norse defenders were taken badly by surprise. Many of them were hacked down to the boards before they had a chance to protect themselves.

It was no small guerrilla raid.

Ryan spotted at least four of the muties' boats, hooked with grapnels to the long ships, and he guessed there had to be one more on the far side of the second of Jorund's tethered vessels. As far as numbers went, it was impossible to make a guess. He knew only his own fights, isolated in the clutching hands of the fog.

His first clash was against a mutie who had two heads. One was red-bearded and wild-eyed, but the other lolled on the wide shoulders, mouth sagging open and a thread of mucus crawling over the smooth chin. The man was wielding a large ax that looked as if it had been made from a honed-down shovel. Ryan was able to stoop under the first wild swing and deliver a vicious cut across the side of the knee. Bone cracked. The mutie gave a gobbling shriek of pain and fell sideways, dropping the ax. Ryan braced himself against the pitching of the long ship and shot left-handed, putting a bullet through the more active of the heads.

As it began to die, he saw that the other, passive head had come to life. The tongue, gray-blue, was darting between the scummed lips and the eyes were rolling with a wild malice.

It was unusual for Ryan Cawdor, but he used another round on the dying creature. He put a bullet neatly between the eyes of the auxiliary head. "Make sure," Ryan muttered.

Screams of bloody anger filled the air all around him. Someone stumbled into him, and he started to swing the panga.

"It's me, Ryan!" Mildred screamed. "Give me a fucking gun."

"Get someplace safe."

"Where?"

He looked around, seeing the steep prow and the invisible figurehead above it. "There. Can you climb up?"

"If you won't give me a gun, the least you can do is give me a hand up."

Ryan cupped his hands and let her step into them. Grunting with the effort, he heaved her into the air. He felt her take her own weight, her feet scrabbling for a purchase on the wet, slippery wood.

Something plucked at his sleeve and Ryan spun around, hearing a sound like an angered hornet. A crossbow quarrel quivered in the figurehead, inches below Mildred's white sneakers. But when he stared into the fog, there was no sign of who'd fired the bolt.

A squat figure came staggering out of the gray wall, clutching a deep gash in its shoulder. Since it wasn't one of the Vikings, Ryan flicked out the blade of his panga and opened up its throat into a pair of raw, crimson lips. The mutie fell at his boots, long nails gouging splinters of white wood from the greasy deck.

"A stand! A stand! Come to the bow!" The bellow was unmistakably that of Jorund Thoraldson. "By Odin, to me!"

Suddenly there was some little order out of the murderous shambles. The rising wind was beginning to peel tendrils off the surrounding fog, making it possible to see more of what was going on.

The second dragon-ship had been cut clear and was drifting to the north, with two of the muties' boats attached. But the crew had been given a few heartbeats of extra time to repel their boarders. The Vikings were defending solidly, beating the muties back and tipping any dead or wounded straight over the side. Already the slate waters were overlaid with spreading patches of scarlet.

But on Jorund's vessel, the battle was slipping the other way.

The baron, blood streaming from a half dozen gashes, waved his smeared war-ax over his head. To his relief, Ryan saw that Krysty and J.B. were also fighting their way to the bow, back to back. The Armorer used a slim-bladed flensing knife, darting it out at the muties with the precision of a surgeon. Krysty had obtained a short sword with a wide blade, and was using it to keep the enemy at bay.

There was no sign of either Doc or Jak. Ryan glanced around and saw Mildred perched snugly now on the head of the dragon.

The mist came and went, but during a momentary clearing, it was possible to calculate how much the odds favored the muties.

The first wave of attackers had taken a dreadful toll among the Norsemen. Other than Jorund, fewer than ten warriors—including Erik Stonebiter and Sigurd Harefoot—gathered in the bow of the long ship to stand against at least thirty muties, who were mostly toward the stern. The muties controlled all the deck area around the mainmast.

Ryan wished he'd been able to snatch up his rifle as well as the pistol. The cache of their blasters had been his first target when the boats came ramming in. He would have put the Heckler & Koch on full-auto and sprayed the living hell out of the cluster of attackers.

But Ryan had never found spilled milk much worth thinking about. Let alone crying over.

The muties started to edge toward them, grinning confidently, when Sigurd Harefoot, crooning a word-less chant to himself, began to remove his clothes.

"Fireblast!" Ryan exclaimed. "What the—"

"He goes baresark," Erik said at his side. "The frenzy of battle takes over the spirit of a warrior and he fights naked against the foe."

"Berserk," J.B. echoed. "Heard of it. Best stop him, or they'll cut him down."

The young Viking turned to grin through the blood that masked his face. "He would cut down any man who tried to stop him. He does what he must."

Mildred had dropped agilely to the deck once more. "He ain't just talking," she said.

Sigurd had built himself into a frothing anger, and he whirled his ax above his head. He had cast aside the horned helmet he'd been wearing and began to shuffle toward the muties, wearing only his high, laced boots. His chant had become a wild shriek of surging rage. Ryan saw one of the muties at the back of the crowd frantically trying to cock an antiquated crossbow. He leveled the pistol, but Erik gently pushed it down with the tip of his sword. "No. No man must aid a baresarker."

Nobody told Jak that. Invisible to the muties, the boy had suddenly come creeping up over the side of the ship, his lank hair dripping lake water. He saw the man readying the crossbow and reached for one of his own slim throwing-knives. Gripping it underhanded by the hilt, he aimed it with a lightning flick of the wrist.

It parted the misty air and struck the mutie in the side of the throat, its blood spurting like crimson steam from the wound. The creature slid wordlessly to the deck, the weapon falling from limp fingers.

Sigurd didn't see it. Ryan doubted if the man could see anything at all, suspecting that the insides of his eyes were now coated red with insane, bloody rage.

"Ooooooooodin!"

If Ryan had been forced to face the charging man with a blaster, he'd have put six rounds through his head, just to be certain. If he'd only had a panga in his hand, then he might well have dived for the water.

Several of the muties were of the same opinion as Ryan.

Out of the corner of his eye, Ryan thought he glimpsed Doc trying to scramble over the side of the dragon-ship. When half a dozen of the attackers leaped for their lives, they knocked him back into the lake.

The berserker was magnificent. But he was also doomed.

Prevented from helping him by their own rules of combat, the rest of the Vikings could only watch as Sigurd Harefoot trod his own path toward the glories of Valhalla.

He took five of the muties with him, hacking them into tatters of torn flesh with his great war-ax. Arms, full-grown and residual, were lopped off. A head was parted from its neck, yet its body remained upright for several ghastly seconds, while arterial blood spurted high over the filling sail.

Once they realized that this was truly a solo charge, the muties gathered courage and united against the single warrior. The pale flesh became blotched with patches of smeared blood, red mouths dribbling away Sigurd's life. A long spear, hefted by a skinny, nose-less woman, caught him in the groin, its barbed hook tearing at his genitals as the mutie twisted and wrenched at it. The Viking screamed then. Once. A thin cry, like a child wakened by a midnight horror.

The ending was swift after that. Sigurd managed once more to clear himself a space, but the muties surrounded him, their knives pecking out his flesh. He dropped to his knees, a last cry to Odin ringing the air. Then he vanished, and there was only the slaughter-house sound of metal on bone and meat.

There was a moment of stillness on the long ship. Ryan saw Jak, crouched in the stern, heard the noise of men and women swimming for their lives through the fog-layered waters. The second vessel now seemed under the control of the Norsemen, its oars fanning out as she turned toward them.

The surviving warriors stood stricken by their comrade's death, not seizing the moment he had bought for them by his valiant passing.

"Come on!" Ryan shouted. "Now!"

J.B. was instantly at his elbow, as was Krysty. Mildred snatched a battered handmade .22 from the belt of one of the Vikings and was at his heels. Erik Stonebiter was first of the Norsemen to move, followed by the baron. Then the others.

As he charged, Ryan pumped all but one round from his pistol into the mass of muties, seeing several fall back, dead or wounded.

The final phase of the fight was very brief.

Led by Ryan, with Jak waging his own vicious war from the rear, the assault against the muties finally took its toll. The few who fled over the side were picked off by the other Viking ship, which was maneuvering skillfully across the lake.

Ryan was battling a pair of twins, who were joined at the hip, and each had a curved sickle in his hand. He stabbed one through the shoulder, but a flailing blow from the other struck his panga from his hand, sending it thunking into the deck planks.

"Drop, Ryan!" a voice screamed from somewhere behind him.

It wasn't a moment to agonize over the decision. He fell to one knee, hearing the whistle of the scythe as it nicked a lock of curly hair from the top of his head.

There was the sickly crack of an undercharged pistol, and he felt another tug at his hair. He saw the bullet strike home just below the mutie's breastbone, sending it backward, pulling its less wounded half with it.

"Sorry!" Mildred cried. "Goddamned gun fired way low."

This time there was no attempt to take any of the beaten muties prisoner to sacrifice back at the steading. Every man and woman—and some that could have been either—was slaughtered and tipped over into the reddening water.

Not a single one survived the raid.

JORUND THORALDSON spoke to the survivors, as the second long ship heaved alongside. "The losses have been severe, but we have beaten the enemy. It will be many long days ere they come at us again." There was a halfhearted, ragged cheer. He held up his hand, and his wrist and lower arm were sodden with dark, drying blood. "Against the winning cast of the dice, there must be measured the losing side. Many of our brothers sleep with Freya this night, and there is hardly a man among us without a wound."

That was true enough.

Ryan had a cut along the back of his right hand, and something had bitten him in the calf, drawing blood from the ragged wound. Krysty had dislocated a thumb, but Mildred had promptly but it back in place for her. Mildred herself had escaped without a scratch. J.B. had a bruise the size of a large egg across his chin, and more bruising around his ribs, where the tallest of the muties had gripped him in its several arms and hurled him to the deck. But Mildred had pronounced that no ribs had broken in the fall. Jak was furious because one of the muties had tumbled into the water and disappeared with one of his beloved knives still buried in its left eye. Other than that he was physically unharmed.

Doc had been hauled into the long ship, coughing and spluttering, having been pushed into the lake on three separate occasions. His dignity was a little dented, and he was shivering with cold. But he was very much alive.

The companions stood together under the figurehead, waiting to hear what the baron was going to say to them. Mildred was next to Ryan, apologizing yet again for nearly putting a .22 bullet through the top of his skull.

"Doesn't matter," he insisted. "You going to keep the blaster?"

"No way, José. Chucked it straight into Lake Superior, where it belongs."

At last, Jorund turned to them. He looked at each of them, though his eyes skated over Jak's pinched face and completely avoided Mildred. "It is sooth that we have won, partly through your aid, outlanders."

"Now I trust that you will abjure all your suspicions," Doc said in his rich, deep voice, "and allow us to go our way unhindered?"

"Let you go?" Jorund asked in tones of utter disbelief. "After this and these deaths? Oh, no, outlander. No!"

CHAPTER THIRTY

I T WAS LATE AFTERNOON when they eventually reached Markland, and the sun had vanished behind fresh banks of swelling fog.

There were more funerals to arrange, and the keening of the women rose above the small ville. Since so many dead were warriors, Ryan wondered whether the Vikings would deplete their shrinking number of slaves still further by butchering thralls to accompany their free-born masters on their last journey.

As the six friends were being escorted ashore, Ryan made another effort to speak to the baron about their discoveries along the coast, and what that horror would inevitably mean to the survivors of the steading. But the big man resolutely turned his face away from him and marched up the beach toward his large hut.

Ryan beckoned to Erik Stonebiter. Glancing around at the other men, the youth moved a few reluctant steps closer. "What?"

"We found something very important."

"You broke faith. Nothing you can say is important to us."

"Wrong. We know what killed the children and the man who made the beer, and what's probably killed many others in the ville."

"We know, too."

Ryan was taken aback. "You know! Then why the dark night don't you do something about it? Why don't you move from this place?"

"No. The gods punish us. That is the sickness. And you . . . you outlanders are part of it. Sent as messengers of evil. Storm crows, all of you. All but the white-hair."

"Bullshit, you bigoted little asshole!" Mildred exploded.

Erik held his hands before his face, sticking out the index and little fingers at her, like twin forks.

She laughed, throwing her head back. "Think I have the evil eye, do you, you sniveling little wimp? As far as I'm concerned, you and your whole damned Viking theme park can go vanish up its own ass. And I'll stand and blow you kisses as you sink in the west."

"You aren't helping, Mildred," Krysty said, shaking her head with exasperation.

"Listen, lady. This bunch of mock-macho creeps aim to see us all turned into blue cheese dip for their gods. Being all lovey-dovey and kissing ass won't change that!"

Erik Stonebiter had moved back, eyes flickering nervously at her wrath. He stumbled over his feet and nearly fell. He righted himself and ordered Ryan and the others to be taken to their hut and kept under a close, armed guard.

"TIME TO MOVE ON, folks," Ryan said as soon as the door of the hut was slammed shut.

There was a general murmur of consent.

"When should we make our move this time?" Doc asked. He'd sat on a bed and pulled a blanket around his shoulders, shivering with cold from his repeated immersions.

"They'll watch us tight," J.B. said, carefully honing his knife against the sole of his boot.

Krysty was looking at the rear wall of the wattle and daub building. "This opens clear toward the forest, doesn't it? All we have to do is kick it apart and do a runner. Wouldn't need me using the Earth Mother's force on it."

"They'll watch front and back real tight," Ryan replied. "If it hadn't been for that triple hot spot we'd have been away clear over the ridge. Be close to the redoubt by now."

Mildred said nothing. She sat on the packed-earth floor, head on her hands, staring blankly into space.

Krysty asked her if she was all right, and the woman looked up with a faint smile that never got within a mile of her eyes.

"I'm fine, honey, thanks. It's just that I think the cryo-process is sort of catching up on me. My head feels like the inside of a spin dryer and my body's kind of fraying at the edges. I'm real, real tired.'' And very quietly she began to cry.

Krysty went to her and knelt at her side, laying an arm across Mildred's shoulders. Sobbing, the woman threw her arms around Krysty and pressed her face into the side of her neck. The others looked away, busying themselves with cleaning their knives, allowing Mildred the time to recover control.

Eventually the racking sobs ceased, and she began to weep more softly. She pushed herself away from Krysty and wiped her nose on her sleeve, summoning up a more convincing grin at the rest of the friends. ''There, Mildred is herself again. Sorry about that. Won't happen again.''

Ryan helped her to her feet and patted her on the shoulder. ''If it does, then it does. Nothing to worry about, Mildred.''

An hour or so later, food was brought by a wizened old woman, whose iron collar had been worn for so many years that it had become wafer-thin.

''When will the funerals be? Will they do it tonight?'' Ryan asked her.

''No, masters, no. Oh, there's too many of the dear ones been taken across the saddle horns of the Valkyries.''

Ryan's rough body count said that around a dozen of the Vikings had been chilled, with at least two more likely not to see the next dawn.

''When?''

"On the morrow." She looked around as if she were scared of being overheard. "But the wisewoman's all taken with a fury."

"Why?" Ryan asked.

"Too many dead, masters."

He didn't understand what she was driving at. "Too many?"

"Dead. A free-born warrior will have company as he rides to Valhalla. It has always been the way in Markland."

Krysty understood first. "She means the slaves, lover, the girls who were throttled for the fire ship funeral the other night. So many were chilled this afternoon on the lake that—"

"There aren't enough slaves to go around," Ryan concluded. "With the sickness and all, the ville must be shrinking around its own ears."

"Vanishing up its own..." Mildred began, shutting her mouth as she caught Ryan's glance.

The crone nodded. "That's correct, masters. Not enough thralls. So bad a murrain for the steading these past weeks. So many gone."

"What'll happen," Krysty asked, "if there aren't girls to sacrifice?"

"Oh, the wisewoman has a plan for that. Young godling there—" she grinned gap-toothed at Jak "—he'll provide what... Oh, Freya's tits! I wasn't to speak of that. I'll be given a good beating if they find out I spoke what I shouldn't."

"We won't tell anyone. But what did you mean about Jak?" Ryan asked.

But the slave woman had terrified herself by her indiscretion. Nothing could persuade her to open her mouth again, and she darted from the hut in a flurry of torn skirts and ragged shawl. The door was closed firmly behind her by one of the young sentries outside.

IT WAS almost midnight. Ryan and J.B. sat close together, one on each side of the single candle they kept burning. They talked about old times, half-remembered, part-forgotten: good times and bad; friends dead and lost; women they'd known in a hundred frontier gaudies; men they'd fought and chilled; men they'd fought who'd then become friends. Sometimes the silences crept in from the corners of the hut, bearing fragments of memory.

They kept their voices quiet, to avoid disturbing their sleeping companions. Eventually the talk came reluctantly back to the present.

"Not good, Ryan."

"No."

"I figure they'll chill us all. Except, mebbe, the kid." J.B. looked around from habit, knowing how much Jak hated being called "kid". But the boy was still locked deeply in sleep.

"Wish now I'd never gotten us into this crock of shit."

J.B. waved a dismissive hand. "Black dust! Not like you to worry about what you might have done." He pushed the fedora back from his temples, the candle-light playing on his narrow, sallow face. His eyes were invisible behind the polished lenses of his spectacles. "No jack in that, Ryan."

"Sure." He sighed. "But there's been chances, times I could've pulled the trigger and I didn't. Odds weren't really good enough. But now—"

"Now we'll have to move with the odds stacked against us. Rad-blast it, Ryan! You think you and me haven't done that before? A whole load of times before. Sure."

"Yeah. Late. Reckon to get some sleep now, and then we—" He was interrupted by the sound of the bolts of the hut door being slid quietly across.

Without a word, both men drew their knives. J.B. padded silently to the side of the room near the door. Ryan blew out the candle and crept to flatten himself against the opposite wall.

The door opened, admitting a rectangle of watery moonlight.

"Ryan Cawdor? Outlander One-Eye? Are you awake in there?"

It was the voice of Jorund Thoraldson. Ryan, staying where he was, whispered his reply. "What d'you want?"

"To speak with you."

"Me? Or all of us?"

"You. You're the leader of the outlanders. Just you."

"Now?"

"Yes. Out here. Just the two of us. You have my word you will not be harmed while we speak."

In the darkness, Ryan could just make out the pale blur of J.B.'s face. Since the Armorer wasn't shaking his head, Ryan figured he must think it would be okay to go out.

"Coming," he said.

TALL THOUGH HE WAS, Ryan felt dwarfed by the giant figure of the baron. The two sentries closed the door when he left the hut and slid the bolts across. The baron beckoned to Ryan and the two men walked together through the sleeping ville, toward the beach and the calm, mirrored expanse of the lake.

Neither spoke until they stopped a couple of yards from the tiny, breaking waves.

"This is a hard talk, outlander," Thoraldson began, "yet I must speak it."

"Go ahead."

"The first fight against the evil ones. You aided us. And on the water, you all fought bravely. And in the tests, you did much to shame the finest warriors of this steading."

"But?" Ryan could still smell blood and sweat on the massive Norseman at his side and almost taste an odd kind of nervousness.

"But...the wisewoman has been warning for weeks that there was a plague coming toward us. When the first child became sick of the bloody flux she said it would be worse. Now she swears the omens blame you and your friends, particularly the black-skinned woman."

"You believe her?"

Jorund's shaggy head swung slowly toward him. "No. I think you and your brothers are true fighting men of courage. But since you came, there have been so many deaths. I cannot stand against the wise-woman and all the steading."

"She wants us all dead?"

"Truly. All but the white-haired one. She says we must adopt him into our family, and he will lead us from the darkness."

"The darkness is what I've been trying to tell you about. Along the coast we found undeniable evidence of a dreadful rad leak, and that's what's chilling your folks. The rashes and the sickness and—"

"No, no! I must not listen to this. She made me swear to speak only as she had told me."

"She runs this? She's the fucking baron is she?" Ryan felt his anger misting his mind, and he tried to control it. "You're the baron, aren't you?"

"Aye. I am. Yet the wisewoman has the minds and souls of my people. But I have spoken against her. I have tried. And she has agreed that I shall make you this offer."

"Go ahead."

Ryan felt the faintest tremor from the restless earth beneath his boots. But Jorund said nothing, and Ryan wondered whether he'd even noticed it.

"The outlander you call Jak Lauren?"

"Sure. With the white hair. What about him?"

"If you will agree to this, then he must stay with us."

"And the rest of us go free?" Ryan had enough confidence in Jak's cunning to be certain that the teenager would find a way of escaping within a day or so.

"No. All but one of you."

"Mildred?"

"This is the only hope I can give. You refuse this, and you will all pay the price."

"Jak stays. Mildred dies. The rest of us walk?"

"Aye. And Jak will sacrifice the black woman to our gods before you go free."

CHAPTER THIRTY-ONE

"YOU SAID WHAT?" Krysty shouted, raising her hands to her forehead to try to calm herself. "What did you say to him, Ryan?"

"I told him I'd think about his suggestion and give him my reply before noon."

His short conversation with Jorund Thoraldson had ended a quarter of an hour ago. He'd gone straight back into the hut and been locked in. It hadn't taken long to shake the others from sleep and tell them what had happened.

"You'll think about it!" Mildred exclaimed. "Terrific, Ryan."

"You think I should have looked him in the eye and told him to fuck off? Think that would have been a real clever idea?"

"I guess not. No. Sorry."

"What else did he say?" J.B. asked.

"Said that any more attempts to escape by any of us would mean flying eagles all around. One chilled, all chilled."

The Armorer nodded. "It'll be harder to make the break this time. Lot harder."

"Sure. But that's the only choice we have."

"Does it sound dipshit stupid to suggest you could always do like the big guy says? That way I go up the Hudson, one-way, and the rest of you walk clear."

There was a long silence, while everyone thought about it.

If Jorund Thoraldson kept his word, then the death of one man would buy the lives of five. It was a lot better arithmetic than most you got in Deathlands.

Ryan broke the stillness. "Can't argue with odds of five for one. I think we'll take you up on the offer, Mildred. After all, we pulled you out of the ice and saved your life. Least you can do is give us that life back again."

Krysty stood up, her finger pointing at Ryan like the barrel of a sawed-off shotgun. "I don't believe what I'm hearing, lover."

Ryan faced her. "Well, you better believe it, lover, because I'm the man in charge here and I say what happens. And what's going to happen tomorrow evening, is that Jak does what they want and takes Mildred's life. The rest of us'll walk free. That's the way it'll be."

Doc leaped to his feet, his face glowing with righteous anger. "I do not believe that I have been traveling with such an unprincipled scoundrel! If I were a few years younger and more spry I vow that I would teach you a lesson you would not forget in a hurry. Blast you!"

Jak didn't stand, and he wouldn't look directly at Ryan. "Since father chilled, thought you . . . Fucking wrong, Ryan."

"That only leaves you, J.B. Let's hear your thoughts on the matter."

His oldest friend looked at him. "We'll do it like you say."

CHAPTER THIRTY-TWO

THE BARON OF MARKLAND was delighted when Ryan told him their collective decision.

"The black woman will offer herself willingly on the stone of darkness?"

"Sure."

"And the blade of mercy will be wielded by..."

"By Jak? Yeah. And all this'll be tonight, will it?"

"After the sun has set. The whole of the steading will make its way in a procession of flaming torches through the forest to the arena of seeing. And there it will be done."

"And the rest of us can go free?"

Jorund nodded solemnly. "I have given my word as karl."

"Can we leave before the chilling?"

Ryan held his breath as the Norse leader considered the question. "No."

"No? But you gave your word."

"And I shall keep it. But the sacrifice to the gods must be completed first. You and the others, but not Jak Snowhead, may leave us at first light on the morrow."

Ryan nodded. "Will you give us food and milk for our journey?"

"We will. And the wisewoman will instruct Jak in the ceremony. It is simple. And the black one will feel little pain. It is swift."

"Glad to hear it."

"JORUND AGREED that we didn't have to actually go along and watch the execution. Says he'll let us stay here in the hut, with just a handful of guards to watch us."

"Ryan?"

"Yeah, J.B.?"

"How many's a handful?"

"Not more'n six, I'd guess. I've promised we'll stay and wait until the chilling's done. I gave my solemn oath on the bones of Odin himself that we wouldn't try to escape again."

Jak had been taken out to be schooled by the wisewoman. By the time he returned, the afternoon sun was already slipping away behind the hills.

"How d'it go?" Mildred asked. "Wouldn't want you to screw up and give me a messy ending. Wouldn't like that at all."

"By the three Kennedys!" Doc said. "I fear that I do not find this a fit topic for merriment. This is life and death for all of us."

Mildred patted him on the arm. "Simmer down, Doc. It's your life and my death."

Ryan turned to Jak. "What did the old woman say to you?"

The boy looked down at his feet. If he'd been able to blush, Ryan suspected there'd have been a pink glow to his cheeks.

"Wanted fuck. Grabbed cock. Lay down, legs open. Wanted."

Krysty grinned. "Gaia! That must be one of the sidelines of being the wisewoman. You get to lay every young god that comes by. What did you say to her, Jak?"

"Said too old."

Mildred laughed. "She must have loved that, honey. Way back when I was alive—when I was first alive— it got to be common for older women to take a much younger lover. They were called toy boys. So the old bitch wanted a blond toy boy, did she? Tough shit, lady."

"Said gods didn't fuck old women," Jak muttered embarrassedly.

"Good one. Ace right on the line for her," J.B. said. "But did she tell you about tonight? What's going to go down?"

"Mildred's on altar. I cut throat. End story."

"Yeah. End of story," Mildred agreed.

THEY CAME AT DUSK, when the gray mist lay upon the sullen waters of the lake and the sun had all but disappeared.

The entire population of the ville seemed to be there, other than a half dozen grizzled warriors left behind to guard the outlanders.

Mildred's farewell to her friends was one of restrained emotion. She hugged them all, one by one, finishing with Ryan. There were no tears from any of them. The Vikings watched approvingly, though the capering wisewoman couldn't hide her disappointment that there was no weeping and tearing of hair.

Jak stood aside from it, simply giving the black woman a cursory embrace, his face set like carved ivory.

Jorund Thoraldson and the senior men wore their greatest finery: horned helmets, the brass glittering like beaten gold; cloaks of leather, trimmed with white fur or with layers of heron feathers; high boots, laced to the knee; their best swords or long-handled war-axes, blades polished like mirrors. But Ryan noticed that very few of them carried blasters to the ritual.

He wondered whether all of their blasters were still stored in the longhouse by the blazing bonfire at the center of the ville. The friends had their knives, but against the armed mass of Vikings, knives would be little use.

"After the..." Jorund hesitated a moment over precisely what he might call it. He tried again. "After the ceremony is concluded, we will celebrate with a great feast. It would be better if you outlanders remained within this hut. Food will be supplied to you. Then, at first light on the morrow, you will all go free.

As we have agreed, Jak will stay with us as a token against further harm to the steading. Is all of this well, Ryan Cawdor?''

Without looking at his companions, Ryan simply nodded his head.

At a signal from the karl, one of the warriors began the slow beating of a slack-skinned drum, the hollow and sonorous sound carrying the melody of death.

Mildred walked into the cool evening air and threw her head back, taking a deep breath. The Vikings surrounded her and led her away. Jak kept pace at the side of the Norse chief. The procession quickly wound its way out of sight. Ryan and the others stood in the doorway until one of the older men gently gestured for them to go inside the hut.

The door was closed and they were left with only the flickering light of the candles.

Ryan looked at his companions. ''Now we wait.''

CHAPTER THIRTY-THREE

TIMING WAS EVERYTHING. Too soon, and Mildred would still die; too late and she would be dead.

The four friends sat in silence, while Ryan kept a careful eye on his wrist chron, counting the seconds away.

"Now?" Krysty asked, breaking the long stillness.

He nodded. "Now."

THE SACRIFICIAL PROCESSION had reached the point on the main trail where the side path wound its way toward the natural amphitheater and the high stone above it. Nobody had said anything to Mildred, and the villagers made sure that they didn't get close enough to accidentally brush against her evil skin or catch a glance from her evil eyes.

The women and children surrounded her, and carried smoky torches that filled the evening with the tang of burned pine resin. Even by the flaring light, she could see in the people more evidence of the dreadful, pernicious seepage from the age-old storage site. It was the children who seemed to be suffering most. Several of them had ghastly sores around their mouths, cracked lips and bleeding gums. Some had weeping chancres near their eyes, and a toddler close to her on the left was struggling to carry his torch, because he'd lost most of the nails from his fingers.

Mildred couldn't see Jak, though she knew he was marching with the baron and the principal warriors of the ville.

As she'd been in this area once before with Ryan and Krysty, Mildred guessed they'd reach the oblong block of bloodstained stone in less than a quarter of an hour.

THE DRIED GRASS AND STRAW that filled the canvas mattresses caught fire easily—dangerously easily. Thick smoke surged to fill the hut, and the bright flames began to catch at the wattle and daub walls.

"Help. Candle knocked over! Fire!" The four companions began to yell and scream for help, coughing and choking in the darkness.

For one heart-gripping moment, Ryan wondered whether the men on guard duty would simply stand by and let them burn to death, deciding it was the safest option. The fire had caught hold with a ferocious intensity. Ryan was almost ready to try to charge through it and break through the back walls.

It wasn't the plan, but neither was being burned alive.

"Help us!"

It might have been Krysty's screams that finally tipped the balance in their favor. The bolts crashed back and the wooden door was flung wide open, showing the darkness of evening beyond.

"Now!" Ryan shouted.

He'd stressed to Doc and Krysty—no need with J.B.—that total violence at the fastest possible speed was their only chance. They knew they had at least six opponents, skilled fighting men, who would be on the watch for an escape.

Ryan had his panga; J.B. gripped his narrow flensing knife, held point up; Doc had dropped the ebony case to his swordstick, and flourished the rapier blade by its silver, lion's-head hilt; Krysty had borrowed J.B.'s broad, saw-edged Tekna knife.

The Vikings stood in a loose circle around the open door, staring at the inferno of flames and smoke. There were six men, the youngest of whom looked at least forty. Two held battered sawed-off scatterguns. The rest carried axes or swords.

Ryan was first out, his fighter's eye spotting the two blasters. He went for the closer bearded Norseman who was leveling his weapon.

If either Viking got off a shot, the noise would carry miles on a quiet windless night. And that would be the end of Mildred.

During their discussions, when Ryan outlined his plan, he'd made it clear that if anything went wrong at this stage in the ville, it would mean every man for himself.

His panga thudded home against the side of the man's throat, with a satisfying jar that ran clear to Ryan's shoulder. The edge of the blade grated between the vertebrae, nearly slicing all the way through.

The carotid artery was severed and hot blood fountained in the air, brilliantly lit by the backdrop of the flames.

J.B. took out the second warrior who held a shotgun. Pushing aside the blaster with his left hand, the slightly built Armorer jammed his stiletto deep into the man's guts, twisting his wrist with a savage determination. A great gash ripped through the man's jerkin, as well as through skin and muscle. J.B. felt the heat of spilled intestines against his wrist as he withdrew the blade and pushed the dying Norseman away from him.

A third man started to back away as he saw the dreaded figure of Doc Tanner, running toward him with his rapier, his frock coat flying open.

Despite Doc's age, the old-timer was fast enough over a short distance. He reached the Viking and killed him with a single, careful thrust through the heart. The man dropped to the earth, his sword falling from his fingers. Doc withdrew his own blade and bowed slightly. "Touché."

Krysty, with hair so red in the glow of the blazing hut that it seemed as if her head were on fire, charged at her chosen victim. Since she was last into the open, the three remaining guards had been given a few precious heartbeats to ready themselves.

But the elderly warrior who faced her was totally unprepared for the lightning speed and demonic ferocity of the tall, emerald-eyed valkyrie who came charging at him. "Odin!" he began to yell, his great ax half-lifted.

Krysty sent him to meet his gods with that prayer frozen on his lips. The Tekna opened him from breastbone to groin. The bloodied blade hacked at his throat as he fell to his knees, clutching his ghastly wound, his ax ringing on stones near his feet.

Krysty stood breathing hard by the dying man, edging back a few paces to prevent the scarlet stream from dappling the toes of her boots.

Ryan had followed through onto the fifth of the old warriors, brushing away the feeble lunge of a shaking sword. He pushed the stubby end of his own blade into the man's open mouth. Teeth shattered like frail icicles. The edge of the steel panga opened the lips several inches wider on the right.

Ryan pulled out the cleaver and aimed a short, chopping blow at the side of his opponent's head. The Viking's skull split open like a dry gourd, and he fell to the ground.

Ryan turned, checking to see if J.B. needed help with the sixth and last of the sentries. The Armorer was kneeling astride his man, cutting his throat as calmly as if he were hacking himself off a slice of breakfast ham at a riverside camp meeting.

"That's it," Ryan said. "Let's go get our blasters."

THE IRON CHAINS were cold against Mildred's skin. The Vikings had stretched her out, ankles secured to the bottom corners of the great slab, wrists pulled far apart and manacled at the top.

She'd been forced to remove her clothes, and they lay on the flattened turf at the head of the altar.

"Nobody's seen me this way since my last gyno checkup," she said. But she was talking to herself only. Nobody was close enough to hear her.

If she turned her head, she could just see Jak Lauren. Jorund Thoraldson had his arm around the boy's shoulders and was giving him something to drink out of an ornate golden goblet.

Mildred felt a shiver of pure terror.

"SO FAR SO GOOD, my dear Ryan," Doc announced as they stepped out of the longhouse into the open center of the steading. They could just make out the large bronze gong that was used to signal mealtimes for the people of Markland. And beside it stood the frail, bent figure of an old man they'd all seen hobbling around the place. Almost blind, hands clawed over his walking stick.

"Fireblast!" Ryan breathed.

The old man also held the long padded stick that was used to beat out the signal. They'd all previously heard the deep, thrilling sound of the gong, ringing across the ville and way up into the hills when it was beaten. If the old man struck it a single blow, the noise would surely carry up to the hillside where the entire population of Markland was gathered.

The gong was about one hundred paces away from them, beyond the distorting flames of the big bonfire that glowed and crackled.

It wouldn't have been that difficult a shot, normally.

Ryan leveled his rifle, then hesitated, his finger taut on the trigger. Sparks and smoke were billowing up from the fire, making the figure of the old man quiver like a ghost.

"Me," Krysty said quietly. She holstered her pistol and started to walk steadily toward the gong. The old man watched her, the heavy stick still lifted, ready to bring the Vikings down from the mountain.

Ryan began to edge sideways, so that he could get a clear shot, but the elderly Norseman saw the movement and made a threatening gesture toward the gong. Ryan stopped in his tracks.

Krysty closed the gap to fifty paces. Above the noise of the burning logs, the only sound was her boot heels on the shingle.

The great bronze disk remained mute as the woman came within twenty yards. Her hair, reflecting the dancing lights of the fire, looked like a tumbling halo of purest flame.

"Stop, or I will rouse the steading from the sacrifice," the old man called in a frail, quavering voice.

"Please don't make a noise," Krysty urged, "or blood will be spilled."

"You slew the six men set to watch over you," the elderly Viking accused.

"Yes."

"One was my son," he said. The old man was now only a stride away from Krysty, and she saw that his eyes were filled with tears.

For a moment she thought about her own father. Then she thought about Mildred, plucked from the freezing, and about Jak, Doc, J.B. and Ryan.

"No closer, witch woman," the Norseman mumbled, lifting a hand in front of his face.

"I'm sorry," Krysty said, and she meant it.

The blow was inch-perfect. The hard outer edge of her right hand cut upward, striking the old Viking at the base of his nose. Shards of jagged facial bone were driven into the brain cavity, instantly bringing the dark mystery of death.

"Chilled?" Ryan called.

"Yeah," she said, looking down at the twitching corpse.

"Then, let's go!"

CHAPTER THIRTY-FOUR

DOC REMAINED in the deserted ville, with seven fresh corpses for company.

"It's a hard run all the way, and then a sprint for life afterward. Some of them might come after us." Ryan corrected himself. "*Will* come after us. Then it'll be the haul through the zigzag path toward the ridge. Enough moon to see by."

"I could cover a retreat," Doc suggested.

"No time to argue this. Stay here. Listen out. Soon as the crap jams the silo you take off up there. We'll catch up with you."

"What if, perchance, you should fail in this venture?"

J.B. slapped him on the shoulder. "Then you're on your own, Doc. Good luck."

"And you, my friends."

Then they were gone, vanishing like wraiths into the darkness around the ville.

THE LONG CEREMONY was approaching its climactic finale. There had been songs and speeches, and an endless incantation from the old wisewoman, which drew on the names of every Norse god Mildred Wyeth had ever heard of, and a lot more she hadn't. A kind of resinous incense was burned, and the scented smoke drifted around the arena, hanging beneath the dark lower branches of the trees.

Jak had been drawn gradually toward the center of the ritual. A knife had been pressed into his hands, the stubby blade streaked with silver moonlight. With an effort Mildred had been able to squint around and see the teenager sipping from the antique goblet. His eyes were half-closed and he was swaying on his feet, supported now by Jorund on one side and young Erik Stonebiter on the other. Mildred had no doubt at all that the ichor probably contained some opiate to dull the boy's senses.

From her point of view it didn't really make that much difference who slit her throat or what state that person was in. Her blood would still flow over the cold altar stone and down into the waiting earth beneath.

"Odin, great father of our people, we beg you to take this offering at these our hands!" The voice belonged to Jorund Thoraldson.

There wasn't much time left.

DESPITE THE MUFFLING SCREEN of the forest, Ryan could faintly hear the bellowed, echoing words. The friends were off the main track from the village, running fast along the narrower side trail. "Not much time," he panted.

Timing had always been the most difficult element of Ryan's plan. Move too soon and they wouldn't be able to hit the crowd when they were locked into their ritual. Move too late and they'd only be able to mop up the blood. And spill a little in revenge.

The unexpected appearance of the old man by the warning gong had thrown off the timing, and by the sound of it, the ceremony was more advanced than Ryan had hoped.

"Slow down," he said.

"We gotta get there quick," J.B. argued.

"Going t'be shooting. Way I am this second, I couldn't hit a shithouse door, even if I was inside it at the time. Slow down. Jog in careful."

"Will they have sentries?" Krysty asked.

"No reason to. They figure we're sealed up tight. Muties got their asses kicked all the way out. There's no threat to them."

They moved forward more slowly, picking their way between the trees, hearing the sounds of the ceremony growing gradually closer and louder.

MILDRED LOOKED UP into the glowing coals of Jak Lauren's eyes and read her death in them, knowing at that moment that rescue wouldn't come and that her race was run.

"Into thy hands, O Lord, I commend my soul," she whispered through dry lips.

The small red-hilted knife was poised above her exposed neck. Jak's body was trembling, and he looked as if he might faint at any moment.

The wisewoman had plucked a small bird from a tiny wicker cage and brought it to her lips as if to kiss the sharp beak. Then, with no change of expression, she ripped the head clean off, smearing the creature's blood over her own face.

Now it was Mildred's turn.

"Take her evil spirit, Odin, and let your people go free of pain and of the shadow of the grave. Take her, take her, take her!"

Mildred closed her eyes, wondering, oddly, which of her friends back in her earlier life would have acquired her collection of books on movies.

"Now, godling, now!"

The voice of the wisewoman was an eldritch screech that filled the arena, causing every man, woman and child to hold their breath. Jak gripped the knife, high above his head, completely motionless.

IF HE'D HAD TIME to think about it, Ryan would probably have figured it as the best shot he'd ever made in his life.

At more than fifty yards, in shifting moonlight, his target was the four-inch blade of the sacrificial knife. The laser-enhanced sniper scope was steadied, the rifle rock-still, stock against his cheek. Ryan held his breath and squeezed the trigger. The Heckler & Koch was set on single-shot. In the silence, the crack of the assault blaster was shockingly loud.

The 4.7 mm round pinged off the steel, kicking the knife spinning from Jak's fingers, then ricocheted into the trees.

Mildred opened her eyes, staring straight into the teenager's shocked, bone-white face.

"What fuck was..." He shook his head in bewilderment.

Then the world exploded into bloody, screaming chaos.

AFTER THAT FIRST single shot, Ryan had slid the control on the G-12 to triple-shot. J.B.'s MP-7 SD-8 was also on triple, its silencer muffling the noise of the bullets. Krysty's P7A-13 Heckler & Koch pistol filled her right hand, and she was ready to follow the two men as they charged the mass of people.

In the first fifteen seconds, without a single hand being raised against them, they chilled more than twenty of the villagers. All three tried to avoid shooting the children, but it wasn't a time for conventional niceness. The killing floor wasn't a place for careful moral consideration. The Vikings would have wasted them if the roles had been reversed,.

Ryan, firing from the hip, tried to shoot Jorund Thoraldson, but the warrior baron was quick. He dived for cover at the first shot, scurrying on hands and knees into the trees on the farther side of the large clearing. Erik Stonebiter half turned to Mildred, hefting the large, polished ceremonial ax he carried. For a moment she thought he was going to gut her with the heavy steel, but the clatter of the rifles disconcerted him, and he dropped the weapon, joining the screaming rush for cover.

Jak had drawn one of his own knives and stood staring at the naked, chained woman, as if he didn't quite recognize her.

"Jak."

His eyes still seemed blurred and unfocused, and he leaned over her, his breath spiced and bitter on her cheek. "You?" he said questioningly. "Who you? Who?"

"Stop sounding like a goddamned owl and get the chains off me, kid."

"Don't call..." He brandished the knife threatening, then his eyes cleared and a grin slipped into place. "Hey, know you. You're all right, Mildred."

"Sure. Get me out of here, Jak. Please."

"Use ax," he replied. He picked up the weapon that Erik had let fall and he hefted it to shoulder height, grunting with the effort.

Out of the corner of his eye Ryan saw the gesture and began to turn, thinking the albino boy had gone crazed and was about to hack Mildred apart. But he saw in the next moment what was happening.

"Get her free and dressed, Jak! Gotta get out of this place."

"I'll second that," Mildred said fervently, gritting her teeth as the ax blade howled off the iron chain, striking sparks from the stone altar.

J.B. saw the problem and sprinted over to the sacrificial block, hurdling the dead and the dying, blood splashing across his legs. He leveled his rifle and blew apart the links from Mildred's ankles and wrists. He grabbed her by the arm and helped her to stand.

"Good to see you guys," she managed to get out, leaning on the altar to recover her balance.

Miraculously the amphitheater was almost deserted.

Terrified by the sudden appearance of the three outlanders, their blasters providing instant tickets to Valhalla, the Norsemen and their families had fled into the forest. Ryan and his friends could hear them shouting and screaming as they ran deeper into the trees.

"Everyone okay?" Ryan called.

"In another couple of seconds I'd have been the first course in a Viking pizza feast. Jak looked like he was going to go through with it."

The boy nodded. "True, Mildred. Sorry. Gave drink. Fucked head."

"Better now?" Krysty asked.

"Yeah. Better. Where's Doc? Not chilled?"

"He's fine. We got out of the ville all right. Left him to watch out for us. Told him to start off up the trail. When these mothers realize they still have numbers on their side, I reckon they could come after us."

"So we should move more and talk less, lover," Krysty suggested with a smile.

Ryan gave her the finger. "Sure. Ready, Mildred?"

The freezie was dressed again, in the same clothes she'd taken from the cryo-center. "Ready. Any spare guns around? This Deathlands seems a place where the gun rules, yet I can't get my hands on a decent pistol."

"You will, Mildred," J.B. promised. "You will."

Ryan led the way out of the trampled, bloodied circle, leaving behind the moaning wounded. Mildred, walking second, was whispering to herself. "'The woods are lovely, dark, and deep, / but I have promises to—'"

The stunted figure of the wisewoman suddenly rushed out of the blackness at her, screaming, and holding an open, straight-edged razor.

CHAPTER THIRTY-FIVE

IN HER BLACK SKIRT and jacket, the wisewoman was almost invisible among the lowering wall of pine trees. But the razor caught the filtered silver of the moon, giving a moment of warning of the threat behind the screeched attack.

Ryan spun around and Jak, coming next in line, also tried to grab at the wisewoman, missing her by scant inches.

Mildred was able to knock the cutthroat aside with the edge of her hand, but the impetus of the attack bowled her over and she fell down, tangled with the old Norsewoman.

Ryan stepped in closer, the panga glittering coldly in his hand. But Mildred saw him. "No!" she gasped. "Mine!"

It was a short, almost silent fight. Despite the lingering effects of the long freezing, Mildred was an unusually strong woman and quickly managed to shake the razor loose from her opponent's grip. She slapped the hag several times across the side of the head, ringing, jarring blows that quieted the woman and left her like a limp doll in Mildred's hands.

Mildred stood, keeping a hold on the side of the Viking seer's neck, pressing her fingers in just below and behind the ear.

"You evil, blood-eyed old bitch," she hissed, tightening her grip.

None of the others tried to interfere in the chilling process, which was very swift. Mildred's practiced fingers located the arteries and choked off the supply of blood to the brain. The hag's eyes protruded and her tongue, purpling, thrust between her swollen lips. There was a harsh rattle from her throat and she went limp. Mildred opened her hands and allowed the shrunken corpse to drop to the dirt.

She straightened and looked around at the faces of the other four. "She deserved to die."

"Surely," Krysty agreed.

Then the tears came, flowing down Mildred's cheeks. She shook her head, refusing comfort from any of them. "No, I'll be all right. It's delayed shock. Oh, God, but this Deathlands is a dreadful place. Dreadful. I've just killed a woman with my bare hands!"

"But she deserved to die," Ryan protested.

Mildred rounded on him. "But I'm a doctor, for Christ's sake!"

THEY SAW AND HEARD no one as they moved at their best pace down the main trail toward the deserted ville.

The corpses lay where they'd fallen, and the bonfire had slumbered to glowing ashes. Mildred had recovered some of her composure, but the sight of yet more bodies upset her.

"Do flowers die where you set your foot, Ryan Cawdor?"

His anger, short-fused, flared. "Your world wasn't so great, was it? Don't utter your stupid moralizing here, Mildred! These people, like many in Deathlands, dislike outsiders. Outlanders. So far we've been lucky on this jump. None of us have been chilled. But I've lost friends...too many to count. When it comes down to it, you either pull the trigger or you swallow the bullet. That's all there is."

His tirade was followed by silence. Mildred met his gaze and nodded slowly. "Maybe you're right, Ryan. And you saved my ass back there so...so I thank you. But I don't know if I'll ever get used to Deathlands."

Jak was staring past the smoldering ruin of what had been their hut, toward the far hillside. "Coming," he said. "Hear them."

Ryan's worry was that the surviving Norsemen might try to cut them off before they could reach the ridge, or that they knew a quicker route that would bring them into the tropical jungle toward the redoubt faster than the companions could travel.

There hadn't been time to carry out any sort of check on who had been chilled in the brief firefight, but he was sure that the Viking baron, Thoraldson, had escaped. So had the young warrior Erik Stone-biter. He guessed the better part of twenty able fighting men could pursue them.

Then again, after such a devastating defeat and so many lost, it was even more possible that there would be no pursuit at all.

"BY THE THREE KENNEDYS!"

"Hi, Doc."

"Upon my soul, Ryan, I swear that I nearly jumped out of my skin. I never heard you approaching."

"Just grabbing a few seconds of eye-close, were you, Doc?" J.B. asked, his teeth gleaming white in the moonlight.

"When I need your common insinuations, John Barrymore Dix, I shall most certainly ask you for them," Doc snapped.

"What was that?" Mildred asked. "Was that *John Barrymore* Dix? Boy, no wonder you stick with J.B. Gotta remember that."

They'd met up once again with Doc Tanner on the steep, snaking trail that rose crookedly from Markland toward the distant ridge. With the trees closing in around them, it was impossible to see more than a hundred yards in any direction. Both Krysty and Jak were agreed that they could no longer hear any sounds of pursuit, which could mean that the Vikings had chosen to remain behind in their ville and mourn their dead.

A heavy shower of rain began, which in no time soaked them all and dampened their spirits. It also turned the path into a treacherous mud slide. Only Jak and Ryan avoided falling in the greasy furrows, picking their way through virtual darkness. The moon had waned, disappearing eventually behind swooping banks of thick chem clouds that had ridden in from the north.

Another problem that slowed their progress was fog. It lay like a wide ribbon of silver-gray velvet across the expanse of the great lake, below them. But it was also gathering itself above them, near the ridge. It seeped over from the wide valley on the farther side, spilling silently between the trees, softening the stark silhouettes and dropping visibility to close to zero.

Though Jak's eyesight wasn't that great in the brightness of day, he saw better at night than any of them, even better than Krysty with her mutie-enhanced vision. Now he took the lead, making his way cautiously up the slippery track, followed by the rest, who were guided by the beacon of his white mane of hair. But it was painfully slow progress.

After Doc had fallen heavily, nearly spraining his ankle, Ryan called a halt.

"Double-stupe to go on," he said. "Rain's starting again. Can't see properly. Trail's dangerous. Best wait up for first light."

"What about the locals?" J.B. reminded, leaning against a tree and trying to wipe clotted mud off his boots.

Ryan brushed rain from his forehead. "Yeah. Worries me, too. They'll know this place a lot better'n us. They'll know we're making for the top of the hill. Follow our marks easy in this mud."

"Wait ambush fuckers" was Jak's suggestion.

"No. If we were sure—real sure—they were coming this way, we could do that. Chop them down from cover. But we don't. Likely there's plenty of hunting trails up and over the top of the mountain. Who knows which one?"

"Only the Shadow knows," Mildred said in a sepulchral tone.

The combination of rain, driven from over the water on the teeth of a rising wind, and drifting slabs of bitter fog, made it a thoroughly miserable night for all of them. The temperature fell sharply after midnight, and Ryan insisted that they huddle together for warmth and protection.

"If those mad Vikings want to come up in this weather and try and take me," Mildred said through chattering teeth, "then they're goddamned welcome to me."

THE DAWN'S EARLY LIGHT brought virtually no improvement to conditions. The wind was close to gale force and carried the stinging bite of acid rain. Not the most acidic Ryan had ever experienced, but bad enough to irritate the eyes and taste sour on the skin. The fog had cleared, but the sun wasn't able to cut through the swaths of dark cloud.

Parts of the path were sheeted in orange mud, and it took the companions another three hours to get close to the top of the hill.

The tight mass of conifers had gradually thinned, and mud was replaced by loose stones. Out on the exposed flank of the mountain, the wind had risen to a ferocious howling that plucked at the clothes and made breathing difficult.

"Once we get over the ridge," Ryan said, "it should ease a whole lot."

Doc was doubled over, hands on knees, hawking up strings of pale spittle. He coughed, rackingly, his shoulders shaking. "I confess that I did not care overmuch for that fetid heat we encountered when we first came to Minnesota. Yet it would be thrice welcome after this damnable piercing wind." He turned to squint up the path. "How much farther, Ryan?"

"Not far, Doc. Mebbe another quarter hour, and then it'll all be downhill."

He was a touch optimistic. The last hundred yards had to be covered on hands and knees, the gale tearing at them, driving them toward the spine of the hill.

One by one they crawled over the top, grateful to see the lush jungle ahead. Ryan was last over, gasping for breath. Even twenty feet down the other side, the lee of the slope protected them and life was hugely easier.

"Yeah," Ryan said. "All downhill now."

CHAPTER THIRTY-SIX

"THIS CLIMATE's like being in a Holiday Inn sauna," Mildred said. "But in a Holiday Inn it's a lot of fun."

"I've stayed places like that," Doc told her, wiping sweat from his forehead with his swallow's-eye kerchief. "I recall that the best surprise was no surprise. Was that not their slogan? Or was it that they tried harder? I fear that all of this excitement has somewhat addled my brain."

Ryan held up his hand to call a halt to the group. "Not far from the real serious jungle. This scrub's okay for safety. No chance of an ambush here. Coupla hundred feet lower down the path, things could get nasty."

"And there's all kinds of wildlife in the forest down there," Krysty added. "Not home and safe yet. Double-care."

"Make it triple," J.B. said.

After the chill air near the lake and the banks of icy fog, the tropical heat farther down the trail was overwhelming. The sickly scent of exotic flowers swamped everyone's breathing, and the sweltering humidity reduced the friends to sweating misery.

As soon as they reached the point where the path grew less steep and the lush foliage met in a dark green ceiling, it became an effort to continue walking. The butterflies were everywhere. Turquoise and gold. Maroon and dazzling green. Some of them as large as dinner plates, fluttering between the flowering shrubs that covered so much of the ground in the clearings.

"No sign of the Vikings," Krysty said to Ryan.

"If they came over the top on a different path, they'll likely not come at us until we reach that river near the freezie center."

"Can we try and find a sidetrack?"

"Yeah, but I guess we could be lost within fifty strides. jungle like this seems to grow while you watch it."

Mildred called out to Ryan. "Can we take a break? Doc's kind of frayed around the edges."

"If you want a rest, madam, then I suggest you ask for one for yourself. I can keep going as long as you can."

Ryan grinned at Doc. "So you don't mind if we don't take a halt?"

The old man shrugged his shoulders with a studied casualness. "A matter of scant concern to me, my dear fellow. But if the good lady here is feeling a touch frail..."

Mildred flopped to the ground and lay on her back, staring up at the sky through the thick green leaves.

"All right, Doc. I'm bushed. At least I'm man enough to admit it."

Doc folded himself beside her, knees cracking like small-caliber pistol shots. "I would confess that the heat is somewhat oppressive. How long before we reach the water, Ryan?"

"It's late morning. I recall the river's not that far from here. But we have to be real careful."

"Killer fishes?" Jak asked, tugging at the strands of hair that had become pasted across his face with perspiration.

"Place like this could have fish, insects, animals, birds, snakes..." Ryan started to run out of breath. "You get the idea, folks. Just be careful about everything!"

"LISTEN!"

"What?"

"Thought I... Quiet, everyone!" Krysty held up her hand, her head on one side.

"Behind us?" Ryan asked.

"No."

"Ahead? Side?"

She shook her head in irritation. "Can't tell. I can hear the river, close now. But I heard something else."

Ryan pressed her. "But it wasn't behind us? You're sure on that?"

"Think so, lover. But I can't swear to it. Guess it might have been a deer or something, moving through the brush."

"Patrol red," Ryan said, glancing at Mildred. "That means we—"

"My mother didn't raise any stupid children, Ryan."

He smiled. "Sure. Sorry. I go first. J.B. comes last. Jak second, then you. Doc and Krysty at four and five. Blasters ready."

"I'll be damned glad when you get me a decent gun, Ryan," she said. "I never was much into the NRA and all that God-given-right-to-bear-arms stuff. But I sure as hell feel naked without something on my hip around here."

They soon arrived at the river. One thing Ryan had noticed was that the swath cut through the jungle by the marauding army of ants had almost totally disappeared under fresh, green growth.

From there to the ruins of the Wendigo Institute of Botanical Research, incorporating the Blackwood Center for Chemical and Neurological Research, Military Division, with the Shelley Cryonic Institute—Private, wasn't all that far.

They saw few signs of life: a glimpse of what could have been a small pig or a large rodent, scurrying about its business, rooting among the leaf mold; fresh, seeping tracks of a massive snake, winding sinuously across their trail, so recent that water still oozed into the long furrows.

As they moved down from the higher part of the mountain, they'd seen a lot of birds, including bright parakeets and tiny, darting budgerigars. But in the past ten minutes the birds had disappeared and the vast tract of jungle had fallen silent.

Ryan held up his hand again. "Got a feeling there's company around."

"We don't have a lot of time to wait them out," J.B. said. "We need water. If they hold the river, we're in serious trouble."

"Can't we loop around them, if they're near that small bridge?" Krysty asked.

Ryan shook his head. "One way or another we have to get over the river, and I'm not going to try swimming it. I'll go ahead on my own. See if I can spring the trap. Rest of you stay close, but not too close."

"We got double-blaster on 'em," Jak said. "Chill 'em up front."

"No. If it's Jorund and the rest of his men, they'll have picked up all their blasters from the ville on the way through. If we'd had time I'd have got them and heaved them all in the lake. The Vikings could've got over the ridge before the worst of the weather."

J.B. agreed. "And in this kind of hostile terrain they could be dug in well. Sure, we got the firepower, Jak. But we won't have the chance to maximize it. Time and place give them the megacull facility over us. Ryan's right.''

"Why can we not attempt to sneak up behind them and ambush the ambushers?" Doc asked. "Hoist them with their own petard, as it were?''

"Look at you, Doc. Look at Mildred. Look at all of us. We're real tired. Tired man makes mistakes. Make a mistake in this forest and it's your last. No. I'll go ahead. J.B., give me a word."

The two men stood together, talking quietly and earnestly. J.B. took off his glasses and wiped them on his sleeve, looked up at the pink sky through them, then replaced them on the narrow bridge of his nose. He burrowed his hand into one of his deep pants pockets, then gave something to Ryan.

Ryan took it and nodded, and they walked back to the others. "This is it. I go ahead. J.B. leads the rest of you behind. Keeps as close as he thinks safe. I'm gonna try to talk to them. Seems there's been enough chilling, and they may listen and let us go through. We'll see."

Ryan half turned away, but Krysty took him by the arm. "Don't ever do that, lover."

"What?"

"Go someplace you might not come back from and don't at least say 'bye' to me."

He half smiled, took her in his arms and kissed her very gently on the lips, the tip of his tongue just probing against her teeth. Then he broke from her. "Bye, lover."

Ryan walked away, his rifle over his shoulder. The path cut to the left, and within seconds he was swallowed up by the dark green warmth.

HE COULD SMELL the water before he actually saw it, a soft, earthy smell, sweet with long years of decay.

Now the jungle was utterly silent. He stopped for a moment and listened. Not a breath of wind stirred the palmlike leaves of the trees around him. Not an insect buzzed after the rich pollen in the brilliant banks of flowers.

Ryan had lived long enough in the Deathlands to be deadly sure that his life could now be measured in seconds. His sixth sense warned him of someone hiding in the undergrowth, twenty yards to his right. But he ignored it, carefully not looking in that direction. He continued to walk steadily ahead.

Ryan paused when he finally caught a glimpse of the sullen sheen of muddy water. To his left, clear as a breaking twig, was the sound of someone belatedly cocking a cap and ball musket.

"I'm here, Thoraldson!" Ryan called, stepping out into the clearing that overlooked the ruined bridge.

Nothing happened. No shots were fired.

"Come on! We're all wasting time. We know you and your men are in hiding. We knew it all along. Better talk first?"

He waited, conscious of sweat trickling down the inside of his collar, running along his spine to the small of his back. Despite the oily brown sheen to it, the water looked tempting. Ryan swallowed hard, licking dry lips.

"Nobody else is coming, Jorund Thoraldson. Not until I say so."

"We could shoot you down, and they could do nothing to help you."

The voice came from ahead of him, behind some thick shrubs, decorated with yellow bell-like flowers.

"True. And how would you get back to your ville, past five blasters?"

This time there was a long stillness. Then Ryan heard other voices whispering. It seemed that one of the loudest was Erik Stonebiter's.

Eventually Jorund spoke again. "This place is filled with dread, Outlander One-Eye. Perhaps you and I should talk."

"Face-to-face. Let's see you. And the others. Unless you're frightened of one man."

The long fronds of leaves trembled and quivered, and out stepped the baron of Markland. At least twenty of his men surrounded Ryan, each holding a blaster.

CHAPTER THIRTY-SEVEN

THE NORSEMEN STILL WORE their ceremonial clothes, which were badly stained with clotted mud, an indication of their haste in leaving their ville and their desperate speed over the mountain to get ahead of Ryan and his companions.

There'd been times in Markland when Ryan had regretted that he and his companions didn't have warmer clothes. Now he was relieved to be wearing more comfortable clothing than the sweltering Vikings.

"Hail, outlander."

Ryan nodded. "You willing to let us pass, or will there be more chilling?"

"You have destroyed all our happiness. You and your friends, the false godling and the black woman of evil."

There was a hysterical note to Jorund's voice, and his eyes were wide and staring. Ryan realized at that moment that he'd misjudged how this confrontation would go. It hadn't entered his calculations that the baron had gone mad.

"Your ville was doomed," Ryan replied, still trying for sanity and balance.

"Lies."

"No."

"Yes, lies. Nothing was amiss with us."

Erik Stonebiter, who stood at his karl's side, spoke up. "There was sickness before the coming of these outlanders, Jorund."

The taller, older Viking swung around, his mouth working, the twin barrels of his scattergun aimed at Erik's midriff. "And you also lie!"

"It's the water you drink and fish in," Ryan said, sensing the futility of it all. "Biggest hot spot I ever saw. Rad count off the scale. Move your ville, and some of you could still live."

"Lies!" the baron screamed at the top of his voice. Ryan saw his finger whiten on the trigger of the scattergun and reached into his own pants pocket.

Before he could act, one of the older Norsemen, on the far side of the clearing, threw his own dice into the game. And found snake eyes.

"Harald said the water for his ale seemed to be fouled and—"

The boom of the double-barrel was deafening. A gout of powder smoke erupted from both muzzles. The Viking who had just spoken was hit in the lower chest and stomach by the double charge, the impact lifting him off his feet and throwing him screaming and torn, ten paces back in the undergrowth.

"No!" someone shouted, but Jorund was too deep in blood. He flicked out the spent cartridges and jammed in another pair, before anyone had properly registered the reality of the brutal chilling.

Anyone but Ryan.

He knew that the shouts and the thunder of the 12-gauge would have been enough to bring the other five at the run, and it was obvious that Jorund Thoraldson wasn't in the mood for further discussion.

"Jorund!" he called, loud enough to attract the Viking leader's attention. "Here! Catch this!"

"This" was a small, heavy egg-shaped object that had a colored band around one end. Jorund, surprised, reached automatically and grabbed it in his right hand, still holding the scattergun in his other.

Without another word, Ryan threw himself to the ground, pressed his hands over his ears and opened his mouth wide. Hardly any of the Vikings moved, though Erik and two of the younger men reacted quickly enough.

The karl blinked, bewildered, and brought the object nearer to his eyes to try to work out what it was.

J.B. had set the fuse on the implode gren, at Ryan's request, to a minimal five seconds.

"Why do—" Jorund began.

The gren detonated.

The force was directed inward, creating a brief but devastating vacuum. Ryan, squinting behind his arms, winced at the effect of the gren. It sucked the skin off the Norseman's face, sucked flesh from bone, sucked eyes, which popped from their sockets, sucked lips from teeth. Arteries and veins were destroyed by the unimaginable force of the small gren, and tendons and ligaments snapped like whipcord.

Jorund didn't have time to scream. He had barely enough time to die.

The implode worked over a small area, but its power became translated into a more conventional explosive force. Several of the nearby Vikings went down, yelping in pain, bleeding immediately and profusely from eyes, ears, noses and mouths.

Ready for the shattering effects, Ryan was up on his feet in a fraction of frozen time, his rifle leveled at his hip. He looked grimly at the horrific sight of Jorund's body, some residual nervous reflex keeping it on its feet and staggering toward the river. His skull was bare bone, streaked with smears of blood and gristle, and one hand was also fleshless. The other still gripped the shotgun, its stock splintered and stripped.

As Ryan and the surviving Vikings watched, the corpse took a last tottering step and splashed into the muddied water. For a moment it floated there, arms and legs twitching spasmodically. Then there was a flurry in the wide, slow stream, and the water began to boil with a frantic, crimson feeding frenzy. Ryan's fears about swimming in the river were all too graphically justified.

"Here, brother," J.B. called, appearing from the fringe of the jungle, his Heckler & Koch rifle at the ready. Jak was on one side of him, Krysty on the other. Doc and Mildred stood just behind them.

Barely a dozen of the Norsemen were on their feet, the others still moaning in pain and shock from the implode. Erik seemed to have assumed command of the ragged remainder.

"You win, outlander. We are leaderless and quite beaten."

"Looks that way. I swear I'm sorry there's been so much chilling. It wasn't of our choosing."

The young man nodded. "I know that, Ryan Cawdor. When the runes of life are cast, then we are but the creatures of the gods in this matter of life."

"Our quarrel's over?"

"Aye."

"So we can pass through?" Krysty asked.

The young Norseman hesitated. "You know a way to get out from this part of the land?"

Ryan nodded. "Yeah."

"Take us. Take us who are left and our women and children, before we all sleep the long darkness from which there is no wakening."

"Sorry. We can't. Where we go, we go alone. Sorry."

Mildred stepped to the front of the group. "If you think I'm the wicked witch of the west, then forget all this. But I can truly give you good advice—advice that will save the lives of some of you.''

''Some?''

She smiled at him, a little sadly. ''A few weeks earlier I might have said all of you. Now, there's some with bone-deep sickness, carcinomas breeding away like maggots in rotten fish. But there's still time to save some. Move away down the coast, away from the radiation.''

Erik smiled at her through his broken teeth. ''We must go how far?''

''Fifty miles, at least. And find some good fresh water.''

''And some will live?''

''Yes, son, yes. Some will live. If you're lucky, then most will live.''

''It shall be.'' He turned to his comrades. ''Come, give help to those who are hurt. Let's say farewell and be away, and meet perhaps some happier day.''

BEFORE MAKING THEIR WAY to the gateway, the companions rested in the redoubt and ate and drank their fill. They took a full day and night to ready themselves for the jump.

J.B. had taken Mildred into the section of the redoubt where the arms and armaments were stored. He encouraged her to pick out a good, workmanlike blaster for herself.

She chose a Czech six-shot revolver, the ZKR 551, which was based on designs originating in the Zbrojovka Works at Brno. Specially designed by the Koucky brothers, the ZKR 551 was chambered to take the Smith & Wesson .38 round and had a solid frame side rod ejector and a short fall thumb cocking hammer.

Mildred picked it because it had been a leading weapon in small-arms shooting competitions, and she liked the balance. And also, as J.B. pointed out, because the blaster was a serious man-stopper.

EVEN THOUGH they'd been away only a few days, there were clear signs of deterioration within the gateway's main control rooms. Several sections of panel lights were out, and one of the big comp-tape spools had broken.

It was a manifestation of something Ryan had noticed several times. The gateways, with their reliable nuke-power units, were self-sustaining and had been kept ticking over, unused, for a century. But when a jump was made, it seemed to trigger a process of disintegration within the delicate machinery.

"Is this going to work, Doc?" Mildred asked as they entered the red-walled chamber.

"More or less, my dear."

"More or less! Jesus, didn't any of you guys ever see a movie called *The Fly*? No? So forget it. Let's go."

"Everyone sitting down ready?" Ryan asked, glancing around the arma-glass, six-sided room. "This is going to make your head spin, Mildred," he warned.

"I rode Colossus Three at Magic Mountain, buddy. So this ain't nothing. Shut the door, it's getting too hot in here."

Ryan slammed the door and sat next to Krysty, resting his head against the cool glass. He stretched his legs in front of him as the metal disks in floor and ceiling began to glow and the faint shreds of white mist began to appear around them.

"We won again, lover," Krysty whispered, holding his hand in hers.

"Times like this I'm not sure I can tell the difference between winning and losing anymore," he replied, feeling the first tingling of darkness at the front of his brain.

"We're alive, lover. And that means we won."

"Yeah," he agreed. Or thought he did.

There was blackness.

Blackness.

Black . . .

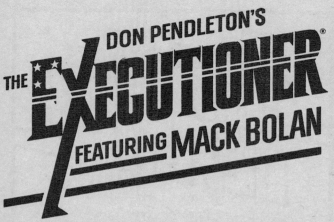

DON PENDLETON'S
THE EXECUTIONER®
FEATURING MACK BOLAN

Baptized in the fire and blood of Vietnam, Mack Bolan has become America's supreme hero. Fiercely patriotic and compassionate, he's a man with a high moral code whose sense of right and wrong sometimes violates society's rules. In adventures filled with heart-stopping action, Bolan has thrilled readers around the world. Experience the high-voltage charge as Bolan rallies to the call of his own conscience in daring exploits that place him in peril with virtually every heartbeat.

'Anyone who stands against the civilized forces of truth and justice will sooner or later have to face the piercing blue eyes and cold Beretta steel of Mack Bolan . . . civilization's avenging angel.''
—*San Francisco Examiner*

ABLE TEAM

DICK STIVERS

Action writhes in the reader's own streets as Able Team's Carl "Ironman" Lyons, Pol Blancanales and Gadgets Schwarz make triple trouble in blazing war. Join Dick Stivers's Able Team—the country's finest tactical neutralization squad in an era of urban terror and unbridled crime.

"Able Team will go anywhere, do anything, in order to complete their mission. Plenty of action! Recommended!"
—*West Coast Review of Books*

GOLD
EAGLE®

Able Team titles are available wherever paperbacks are sold.

AT-1R-A

by *GAR WILSON*

The battle-hardened five-man commando unit known as Phoenix Force continues its onslaught against the hard realities of global terrorism in an endless crusade for freedom, justice and the rights of the individual. Schooled in guerrilla warfare, equipped with the latest in lethal weapons, Phoenix Force's adventures have made them a legend in their own time. Phoenix Force is the free world's foreign legion!

"Gar Wilson is excellent! Raw action attacks the reader on every page."
—Don Pendleton

Phoenix Force titles are available wherever paperbacks are sold.

PF-1R

PHOENIX FORCE

GOLD
EAGLE

Out of the ruins of civilization emerges...

DEATHLANDS®

The Deathlands saga—edge-of-the-seat adventure not to be missed!

Introducing Max Horn. He's not your typical cop. But then, nothing's typical in the year 2025.

HORN

HOT ZONE

BEN SLOANE

The brutal attack left New York Police Detective Max Horn clinging to life and vowing to seek vengeance on the manic specter who murdered his wife and young son. Now, thanks to cold hard cash and the genius of an underground techno-doc, Max is a new man with a few new advantages—titanium skin and biomechanical limbs hard-wired to his central nervous system.

On an asteroid called New Pittsburgh, Max walks a new beat...and in a horrible twist of fate comes face-to-face with the man who killed his family.

Look for HORN #1—HOT ZONE in March wherever paperbacks are sold because once you meet Max Horn, you'll never forget him.